M000032895

PROJECTOR FOR SALE

A Novel about Dreams

Steven Decker

Printed in the United States of America
Published in Hellertown, PA
Cover and interior design and illustrations by Leanne Coppola
Library of Congress Control Number 2021917751
ISBN 978-1-952481-55-0
2 4 6 8 10 9 7 5 3 1 paperback

For more information or to place bulk orders, contact the publisher at Jennifer@BrightCommunications.net.

For Paige

Prologue
February 2010

Projector for Sale. Brenkert BX-60 in
perfect working condition. Manufactured in
1951 and used in the famous but now closed
Palladium Movie House in downtown Denver.
This projector is one of a kind. Serious calls only
please. 303.212.8602.

—Classified ad from the *Denver Post* that had
been running continuously since 1985.

Chapter 1
February 2010

As the chair approached the 12,060 foot summit of Mary Jane Mountain, Emily Noland glanced down at her right arm to make sure the thermal sock was secure. An old habit. When the chair leveled off, she shoved herself away with her left hand, got a little speed coming down the ramp, glided past the unloading zone and brought her board to a stop. It was fairly cold this high up, around zero that morning, and the wind was howling, plunging the windchill way into the negative. Emily and her two friends, Tommy and Brian, were all wearing face masks to protect their skin from the piercing, frigid wind, and goggles to keep the swirling snow out of their eyes. Emily used her left hand to anchor her free boot into the snowboard binding and waited for the guys to get ready.

Tommy and Brian weren't snowboarders—they were skiers—and today they had outfitted themselves with mountaineering skis and poles to tackle the upcoming traverse, and to help their snowboarding friend, who couldn't use two poles even if she wanted to. They were headed to the

Cirque, about a mile away, the most challenging and dangerous skiing on the mountain, but no lift could take you there. Ski Patrol had told them earlier that the Cirque was still open because the blasting to prevent avalanches had been successful earlier in the morning, but they warned that if the snow kept up, it would probably be closed.

The snow was deep, about 18 inches of fresh powder so far, with more on the way, so walking the mile over to the Cirque was out of the question. Emily had on a harness that had a hook in the front. Tommy and Brian were both wearing harnesses that had a metal connector ring in the back. They lined up side by side, just in front of Emily. She reached out with her left hand and removed a cable from Tommy's pack. The cable was a single on one end and then forked and became a double strand on the other end. She hooked the single strand to her harness, then latched one of the double cables to Tommy's connector ring and the other to Brian's.

"Okay!" she yelled. "Let's try this!"

The two young men didn't hesitate. No reason to hang around in these conditions. They pushed off with their poles and started pumping their powerful skier's legs, driving themselves forward. Emily leaned back as the cable rose up from the snow, and when it was taut, she started to move. The guys got into a slow cross-country cadence. Their mountaineering skis allowed their heels to come up, and the underside of each ski was configured to allow them to gain purchase on the snow when pulling the ski backward, while sliding with minimal resistance when pushing the ski forward. They were well above the treeline, so there were no natural barriers to protect them from the wind, but they ignored the conditions, curling slowly around the upper edge of the ski area boundary. They kept close to the boundary markers, not wanting to lose any vertical before they arrived at the Cirque. This meant that at times they were moving in a slightly upward direction, challenging their legs even more.

Emily continued leaning back to keep the cable tight and to maintain her balance on the slowly moving board. It was a rare thing for her to accept help from others in anything she did, but she'd known Tommy and Brian for the entire four years she'd been living in Winter Park, and she was willing to listen when they'd come to her with their idea. Tommy was a California surfer dude, tall and blond, who'd fallen in love with the mountains during a trip to visit friends, and never left. He'd been at Winter Park for seven years. Brian was from Wisconsin and had that humble, unassuming personality of a Midwesterner. He had dark hair and was a few inches shorter than Tommy but was firmly built from his years as a wrestler. Brian had arrived the same season Emily had moved up from Boulder after she graduated from the University of Colorado.

Tommy and Brian had approached Emily with their idea the night before at the bar, basically begging her to let them try, and she'd eventually agreed to it. Her rationale was twofold: One, she needed to begin dealing with her extreme reluctance to depend on others, for *anything*, and two, in all her years skiing at Winter Park, she'd never gone down the Cirque in deep snow, on a board or on skis. The guys knew her situation well and respected her for all she'd accomplished in spite of her "limitation," and they were really pumped up about the three of them working as a team to make something awesome a reality. They were also aware that the word "limitation" was not part of Emily's vocabulary, and they would never speak that word out loud in her presence.

It took about half an hour for the three to reach the Vasquez Cirque area. When they did, Emily quickly unhooked the cable ends and secured the cable back into Tommy's pack. The guys secured their heel bindings in preparation for some serious downhill skiing. The three of them then huddled together as closely as they could, knowing it would be difficult to hear each other over the relentless wind.

"Alphabet?" screamed Brian.

"Oh yeah!" shouted Emily.

"Let's do it!" yelled Tommy, pointing his skis downhill.

Alphabet Chutes was the steepest run on the entire 3,000-acre resort. With a slope of 50 degrees, it was one of the most challenging runs you could find in North America. And it wasn't really a run. It was a piece of backcountry that had been brought within the ski boundaries in the late '90s. The managers of Winter Park had wanted to provide literally every kind of skiing experience on the three peaks that composed the resort—Winter Park, Mary Jane, and Vasquez Ridge. Winter Park was known for its intermediate cruiser runs, with a sprinkling of advanced trails; Mary Jane was a serious bump mountain with some great tree skiing and some bowls up top; and Vasquez Ridge was composed of backcountry up above, known as the Cirque, with plenty of glades once you got down to the treeline and some nice advanced and intermediate runs lower down.

Very few ventured over to the Cirque, even on sunny days, because it was a long trek, and getting down was a treacherous proposition for most. The first descent was above the treeline, so it was normally rough, ungroomed snow, but now that a blanket of powder 18 inches deep had fallen, it was heavenly, for those who could get there and for those who could handle it. Alphabet Chutes was a "Double Black Diamond," meaning it was truly for experts only, and all three of the friends standing above Alphabet that day were definitely experts. They counted themselves among a small core of local powder hounds who were braving the elements that day while more recreational skiers stayed at the lower elevations or warmed themselves by the fire inside.

Emily turned her board downhill and slid into a chute that was so steep it was almost like jumping off a cliff. But the powder and her skill kept her under control. As she S-turned her way down Alphabet, the sensation of floating became predominant. It was a feeling all powder hounds covet, just as surfers seek the rare, indescribable feeling of being inside the tube of a curling wave. Tommy and Brian were right beside her, all three seeking the additional thrill of being so close together, on such a dizzyingly steep hill, that a powerful feeling of trust is achieved, which is also quite exhilarating.

It wasn't long before they reached the treeline. They didn't hesitate as they floated into a dense glade near the Eldorado Trail. The trees here were tight, but none of the three had any difficulty maneuvering through them. Tommy was slightly ahead, and when he found the spot they were looking for, he came to a stop. It was a relatively flat patch of snow that was surrounded by trees, so it was well protected from the wind. Tommy removed his gloves, reached into the pocket of his jacket, and pulled out a lighter and a joint. He cupped his hands and quickly lit the joint, inhaling deeply, then put it up to Emily's mouth. She drew in the smoke, holding it as long as she could, then blew it out, a cloud escaping from her mouth. Tommy repeated his favor with Brian, enabling both Brian and Emily to keep on their gloves, then put it out and returned it to his jacket pocket. The whole process had taken less than 30 seconds, so Tommy was able to get his gloves back on before his hands got too cold.

"Whoa, that was awesome," said Brian, exhaling.

"It *was*," replied Emily. "I'm so happy you guys had this idea."

"Wouldn't be the same without you, Em," said Tommy, and he meant it. They loved Emily like a sister, as did all who knew her well.

"What up next?" asked Brian. "Catch Eagle Wind back up?"

"What time is it?" asked Emily.

"Don't know," said Tommy. "Why?"

"I've got a lesson at 10," she replied.

"Dang," said Brian. "We're just getting started."

"You guys keep going for it. I'm gonna head down to the base and get ready to go."

"They can't be doing much on a day like this, can they?"

asked Brian.

He was referring to the National Sports Center for the Disabled, where Emily was a volunteer, helping disabled people of all shapes and sizes learn how to ski and board.

"Oh, there are always some hearty souls who want to give it a go in the powder," she answered. "Just 'cause they're disabled doesn't mean they don't like a challenge."

"True," said Brian. "My bad. But what say we hang together till we get to Eagle Wind, 'kay?"

"Cool," she said.

"Let's tear it up!" yelled Tommy, turning his skis downhill and bolting off.

The others followed, and they soon emerged from the trees and took a hard left, working their way down to the Eagle Wind lift. There was no lift line, so the guys kept skiing until they got in front of the next chair and were scooped up. They raised their poles in the air as they were carried back up the hill.

"Later!" Tommy and Brian yelled to Emily, in unison.

"Later!" Emily called back, kind of wishing she could go with them, but also excited about what she'd be doing next.

Chapter 2

Emily worked her way down the mountain to the Winter Park side of the resort, which had evolved into a complex beehive of activity since its humble founding in 1939 by the city of Denver. In 2002, the city had sold the resort to a private developer, and lots of expansion had taken place since then. The National Sports Center for the Disabled (NSCD) had been founded in 1970 by Hal O'Leary, not long after he taught a skiing class to 23 amputees, which inspired him to do more. The NSCD had gone on to become one of the largest therapeutic recreation organizations in the world.

The vast majority of people working at NSCD were highly trained volunteers. Emily was one of those. She volunteered two days a week at NSCD and cherished the opportunity to help people who needed just a little guidance to find the "able" in the word disabled, just as she had done.

Emily took off her board, leaned it up against a ski rack, and made her way to her locker, taking note of a wall clock that read 9:35 a.m. She removed her helmet and mask, putting the mask in the locker because it wouldn't be needed any longer. The wind and the cold were not nearly as severe down at the lower elevations. She placed the helmet on the bench in front of her locker, took off her harness and put it in the locker, then removed the thermal sock from her right arm and positioned the end of the arm against the edge of the glove on her left hand. She used the end of her arm to slowly work the mitten off her hand. It fell to the floor, and she leaned down to pick it up, then stuffed it and the thermal sock in her pocket.

Emily sat on the bench, removed her snowboard boots, and put them on the floor next to her. She retrieved her ski boots from the bottom of the locker and filled the space they'd occupied with the snowboard boots. She put the ski boots on, stood up, closed the locker, slipped the helmet on and made her way to the cafeteria. She got in line and looked for something that could be eaten quickly.

"Hey, Jayden!" she said to the food server behind the counter.

"What up, Em?" asked Jayden.

"Getting ready for a lesson over at NSCD. How've you been?"

"Been better. It's killing me to be in here when the fluff is falling, you know?"

"I hear you, dude. But some good stuff will still be there when your shift ends."

"Your mouth to God's ears, Em. What'll you have?

"An egg sandwich and a bottle of water, thanks."

"You got it. Here you go."

Emily thanked Jayden for the food, paid for it, found a seat, took off her jacket, and sat down. She gobbled up the sandwich, drank the water, and got ready to leave. First, she put the thermal sock back on her right arm. Then she stood up and put on her jacket. She worked the mitten back onto her left hand, clawing at the inside of the mitten with her fingers while pushing on the outside with the end of her right arm. Finally, she put on her helmet and headed outside. The wall clock said 9:50. Once outside, Emily made her way to the NSCD office and went in. She saw her friend Reenie behind the counter.

"Hey, Reenie," said Emily. "How you doin'?"

"Awesome," said Reenie. "You get any of that powder yet?"

"A little bit," said Emily. "Got one run down the Cirque with Tommy and Brian."

"Whoa! How'd you manage that?"

"Creatively," said Emily. "I'll tell you more later. You got my wide boards back there?"

"You bet," said Reenie. She turned to grab a pair of short, wide skis and handed them to Emily. Emily kept several different skis at the NSCD, choosing the ones she needed to fit the conditions of the day. Today, the short skis would let her stay close to her student, and the width would help keep the skis on top of the deep snow.

"Thanks," said Emily. "Is Hannah here?"

"Outside, waiting with her mom and dad. She can't wait to ski powder!"

"And ski powder she *will*!" said Emily, turning and heading toward the door. "Catch you later, Reenie."

"See you at the Oasis later?"

"For sure. I'm working tonight."

Chapter 3

Emily exited the NSCD office, stepped into her skis, and skied out to the area where the lesson participants were gathered. Today, Emily was giving a private lesson to an eight-year-old girl named Hannah Baxter. She looked around and spotted Hannah with her parents. The snow cats had done a good job of grooming certain sections of the base area so people wouldn't have to trudge around in nearly two feet of snow. Hannah and her parents were standing in one of those sections.

"Hi there!" said Emily. "How's the Baxter family today?"

"We're great!" said Hannah excitedly. "Am I gonna ski powder today?"

"You sure are, honey!"

"Yay!"

"How was the drive up?" asked Emily, addressing Hannah's parents.

"Actually, we drove up yesterday, before the storm hit," said Mrs. Baxter.

"No way Hannah was going to miss a chance to ski powder!" said Mr. Baxter.

"Great move!" said Emily.

Emily had been giving ski lessons to Hannah all winter long. Her parents normally drove her up from Denver every Tuesday morning. They had told Emily that Tuesdays were the highlight of Hannah's week. Emily had responded that Tuesdays were the highlight of her week, too, and she meant it with all her heart.

Emily had been volunteering at the NSCD for seven years, having started when she was a sophomore at the University of Colorado. She was now one of the most experienced, trusted instructors in the NSCD. Not one of her students had ever suffered an injury during her classes, and she was given more discretion than most in deciding the best way to approach a lesson on any given day. For today's lesson, she'd come up with an interesting approach, which she'd cleared with her manager the prior day. But she knew she'd have to convince Hannah's parents that it was a good idea.

Emily noticed that Hannah was wearing her outrigger skis on her arms. This type of ski is used by people with balance issues in place of ski poles. They attach to the arms and have hand braces to lean on. For Hannah, they were very helpful in allowing her to ski on one leg. Hannah had been born with a deficiency in her lower right leg that resulted in it being amputated below the knee when she was still an infant.

Emily was inspired by the courage of the little girl, and also by Hannah's parents' unwavering support of their daughter. This reminded Emily very much of her own parents, who had always encouraged her to try everything and anything after the accident that had led to the loss of her right hand when she was 11 years old.

Today, Emily planned to ditch Hannah's outrigger skis because they would be virtually impossible to maneuver in the deep snow. Emily herself would serve as Hannah's outrigger. Most of the runs on the lower mountain would be groomed, meaning the fresh, deep snow would be flattened or pushed aside, but if Hannah wanted to ski powder for the first time, Emily would find some powder, and the outriggers would be of no use when she did.

"Hey, folks," said Emily. "I think today we should ski without the outriggers, okay?"

"How come?" asked Emily's dad.

"If we get into the powder, the outriggers won't work so well," replied Emily.

"So, you're *really* going to ski powder then?" asked Hannah's mom.

"You bet!" said Emily. "And we'll ski on some groomed trails as well. Maybe you guys don't know it, but Hannah can ski without outriggers when she wants to."

"Oh, we *know*," said Hannah's dad, smiling with pride. "You think she'd keep such a great accomplishment a secret from us?"

"Okay, let's go!" interrupted Hannah. "I wanna ski powder!"

"No problem, honey," said Emily. "But we have one more thing we need to do."

"What?" asked Hannah, frustrated by the delay.

"We need to give you one of my skis," said Emily.

"Why would you do that?" asked Hannah's mom.

"These are powder skis," said Emily. "*Short* powder skis, but powder skis, nonetheless. Hannah's ski is a regular ski, mostly for hard-packed conditions."

"But can *you* ski on one ski?" asked Mrs. Baxter.

"Of course!" exclaimed Emily. "And so can Hannah. But today, we're going to be a team and use our two skis together, okay folks?"

"I'm fine with it if you are, Mary," said Mr. Baxter to his wife.

"Sure," said Mrs. Baxter.

"All right then. Hannah and I will take a quick trip into the shop to get my left ski fitted to her boot."

Emily helped Hannah out of her ski and removed her own skis. She left Hannah's ski with her parents, keeping her own skis with her, clamped tightly between her right arm and her body. Then she and Hannah walked over to the ski rental shop. Hannah used her outriggers to support her weight while she pushed herself along with her left leg. Normally, Hannah wore a prosthetic on her right leg that allowed her to walk, but her father had removed it when they were getting her ready to ski because the prosthetic didn't perform well in the motions needed for skiing.

When the pair arrived at the ski rental shop, Emily helped Hannah remove her outriggers. She placed the outriggers on a rack nearby. She supported Hannah's right side by wrapping her left arm and hand around Hannah's waist and having Hannah hold onto Emily's waist with her right arm and hand.

"Okay," Emily said. "Let's practice walking together. You step with your left leg, and I'll keep pace with you." Emily stepped with her left leg when Hannah did, then Emily stepped with her right.

It was a little awkward at first, but the two found a rhythm and made their way into the shop. Emily walked them straight into the back of the shop, where the technicians were located.

"Can you fit Hannah's boot to one of my skis?" she asked one of the guys.

The technician nodded. Everyone knew Emily, and no one would ever refuse her. She gestured for Hannah to sit on a bench, took off her boot, and handed it to the technician. The binding adjustment was completed in less than two minutes.

"Thanks!" Emily said to the technician. "You've earned a beer on the house the next time you come to the Oasis and I'm working."

Emily helped Hannah put on her boot, then together they made their way back outside. Emily helped Hannah step into the powder ski. She put her remaining ski on her right leg, then got on the right side of Hannah and wrapped her left arm around Hannah's waist. She used her free left boot to push them across the recently groomed snow, letting the child get a feel for her new ski. They soon arrived back with Hannah's parents.

"Okay, we're good to go!" said Emily. "If you two would hold onto Hannah's old ski and go grab her outriggers from the rack over there, that would be great. We're gonna head over to the lift."

"What time will you be back?" asked Mrs. Baxter.

"I know the lesson is only supposed to be an hour and a half," said Emily, "but for us to get to some good powder, it'll take a little longer than usual. Can you meet us back here at 12:30?"

Mr. and Mrs. Baxter looked at each other, appearing to be happy that their daughter would get to spend more time than usual with Emily. They'd arranged with Hannah's school for Tuesdays during the winter to be special physical education days for Hannah, so there was no rush to get back to Denver, especially because Mr. and Mrs. Baxter ran their own small business from home.

"Great!" said Mrs. Baxter.

"Can we go now, please?" asked Hannah, impatient to get started.

"Let's go!" said Emily.

Chapter 4

Arm in arm, Emily and Hannah made their way over to the Gemini Express lift. There was a line, but because this was a lesson, they used the dedicated lesson entrance and went right on. The lift operators were trained to take special precautions when students from NSCD were boarding the lift, so they slowed it down to allow Emily and Hannah more time to properly position themselves for boarding. The lift scooped them up, with Hannah on the left and Emily on the right, and they were on their way.

Emily glanced over at Hannah. She was beaming. Strands of her blonde hair came out from under her helmet. Her face glowed red from the cold, and she looked beautiful to Emily, so happy and excited.

"How've you been doing lately?" asked Emily.

"Good," said Hannah.

"What about school?"

"I got my report card and got all A's!"

"Awesome! And how are other things at school?"

"Some of the kids still make fun of me," said Hannah,

her mouth turning down.

"Yeah, that happens. Happened to me, too."

"It did?"

"Yeah, at first, after my operation, everybody felt sorry for me and was nice. But as time went by, people who didn't know me would stare and make comments behind my back about my missing hand."

"Yeah, that's what they do to me, too," said Hannah.

"I understand. It makes life a little harder, doesn't it?"

"It makes me sad."

"Yep, I felt that way, too. But I never let people know it. I always made a point of going up to the ones who were snickering, a big smile on my face, making small talk, like I was a regular person, which I am. I wanted them to understand that."

"Really? That seems scary."

"It takes a little bit of courage, but no more courage than what we're going to need today, right?"

"Right! Skiing powder takes a lot of courage!"

"It *does*, when you haven't done it much," said Emily. "But after a while, it gets a lot easier and is something to look forward to."

"Yay!"

Their chair approached the unloading point, and Emily placed her left hand under Hannah's right arm, just above the elbow, squeezing firmly.

"Okay, so remember: You're our left ski, and I'm our right ski, okay?"

"Yep!"

"There won't be any powder on the ramp, but we'll hit

patches of it here and there. Keep your knee bent; that will help us keep our balance when we hit a patch of powder, okay?"

"Yep!" Hannah's eyes were wide, but she was still smiling.

Their skis touched the snow. Emily pushed them away from the chair, still holding tightly to Hannah's arm. They skied down the ramp, and Emily guided them off to the right side.

"Okay, this is going to be a short, easy run. We're going to ski down Bill Wilson's Way to the Prospector Express lift. This run has been groomed, meaning it doesn't have any good powder."

"I want to ski powder!" whined Hannah.

"Oh, we *will*, honey. We will. But anything worth doing is worth working for, right? Most of the runs down here have been groomed, so we have to take a few lifts to get up to the good powder, okay?"

"Okay," said Hannah, resigned to the fact that she'd have to wait a little longer.

"This is a good chance for us to practice skiing together anyway," said Emily. "For this first run, when I say 'right', turn your ski a little to the right, and when I say 'left', turn your ski a little to the left, okay?"

"Yep."

"Off we go!"

Emily pushed them forward with her left leg, then pulled it off the ground and held it there after they worked up enough speed. Emily knew that Hannah was a good athlete and was confident they could pull this off. She gave the "right/

left" commands to Hannah, and they made it easily down Bill Wilson's Way, which was a beginner's run, then boarded the Prospector Express lift.

On the ride up, Emily explained to Hannah that there were two intermediate runs on the far side of the mountain that wouldn't have been groomed yet and *that* was where they were headed. When they got off the lift, they skied down Tweedledum and Wagon Train and got on the Pioneer Express lift.

"Okay," said Emily. "This is the lift that will take us to the powder!"

"Yay!" said Hannah. "But now I'm scared. What if we fall?"

"Then we'll be covered in fluffy snow! What's so bad about that?"

"Yeah! What's so bad about that?"

Before they exited the lift, Emily reminded Hannah to keep her knees bent because they would be in the powder as soon as they got down the ramp. They came to a stop a lot sooner than they would have if there were no powder.

"You see," said Emily. "The powder really slows you down, so there are two challenges when you ski powder. First, you can't be afraid to point your ski down the hill and *keep* it pointed down the hill until you get enough speed to start making turns. Second, you need to keep the tip of your ski up a bit. The easiest way to do that when you're learning is to lean back a little more than normal. Okay?"

"That's a lot to remember," said Hannah, her mouth turning down. She was looking down the hill with fear in her eyes, but Emily had seen this many times before in her students.

"Yeah, you're right," she said. "Let's just do this. Let's not even worry about turning. Let's just ski straight down, and I'll bring us to a stop with my left leg before we get going too fast, all right?"

"I guess so," said Hannah, still a bit fearful.

"All you have to remember right now is to lean back, just a bit. I'll hold your arm, and I'll squeeze when you've got it just right, okay?"

"Okay," said Hannah, gaining courage.

"Here we go!"

Emily pushed off with her left leg and kept pushing until gravity took over. They picked up speed, and their skis found their way closer to the surface of the snow. They were on the Sundance trail, classified as intermediate, although it was a little steep at the top.

"Yippie!" yelled Hannah. "I'm skiing powder!"

"You sure are!" shouted Emily, excited that her plan was working. "Hey, since we're doing so good, why don't we start making turns. You ready?"

"Yep!"

"Okay, point your ski a little bit right."

Hannah pointed her ski right, as did Emily, and their direction changed. When they got close to the right side of the trail, Emily gave the "left" command, and they redirected themselves toward the left side of the trail. They did these wide S-turns all the way down, without stopping, until the Sundance trail merged with Big Valley, a beginner's run that took them all the way down to the Prospector Express lift. They got on the lift and started the ride back up.

"So, what do you think?" asked Emily.

"I love powder!" Hannah screamed, pure joy in her voice.

"Me, too."

The reality was that Emily was pretty worn out already. Skiing on one leg, holding the other leg up in the air, fighting the weight of a boot tugging it down, and guiding a novice skier, all at the same time, was a challenge. But Emily was always up for a challenge, especially when the reward was giving a child the thrill of doing something that very few people, of any ability, get to experience. Emily also believed that the confidence their time together would cultivate in Hannah would be even more beneficial to her in other aspects of her life.

"Want to do another run in the powder?" asked Emily.

"Yessss!!!" squealed Hannah.

They completed another run, down Stagecoach this time, then rode the Pioneer Express lift up and slowly worked their way back to the Winter Park base area. They spotted Hannah's parents and made their way over to them. Hannah was shouting before they even got there.

"I skied powder! I skied powder!" she yelled. The smile on her face was a prize that Emily wished she could take home with her, keeping it forever on a shelf where she could look at it whenever she wished. A swell of emotion rolled up inside her. She worked hard to maintain her composure, but a few tears leaked from her eyes.

"She was awesome," said Emily. "*So* awesome."

Both parents hugged and thanked Emily. She said her goodbyes, finishing up with a long embrace of Hannah. She turned away quickly and made her way back toward the NSCD office, tears flowing fully down her face.

Chapter 5

Emily's shift at the Oasis in the Cold began at 6 p.m. and would end at 2 a.m. The Oasis was located in Fraser, the next town over from Winter Park, and was several blocks off Route 40, the main drag. Because it was more remote than most bars and because a lot of locals lived in Fraser, where the rent was less expensive than Winter Park itself, the Oasis was primarily a locals' bar.

Emily lived in a tiny studio in Fraser, which was fine with her. It was warm, and warmth was the number one priority in Fraser, which had been documented by the weather service to be the coldest incorporated town in the lower 48 states. Fraser was as cold as towns in northern Alaska, which was saying something. Temperatures in Fraser at night were below 32 degrees Fahrenheit more than 300 nights per year. They were below zero 79 nights a year. It was common to experience nights at 30 below, and there had been a few instances in Fraser's history when the temperature had dropped to lower than 50 below in December and January. All the locals understood that you had to prepare for the cold and respect it. They kept sub-zero sleeping bags in their cars in the event they had a breakdown on a cold night, and they dressed properly for the cold, in lots of layers.

The afternoon had been melancholy for Emily. When she had left Hannah and her parents earlier in the day, she'd experienced mixed emotions. The tears she had shed were multifaceted. Without question, the predominant emotion was an outpouring of sheer joy for the happiness she'd brought to Hannah *and* for the lessons conveyed, not only about skiing, but about making your way through life as a disabled person.

But the tears were also a manifestation of great sadness because Emily knew how hard life was for a person like Hannah, *and* her family. Emily wished more than anything that the world would be more understanding and supportive of people like her and Hannah.

And then there was the regret and anger of what had happened to her when she was 11, a transformational event that could have been avoided if Emily had been more cautious. But that was not her way. Risk-taking seemed to be in her blood, and even though it had cost her a hand when she was 11, she refused to let her loss change who she was after she recovered from her accident.

Emily had been fortunate to stumble upon Winter Park and the NSCD. She'd developed a wonderful support system way up here in the mountains, with many close friends, and her volunteer work was the most rewarding thing she'd ever done. But she feared it wouldn't last. Hers was a restless soul, always seeking more. She didn't understand why it was so hard for her to be content, and this continuously frustrated her.

Normally, Emily wore no makeup and dressed practically, for comfort and for warmth. That afternoon, however, she had chosen her outfit more for looks than for comfort, and she spent some time applying a little eye liner and lipstick. Even though it was still late-February, she decided to wear a spring dress to work. It was an off-white cotton fabric that hung loosely on her body, coming down to mid-calf, with short sleeves that had a folded-over hem. Her cowboy boots, once she put them on at the door, would come up all the way to the bottom hem of the dress.

Emily lived a five-minute walk from the Oasis, and if she drove, which she would do tonight, it took only a minute or two to get there. Plus, she owned a long, down coat that would cover her legs when she was outside. And she wasn't worried about getting cold at work because the owner always kept the place really warm. But she'd never worn a dress to work, and she wondered if anyone would notice.

Emily never made any attempt to disguise the fact that she was missing a hand. It was part of who she was. And she had many attributes of an attractive person. She was 5 feet 7 inches tall, with a shapely, muscular body, and sparkling blue eyes. She kept her dark hair short to avoid the hassle of putting her hair up or in a ponytail, with only one hand to do it with. Her hair curled forward just above her shoulders, and it had a natural shine to it.

Emily was aware that some men, *and* women, were attracted to her, in spite of her obvious deformity, but she always deflected the advances of others. On the outside, she was a talented, confident person, with a lot to give to the world. But somewhere deep inside, she felt shame and embarrassment about her missing hand.

Emily arrived at the Oasis right on time at 6 p.m. Her partner behind the bar that night was Russ Temple. Russ lifted weights and was well built. He also liked to ski, as did most people who lived in Fraser. He was dressed in a flannel shirt and jeans, which was what Emily normally wore as well. When he saw her, he didn't hesitate to comment.

"Whoa! What gives?" he asked, raising his eyebrows.

"I don't know what you're talking about," she replied.

"I wish you'd dress like that every night. Our tips would double!"

Russ was a good bartender, but he *really* didn't understand people, especially women.

"I'll make a deal with you," said Emily. "You wear a tight shirt that shows off your big biceps, and I'll wear this every night, okay? After all, we're a team, right? We both need to pitch in."

Russ got the point.

"My bad," he said. "I should have just said you look nice, which you do."

"No worries," said Emily, smiling. "We're good. Thanks for the compliment."

Emily got ready to work. It was a Tuesday, so the crowd wasn't too bad, but there *were* a healthy number of "après-ski" customers, most of them locals, swapping stories of the powder they'd found in places that others wouldn't even think to look. The Oasis was a medium-sized establishment, bordering on small, seating about 50 people, with a bar that had stools for a dozen patrons.

The door to the bar opened, and Emily watched her best friend, Woha, enter. Woha was a Native American from the Cherokee Nation. He was 6 feet 2 inches tall and had long, straight, jet-black hair. His skin was a warm brown, and he had a wide nose and medium-sized lips. He was one of the most attractive men Emily had ever known.

The two had become friends when they met at a film class at CU in Boulder. Emily was a cinema studies major, while Woha was just taking the class for an art requirement, but they both enjoyed the class because it focused on the golden years of cinema, back in the '30s, '40s and '50s. They learned how films were made and shown and were amazed at how tedious it had been compared to today's digital technology, yet the films produced back then were exceptional. Emily and Woha had watched *The Wizard of Oz*, *Citizen Kane* and *Casablanca* dozens of times over the years.

Woha ambled over and took a seat at the bar, looking over at his best friend.

"Yo," he said. "Good powder today?"

"The best," she replied. "What'll it be tonight, dude? Club soda?"

Emily was still angry with Woha for what had happened the past Saturday night. Woha was normally a gentle, philosophical person, deeply spiritual in many ways, but every now and then, he drank more than he should. Woha was an angry drunk, and this sometimes led to altercations. *That* is what had occurred last Saturday night. If Emily hadn't gotten in the middle of it and somehow reasoned with Woha through his drunken haze, it could have gotten ugly. The owner of the bar wanted to ban Woha, but Emily had talked him out of it. And it hadn't been the first time.

"I'll have a Coors," said Woha, ignoring her slight.

Emily turned around, grabbed a beer mug off the shelf with her left hand, held the mug under the Coors tap, pulled the tap forward with her right arm, waited for the beer to fill the mug, then shut off the tap. She set the beer on the bar in front of Woha.

"How was work today?" asked Emily.

"Sucked," he said. "Spent more time shoveling snow off lumber than pounding nails."

Woha had become a carpenter's helper when he and Emily moved up to the area after graduating from CU nearly four years ago. Because of the shortage of help for outdoor work up in the mountains, it didn't take long for him to become a full-fledged carpenter. Now he had his own crew. They built mostly condos and single-family homes, which seemed to be in endless demand as the popularity of the resort continued to grow.

"What's the occasion by the way?" asked Woha, gesturing to Emily's dress and makeup.

"Just needed a change of pace, that's all," she said.

Woha crinkled his lips.

"What's the matter?" he asked.

Woha was probably the only person who knew Emily well enough to understand that Emily dressing up meant something could be amiss with her. He was also well-qualified to help her sort through it. Woha might have a drinking problem, but he was still a man of great wisdom, and Emily often relied on him to help her wrestle with difficult subjects in her life.

"I'm not completely sure," she said. "But I think I need a change."

"What kind of change?" Woha had a concerned look on his face.

"I think I need to try something new," she said.

"Why?"

"I'm not sure. I just have this feeling."

"Where did this come from?"

"Not sure. I gave a lesson today to a little girl with only one leg, and I was really happy, but also sad. I've been working with Hannah all winter, and we talk about a lot of things. I want to teach her that she can do *anything*—that she doesn't have to limit her choices because of her disability."

"Makes sense. But what's that got to do with you wanting to make a change?"

"It got me thinking that I should do more, I guess. What do you think?"

Woha took a deep pull from his beer, then set the mug down. He looked up from his beer and stared directly at Emily. His gentle, brown eyes conveyed a sense of peace as he entered what Emily liked to call his "philosophical mode." His placid gaze captured her full attention.

"My people believe in balance," he said. "We believe that all living things—plants, animals, people—have an intelligent spirit, and that they *all* make important contributions to the balance of the world."

Woha had come to CU directly from the Cherokee Nation in Tahlequah, Oklahoma, where many of their nearly 400,000 members still lived. The Cherokee people had originally lived in the southeastern United States, and some tribes still did, but the seat of government for the Cherokee Nation had been established in Tahlequah in 1839, not long after many Cherokee were relocated as part of the Indian Removal Act.

The Cherokee Nation government worked hard to preserve the old ways, and Woha's family was very respectful of this. Woha's full given name was "Wohali," which means *eagle*. The eagle is a sacred symbol in Cherokee culture, and great things were expected of anyone who was given that name. There were expectations back home that Woha would go to college for an education, then return home and work his way up in the Cherokee Nation government. Woha had chosen not to return, for now, and he bore the weight of his people's expectations unsteadily.

"You know well that I have not yet achieved balance," he said. "But one day, I will. It is my destiny. As for you, I have believed since we came up here that this was a place of true balance for you, that you had found your own unique way to contribute to the world. So, I must admit, I'm surprised to hear you say this thing."

"I know. I'm surprised, too. But let me ask you this: Isn't it also accepted in your culture that people will sometimes go out into the world in search of their destiny before returning to the tribe and fulfilling their responsibilities?"

"Of course," he said. "You know this. You know that is what I'm doing right now, and you're also aware that my time here is short because it is clear to me now that my destiny is with my people."

"I know," she said weakly, not wanting to think about a life without her best friend. "But from what you said, it's okay for me to go out and seek a new destiny if that is what I'm called to do."

"Yes, of course," said Woha. "All I've said is that I'm surprised you would do this because it seems you've already achieved the balance in your life that all humans seek."

"Maybe," she said. "But if I leave this place after the season, will you be okay? What will you do?" Emily already knew the answer to this question. She knew that Woha loved her and that he'd always wanted more than friendship with her, but she had never been able to take that step. She wasn't sure if it was because of her insecurities about intimacy or because he wasn't the right partner for her, but she was steadfast in her refusal to let their relationship go in that direction. He had accepted this.

Woha picked up the mug and drained his beer.

"Of course, you know the answer, but if hearing it helps you in some way, then I will say it. If you leave, the time for me to return to my people will have arrived," he said. "On a less serious subject, may I please have another beer? I promise, I will have only one or two more."

"Your wisdom has earned you a beer or two, my friend."

Emily always appreciated Woha's counsel and often ended up following his advice. But as the evening dragged on, she couldn't shake the feeling that she needed to make a change. She decided to wait and see how she felt at the end of the winter season.

Chapter 6
Late April 2010

Emily picked up the Sunday *Denver Post* she'd purchased at the local convenience store. It was a thick paper, but the part she wanted to look at was the classified ads. Her feeling about making a change had not dissipated. On the contrary, it had blossomed into a roughly construed plan.

Emily was thinking about applying for a job in the Denver area to give life in the "real world" a try. The winter season was over, and Emily's apartment lease was expiring at the end of the month. If she was going to make a change, this was the time to do it. As she fumbled through the pages looking for the job listings, an ad in the merchandise section caught her eye. It read:

Projector for Sale. Brenkert BX-60 in perfect working condition. Manufactured in 1951 and used in the famous but now closed Palladium Movie House in downtown Denver. This projector is one of a kind. Serious calls only please. 303.212.8602.

Emily was mildly intrigued. She had learned all about the Brenkert Light Projection Company in her History of

Cinema class at CU. What fascinated her most was the concept of "moving pictures," which is what film was called long ago, because that is exactly what film is. It's a series of still shots that are moved by the projector to create movement on the screen. The BX-60 had been a workhorse in movie theatres in the 1950s, but as the use of television had spread, theaters closed in droves, and the use of the machines eventually died out. She knew that many projectors like the BX-60 were now museum pieces, but she'd never seen one that was still in "perfect" working condition.

She noticed the price of the machine wasn't listed but knew from school that projectors like this ranged from $3,000 to $10,000, depending on their condition. She'd saved a lot of money over the past four years. Her tips at the bar ranged from around $200 on weeknights up to $500 on Friday and Saturday nights. But she wasn't sure she wanted to invest in a machine that would be more of a toy as opposed to something productive.

But Emily wanted to see the machine *actually* work. In her classes at CU, she'd seen recordings of old films, but she had never experienced a film played by the projector itself. She thought this might be a chance to do that but decided not to call about the projector until she'd arranged for a job interview or two down in Denver.

By 2010, Denver had developed into a diverse metropolitan economy and was already in a strong recovery after the recession of 2008–2009. Jobs were plentiful, and there were many listings in the classifieds. Emily was looking to expand on her work helping disabled people, and there were several opportunities in the paper.

When Emily thought more deeply about her job search, however, she realized that her contacts at NSCD would be an outstanding networking opportunity. She made some calls, and one of her contacts suggested she apply for a client coordinator position in the Denver office. The job would allow her to speak directly with families looking to enroll their children in the program. Emily's experience in the field working with actual participants would be invaluable in this role, so she updated her resume, made the call to the person her contact had suggested, and was promptly scheduled for an interview this Friday. With her preliminary goal of arranging an interview met, Emily dialed the number on the Projector for Sale ad.

A man answered the phone.

"Fred Watts here. Are you calling about the projector?" The man's voice sounded like he was an older person. It was high pitched and a little crackly, not as smooth as a young person's voice.

"Why, yes, I am," she responded.

"Why are you interested in it?" he asked.

"I was a cinema studies major at the University of Colorado in Boulder."

"Oh, okay. And you know what these machines cost, right?"

"Yes. How much is your machine?" she asked.

"I'm flexible on price," he said.

"Oh, okay, good."

"What do you do for a living?" he asked.

"I'm a bartender up in the Winter Park area."

"You're a ski bum then?"

"Hardly a bum, sir, but I *do* love to ski. In fact, I'm an instructor as well, but I make a good living."

"And you love the mountains, right?"

"Yes, but why does that matter?"

"Doesn't matter," said the old man. "When do you want to come and see the machine?"

"I was thinking this Friday afternoon if that would work for you."

"Around two in the afternoon, then?"

"Yes, that's fine. What's your address?"

"22 Maple Street in Edgewater. What's your name?"

"Emily Noland."

"I'll expect you at two." The line went dead. The man apparently had just hung up on her, before Emily could even ask his name.

Oh well, she thought. *He's old. I'll give him the benefit of the doubt.*

Chapter 7

Emily departed Fraser in her 1999 Jeep Cherokee on Friday morning. The car had 110,000 miles on it, but it still ran pretty well. Four-wheel drive was a necessity where Emily lived because the Fraser Valley received around 200 inches of snow nearly every year.

Emily turned onto Route 40 East and began the 90-minute drive to Denver. She passed Winter Park on her right and began the ascent up Berthoud Pass. Berthoud wasn't the steepest pass in Colorado, but it was one of the most treacherous, with numerous sharp-turn switchbacks on both sides of the pass. Even though it was the third week of April, Emily was relieved that there was no snow in the forecast. It often snowed in April, and one year there had been a big snow in June. *Whenever* it snowed, Berthoud Pass was a very scary place to drive. It was often closed during heavy storms, giving crews a chance to get it cleared without having to worry about oncoming or stranded vehicles.

Emily worked her way up to the 11,300-foot summit

of Berthoud, then weaved her way down, passing by the small town of Empire where a molybdenum mine was located. Emily knew a few people who worked at the mine who came into the Oasis regularly. They made good money, but being deep underground all day wasn't something she would be comfortable with. She passed by the mine entrance and was soon on I-70 East, cruising out of the mountains toward Denver.

Emily's interview at the NSCD office in Denver was at 11 a.m. She arrived on time and had a great interview. They offered her the job as a client coordinator on the spot. She told them she would let them know if she would accept their offer on Monday, found a place to have lunch, then drove over to Edgewater, a diverse community just west of downtown Denver. She found 22 Maple Street and pulled to the curb.

The house was a small, one-story ranch, on a lot that was only about a quarter of an acre. The house was gray and needed a paint job. A rectangular sign was staked in the front yard, close to the road. The sign was made of white-painted plywood mounted to a wooden stake. The sign had tilted quite a bit to the left, as if the stake hadn't been driven in well or the sign had been there for a long time. Emily figured it was probably the latter because the sign looked as worn out as the house.

The sign said, PROJECTOR FOR SALE in big, black, capital letters. In small letters at the bottom, it read, "Call for an appointment," and gave the same phone number that had been listed in the *Denver Post*.

Emily became nervous as she approached the rundown

house, but she *had* spoken on the phone to the old man. He seemed legit, so she continued up the sidewalk and climbed the two steps up to the front porch. Just as she was about to knock, the door opened, and the old man appeared. He had thinning white hair, and was tall and slender, though he was a little hunched over. He appeared to be in his late sixties. He was wearing a white, short-sleeved, collared shirt, with a pocket over his heart. An image of a projector was imprinted on the pocket.

"Hi, I'm Fred Watts," he said, extending his hand. "You must be Emily."

Emily extended her left hand, twisting it slightly so she could grip the man's right palm and gave her version of a firm handshake.

"Oh?" he said, looking at her right arm. "You bartend with only one hand?"

Emily was surprised that the man wasn't self-conscious about referring to her missing hand, as most people were, but this actually made her feel better about him. It was refreshing to meet someone who didn't dance around the subject, handling her with kid gloves.

"For sure," she said. "The key is to be really quick and precise with your motions. I can be just as fast as a bartender with two hands. And my right arm is not completely useless either."

"Interesting," said the old man. "Sounds like you don't shy away from a challenge."

"I try," said Emily.

"Well, you want to go see the projector?" he asked.

"Okay," said Emily. "If you'll just give me a second, I

need to call my boyfriend to tell him where I am. He's on his way over to meet me here now. We're going shopping over in Cherry Hill after this."

"Oh, really?" said the old man. "I guess you *do* have a lot of money saved." Cherry Hill was one of the more exclusive areas of Denver.

Emily held up her left index finger and stepped away from the porch, speaking quietly into the phone. She wasn't speaking to anyone, but she wanted the old man to believe that people knew where she was, just in case he wasn't what he claimed to be.

In addition, she had let Woha know the man's address so he would know where she was in the unlikely event that she didn't return. Woha had offered to take a day off and go with her, but she felt it wasn't necessary.

Emily pushed the "off" button on her phone and walked back up to the house. She put the phone in her left jacket pocket, keeping her hand in the pocket and grasping the pepper spray that was also in there.

"Okay, let's take a look," she said.

"Come on in," said Fred. "It's in the dining room."

Emily entered the home, noticing right away that the interior was furnished in a very spartan way. There was an old sofa and a single lounge chair in the living room, separated by a coffee table. There was no television or knickknacks, not even pictures on the wall. Emily followed Fred through the living room, into a small kitchen, then through a door in the kitchen that led to the dining room, which was in the back of the house. The curtains over the windows in the room were closed, presumably to allow for better viewing of the films.

The dining room was noticeably in much better condition than the rest of the house. She saw the projector sitting on a stand to the left of the entry door from the kitchen, pointing at a screen that had been set up on the other side of the room. There were six very comfortable-looking leather chairs in the room, arranged to allow the light from the projector to reach the screen, three to the left of center and three to the right.

"You want to take a look at the machine before we see what's playing today?" asked the old man.

"Sure," said Emily.

She approached the projector and noticed that it was in immaculate condition. It looked as if it was brand-new.

"This machine was used commercially?" she asked.

"Oh, yes," he said. "For many years, at the Palladium Movie House, before it closed."

"It looks new," she commented.

"Well, I fixed it up real nice," he said, a hint of pride in his voice. "You want to see it work?"

"Sure, what's playing?"

"Not sure," he replied. "I grabbed a small reel from the rack over there and loaded it up."

Emily glanced in the direction Fred was looking and saw a large rack that held dozens of film cases of varying sizes.

"Okay," said Emily. "I guess I should sit in one of these chairs?"

"Yep. Make yourself at home. I'll just dim the lights a little. Won't turn 'em off since you seem a little uncomfortable.

Understandable. But you'll be okay. I promise."

Emily walked over and took a seat in the chair on the far-left side of the front row, where she could keep an eye on Fred in her peripheral vision. The chair was extremely comfortable, and she immediately relaxed a bit, cautiously withdrawing her left hand from its grip around the pepper spray in her pocket.

Fred reached over to a dimmer switch on the wall behind the projector and turned the lights down a little, then he turned back to the projector and flicked a switch on the machine. It rattled to life, running through a few blank frames, then settled into the film. There were no credits and no sound, and the film was in black and white. The projection seemed a little grainy.

The scene that unfolded on the screen was of a man, wearing a hat that looked like a cowboy hat, gripping poles that looked like ski poles with his hands. The sun was shining brightly. The man was walking along a ridge that ran along the top of a beautiful, mountainous landscape. He had well-defined features and was a handsome man, around 30 years old. In the distance, the camera captured a view of a bay down below in a valley. The camera then panned back behind the man and filmed a dozen or so other people, dressed similarly to him and also equipped with poles, trailing behind him in a haphazard line. The camera caught a flock of sheep grazing off to the side of the path, seemingly unconcerned with the nearby humans. Suddenly, like a switch being flipped, the sky darkened, and it started to rain.

The scene then switched and showed the group coming out of the mountains and getting into a van that had a sign on the side that read "Hill and Town Walking Tours." The next scene was shot from inside the van as it entered a busy little town, with shops, pubs, and restaurants along the streets. In the distance was a large body of water, indicating this was a seaside village.

The next scene showed the van pulling up to a curb. The group exited the van and approached an inn with a sign above the door that read "Molly and Dan's B&B." The group entered the B&B. Just then, the film ran out, the loose end of the film making a slapping sound on the bottom reel as the machine continued to run. Fred turned off the machine, and the rotating reels came to a stop. He reached behind the projector again and turned the lights back up.

"What *was* that?" asked Emily.

"Don't know," said Fred.

"But it came from your rack over there, right?"

"Yep," he said. "Never seen that one before. People send me stuff like this all the time because they know I have a projector that can play it."

"But it's not a fully edited film," she said. "It's just some raw footage."

"Yep, that's what it looks like."

"Do you know where it was made?" she asked. "Even though it was black and white, the scenery was beautiful, and that town looked really interesting."

"Don't know," said Fred. "Could have been Ireland. I hear they do a lot of that kind of walking over there."

"When was the film made?"

"Don't know. Probably a long time ago. Most film reels

like this were."

"I'm not sure about that," said Emily. "Some of the cars on the street in the film looked pretty modern."

"Maybe so. Couldn't say."

"How much are you asking for this machine?"

"One million dollars," said Fred. "And I'll throw in the reels for *The Wizard of Oz* as well."

"You're joking, of course," she said, smiling.

"Nope, I'm serious."

Emily scrunched her lips into a scowl and got up, ready to leave.

"I thought you said you were flexible on the price," she said. "You implied you were ready to make a deal."

"I am," he said. "I'll be happy to give you a $10,000 discount and sell it to you for $990,000."

Anger rose up from Emily's gut. She stood, shaking her head in disgust, put her left hand into her pocket again and wrapped it tightly around the pepper spray, striding quickly toward the doorway to the kitchen.

"Thank you," she said. "But I don't have $990,000."

"No problem," said Fred. "But do me a favor, okay?"

"What?" she said, in a hurry to get out of there as soon as possible.

Fred reached into the pocket on his shirt and withdrew a business card, extending it toward her.

"Please, keep my card. Will you promise me you'll do that?"

"Why?" she said. "I wouldn't pay a million dollars for that machine even if I was a billionaire."

"Well, times change," said Fred. "I think you'll want to

come back someday, maybe not to buy the machine, but maybe just to see what's playing that day. Please take it."

"I don't want your card," said Emily, getting even more angry. "I won't be coming back." She strode into the kitchen, turned into the living room, and made her way to the front door.

Fred tried to keep up with her, unsuccessfully, so he called out to her. "If you change your mind, look for the ad in the *Denver Post*. You can get my phone number there, like you did this time. I'm sure you'll want to come back. Absolutely certain of it!"

Emily left the house, shaking her head. She got in her car and drove off, feeling her heart racing in her chest. She was angry that Fred seemed to have lured her there under false pretenses.

After a while, she settled down and began to process what had just happened. It was very confusing. Why would the old man go to the trouble of running an ad and showing the projector to people if he was going to charge a price no one would pay? There was simply no good answer for that. She wondered if Woha would have any thoughts on the matter and looked forward to speaking with him about it at the Oasis later.

She got on I-70 West and headed back up into the Rockies. She took the exit for I-40 and made her way up and over Berthoud Pass, dropping down into Fraser Valley. So far, the day had been a beautiful, partly sunny spring day in the mountains. Suddenly, like a switch being flipped, the sun went behind the clouds, and it started to rain.

Chapter 8

Over the weekend, Emily had to decide whether or not she should take the job at NSCD in Denver. It was a great opportunity to establish a career in a field she loved. It made perfect sense.

She had a shift Friday night, but Woha hadn't come in, which was odd because he came in literally every night she was on duty. She was worried for him but also frustrated that he wasn't there to counsel her regarding her pending decision. During her break, she called him.

"Whatcha doin'?" Emily asked.

"I'm home," Woha replied.

"Are you alone?" asked Emily, concerned. "Are you drinking?"

"Just a little," Woha said, but Emily could tell from his slurred voice that was not the case.

"Why are you drinking at home?" she asked.

"Just need to work through something personal, that's all. I'll talk to you about it tomorrow night, okay?"

"Okay," she said. "But don't go out. Please just stay

home."

"Don't worry. I'm not going out. I promise to come to see you tomorrow night."

They said their goodbyes, and Emily got back to work. As usual after a Friday night at the Oasis, Emily went to bed at 3 in the morning. She woke up around 11 a.m., remembering a dream from the night, which was something new. She normally didn't remember her dreams; in fact, she had *never* remembered them. The dream clearly had something to do with the film she had seen down in Denver, but it wasn't *exactly* the same. She saw the handsome man with the hat and walking poles leading a group of people down a path in the mountains, but these mountains were different from the ones in the film.

Even more confusing was that she saw herself *in* the line of people! She saw herself entering a B&B, although it was a different one from the one in the film. Another difference from the film is that she hadn't seen a van in her dream. She didn't understand why she would have that dream, or why she would remember it.

Emily shook her head to clear her mind. Her unfortunate experience with the projector man, Fred Watts, was in the past, and that's where she wanted it to stay. She wanted to be thinking only about the future, specifically, the wonderful opportunity that NSCD had offered her in Denver.

Saturday evening, Woha came into the bar and sat on a stool in front of her. He looked okay. There were no scrapes or bruises on his face, which meant he hadn't been fighting, and no sign of a hangover, which didn't mean much because Woha never really seemed to suffer from a heavy night of drinking. Emily handed him a mug of Coors.

"What's going on with you?" she asked.

"I'm leaving," he said.

Emily's heart sank. She knew Woha's departure was imminent, but she hadn't expected him to take any steps to leave until her *own* direction was finalized. Hearing him speak of it now felt like an anvil dropped on her toe.

"When?" she asked, trying to keep the panic she felt out of her voice.

"Tomorrow," he said. "I will return to my people."

"Why so quickly?" she asked, forcing herself to maintain her composure.

"It's my way," he said. "If I stay longer, I will doubt my decision."

"I see," she said, pressing her lips together in grim acceptance.

Woha didn't respond. The quiet was like a moment of silence in memory of someone who'd recently passed away. And that is how she felt. He gazed at her with his peaceful, brown eyes.

"I hope you always remember me," he said, his voice steady.

Emily wondered how he could stay so calm during such an emotional moment. She was fighting with all her strength to hold it together, and it took so much effort that she couldn't bring words to her lips. Woha filled the silence.

"I've arranged, with the help of my family, to be placed in a rehab facility near our home in the Cherokee Nation before I return permanently to my people."

"That's good," she said, the words coming stiffly from

her mouth.

"Don't worry, my friend. I'll be fine. This is my destiny."

"I know."

"You can help me in my transition by promising to stay in touch and visiting me when you can."

Emily didn't hesitate to reply. "I promise," she said, keeping her words short, concentrating hard to control her emotions. She refused to allow tears to escape from her eyes. She didn't want anyone, not even Woha, to see her cry.

Woha took a long pull from his beer and placed the mug gently back on the bar.

"That's my news," he said. "Now, what about you? What happened yesterday down in Denver?"

Emily composed herself, glanced over at Russ, her partner again behind the bar, raising her eyebrows to alert him that she needed some time. Russ nodded his head and smiled. He might not understand people too well, but it was obvious that something heavy was going down between Emily and Woha. Russ would handle the bar until they were finished.

"Well, a couple of things happened," Emily began. "First, I got the job offer from NSCD to be a client coordinator."

"Awesome," said Woha, raising his mug to her in congratulations, then taking another big pull.

"I have to decide by Monday if I'm going to take the job. I want to talk it through with you."

"Of course," he said. "But you mentioned a 'couple of things.' What was the second thing?"

"Well, I went to look at that film projector," she said.

"And?"

"The guy wanted a million dollars for it. And he was serious!"

"Wow, that must have been some projector."

"It was nice, but a machine like that is worth about 10 grand. So, either the guy was crazy, or something."

"Did he play a movie for you?" asked Woha. "One of our favorites?"

"He played some raw footage of a guy leading a group of people through the mountains on a hike. He said he thought it was Ireland."

"Hmmm."

"The projector was in great shape, but when he told me his price, I got really angry and walked out. Felt like the guy was wasting my time going over there and looking at his BX-60."

"I see," said Woha. "Anything else?"

"Not really," she said, pausing for a moment, deciding if she should reveal her dream. "Well, there *was* something, but it's weird."

"What?"

"I dreamed about the man hiking, but in my dream, I was one of the hikers following him."

"Ohhhh," he said. "I can tell you what to do about the job then."

"What?" she asked.

"Don't take it."

"Why? It's a great job! Exactly what I want for my future."

"I'll explain," he said, pausing to take another pull from his beer. "My people believe the world of dreams is just as real as the physical world. In fact, some of us believe that the physical world is all a dream as well."

"Oh, wow, you never told me that."

"You never told me about your dreams," he said, calmly.

"I guess that's true. Probably because I literally *never* remembered my dreams before."

"My people are taught from a young age to try to remember their dreams, to learn from them, and to aspire to achieve their dreams in the physical world, when it makes sense."

"But what makes sense about this? Are you saying I should pack up and go to Ireland?" she asked, incredulous.

"Yes," Woha said, "if you can confirm that's where your dream took place." He finished his beer and held the mug out to her for another.

Emily turned around quickly, poured him another beer, swung back around, and placed it in front of him.

"That's kind of crazy, don't you think?" she asked.

"Not to me. The signs are there that this is an important dream. You must go."

"Gosh," she said. "I never expected you to give me that advice. I definitely thought you'd tell me to take the job."

"It's not my decision to make," he said. "But I know that if it was me, I would go. Dreams like that are nothing to trifle with."

"Well, I guess I'll have to think about it," she said. "Thanks for that final piece of advice."

"Not final," he said. "Because you have promised to keep in touch, right?"

"My bad," she said. "Not final. For sure. Not final."

Emily had said the words, but the fact remained that Woha was leaving to fulfill his destiny. She envied his certainty while dreading that *her* life teetered toward increasing uncertainty. The dream of Ireland was the reason. Would there be more dreams? She hoped the answer was no, but she feared it might be yes.

Chapter 9

That night, Emily's dream contained events that hadn't been in the film at all, but they were obviously related. She saw herself getting off a train, being met at the station by the man from the film, and then getting into a smaller version of the van from the film. The van drove through the countryside and stopped in front of a long, white, beautiful B&B, with a sign on the front that read "Glenmalure Lodge." The man got out of the van and carried her bag inside, and she followed him in. That was the end of the dream.

On Sunday morning, Emily woke up, remembered the dream, then got out of bed to make coffee. Sitting at the small table in her studio, she sipped her coffee and went online on her laptop. She tried to remember what had been written on the side of the van in her dream. She remembered "Hill and Town Walking Tours." When Emily typed that into her browser, the website www.hillandtown.com came up as the first choice. She clicked on the link.

Hill and Town Walking Tours was indeed a real company in Ireland that arranged guided and self-guided walking tours. The concept of the self-guided tour was that you would walk from one town, through the hills and countryside of Ireland, until you got to the next town, where you then slept overnight in the B&B that the tour company had booked for you in advance. Each day, the tour company moved your luggage from the B&B you stayed in the night before to the B&B you'd be staying in that night.

"Your luggage will be waiting for you at your next stop," the website promised.

The B&Bs provided lodging and breakfast. Guests were on their own for dinner, although many B&Bs had their own restaurants, and if not, the website explained that nearby pubs served good Irish food.

Interesting concept, thought Emily. *But what should I do with this information?*

She briefly considered calling Fred to ask him some questions about the film. His number was still in her recent call list. But she remembered he'd acted as if he knew nothing about the film, so she concluded that would be a dead end.

But the strange dreams were really beginning to upset Emily. She didn't understand why she was having them, and was especially befuddled that she was remembering them, considering she had never remembered her dreams before.

I wonder if Fred knows more than he was saying, Emily thought. She pulled his number up from her recent call list and created a new contact: Fred Watts (Projector Man) in her iPhone. She wouldn't call him now, but she wanted to keep that option open for the future.

Emily decided to call Woha to tell him about her most recent dream and her web search.

Woha was already on the road, having left at 4 a.m. to begin the 12-hour drive to his hometown, Tahlequah, Oklahoma. But he answered his cell phone, listened to her update, and strongly encouraged her to book a tour with the company and turn her dream into reality.

Emily went back to the Hill and Town website and reviewed the tours they offered. They had tours all over Ireland, lasting from as few as 6 days to as many as 11 days. Emily searched for "Glenmalure Lodge" and found that it was in the county of Wicklow, in the eastern part of Ireland. She went back to the Hill and Town site and saw they offered both self-guided *and* guided tours of the Wicklow Way, the oldest walking trail in Ireland. She honed in on a six-day guided tour in early June, about five weeks away. When she checked the price, she thought it was pretty reasonable.

Emily almost clicked the "Book Tour" button, but then she hesitated. She still wasn't sure. It was all kind of crazy. She decided to wait a day, speak to NSCD on Monday about postponing her start date, and decide about the tour based on whether or not NSCD could accommodate her request.

On Monday, she called the NSCD office and accepted the job, under the condition that she delay her start date until July 1. They told her it wouldn't be a problem. As soon as Emily got off the phone, she turned on her computer, went to the Hill and Town site, signed up for the tour, and paid the deposit. Now she was committed. She made a plane reservation to Dublin and went to find her passport.

Emily was relieved that she could get the Ireland thing out of the way without compromising her career aspirations. And she needed to be moving forward. Now that Woha, her companion for the past seven years, was gone, she felt an emptiness inside that needed to be filled. Even though she had many friends up in the mountains, Woha was the only person she trusted completely. He was like family, more than family in some ways, and the ache of missing him had already taken hold in her heart.

For the first time in a long time, Emily felt very alone. But her lease was expiring at the end of April, only about a week away, so she decided to pack up her sparse belongings, clean up the apartment, and head back East to spend some time with her family. She waited until that evening to call her parents, hoping she'd catch both of them at home. Her mom answered the phone.

"Hello?" said her mom, who always answered the phone with a question, in typical New Englander fashion, seemingly put out by the intrusion. The family lived in a small rural town in the northwest corner of Connecticut.

"Hi, Mom. How are things?"

"Emily! Oh my, so good to hear from you! Is everything all right?"

Emily called home often, but her mother never failed to ask if she was okay to open the conversation.

"Yep, all is good. Lots of changes coming up though."

"Oh, really? Like what?"

"I've taken a job down in Denver with the NSCD. Client Coordinator. A dream job for me."

"Oh, my, that's great!" said her mom.

"Thanks, Mom. But the good news is that the job doesn't start until July 1, so I have some time to come home."

"Fantastic!"

"I have a vacation planned in Ireland for early June, but I'll have the whole month of May there with you guys."

"That's great!"

"Is Dad there?" Emily was well aware that her dad stayed many nights in the city in a small apartment he rented to minimize his commutes home.

"No, he's in the city."

When Emily and her older brother, Sam, were growing up, their dad had worked as a financial advisor for a small, successful local firm. He was always available to take them to practices and to come to recitals. He was a big supporter of Emily's desire to be just the same as everybody else. He strongly encouraged her to continue playing soccer after her accident, and she'd gone on to become a star player for the local high school.

Once Sam and Emily graduated from college and were on their own, their dad had sold his book of clients to a large firm based in New York City and now worked for them. Emily knew that the two-hour commute was a miserable affair and made for long days away from home. But now that he spent many nights at his city apartment, Emily was even more worried about her mother being alone so much.

"Is everything okay between you and Dad, Mom?"

"Why don't we talk about that when you get home, dear."

"All right," said Emily, even more concerned. "But you're okay, aren't you, Mom?"

"Oh, yes. I enjoy my new job working for the town, and I still have my volunteer work and more friends than I can keep up with, so I'm quite busy. Actually, I have to leave in a moment for a meeting. But I'm so glad to hear you'll be coming home!"

"I'll be home in about a week. I'll take my time getting there. I'd like to stop in to see a few friends along the way."

"Sounds great! Call us if you need anything."

"Will do, Mom. Love you."

"Love you, too."

Emily hung up the phone and finished packing, happy to be going home, but nervous about what she would learn when she got there and also anxious about the pending trip to Ireland.

Chapter 10
Early June 2010

Around noon on Saturday, June 5, Emily and her dad loaded her small rolling suitcase into the car and began the drive to Kennedy Airport. Emily's flight to Dublin on Aer Lingus was scheduled to depart at 5 p.m. It was normally around a two-hour drive from their home in Connecticut to Kennedy, so they would arrive in plenty of time, even if traffic interfered.

While Emily was growing up, her family traveled frequently on international trips out of Kennedy, so she wasn't nervous about the flight. What she *was* nervous about was what would transpire when she got to Ireland. The rationale for the trip was hardly sound. In essence, it was based on a strange film she'd seen in an old man's run-down house, and her subsequent dreams, which had been validated by a Native American's belief that dreams were real. Thinking about her trip in this way did not foster confidence in Emily, so she departed that train of thought and pursued a more meaningful undertaking: speaking to her father.

"So, Dad," she said, "are you 100 percent committed to

this new direction in your life?"

A month earlier, soon after Emily had arrived home, she'd been informed that her parents were getting divorced. They sold it as a mutually agreed decision that was the best direction for each of them, explaining that they'd had no difficulties working out a divorce agreement with the help of a mediator. All that remained was to file the documents with the court and make an appearance on July 1. It was not lost on Emily that her parents would officially begin a new era of their lives on the same day she would begin her new life in Denver, working at the NSCD.

"Well, Em, 100 percent is a tough bar to reach for any big decision in life. But I truly believe this is the right thing to do."

"I hear you, Dad. And it *does* seem like it's what you both want, right?"

"From my perspective, it's true. I can't speak for your mother's innermost feelings, although I *can* say I have yet to hear a word from her that indicates any reluctance or doubt on her part. It'll give us both a chance to pursue our individual interests, which have diverged over the years."

"Yeah, I guess." Emily had mixed emotions about her parents' divorce. She was happy for them, if what they were saying was true, but she wondered if she was at least partially responsible for the collapse of her parents' marriage. Her accident had occurred 14 years previously, but she remembered distinctly that things were never the same between her parents after that.

Emily's father was burdened with tremendous guilt regarding what he might have done to prevent Emily being injured, and her mother had done nothing to disavow that notion. In fact, on a few occasions Emily had heard her mother accuse her father of being responsible for Emily's accident. Here was yet another barb that stuck in Emily's heart that exacerbated the anger, and the guilt, over what she had done to herself and to her family.

"But hey, enough of that," said her dad. "You know our love for you won't change at all because of this. And speaking of *you*, you haven't really explained yet why hiking in Ireland is so important. And by yourself no less."

"I know I haven't, Dad. The logic behind the trip is, well, it's somewhat tenuous."

"How so?"

"Well, according to Woha, it's something I have to do to fulfill my destiny."

"Ah yes, Woha. How's he doing?"

Emily's parents had visited her in Winter Park several times during the past four years, both in the winter season and the summer season. Woha had joined them on many of their outings, and they'd all gotten to know each other well. Luckily, Woha had always been well behaved during his time with Emily's parents, meaning he hadn't had too much to drink and gotten into trouble.

"Woha is actually making some changes in his life as well," she said. "He's decided to go back to Oklahoma and take up his responsibilities within the Cherokee Nation."

"I see. What responsibilities does he have?"

"It was always the plan for him to work his way up in the Cherokee Nation government. He decided that he's ready to do that. He wants to help his people—not only his family, but his entire nation."

"Wow, that's a noble cause. Woha always struck me as a man of great integrity."

"He is. And great wisdom as well, at least that's what I believe."

"Hence your trip to Ireland."

"Yep. There's more to it than that, Dad, but at the very least, it should be a fun trip. It's a guided tour, so I won't be by myself."

Her father tightened up a little when she said this. Bill Noland was 55 years old, in good shape, with dark hair, graying at the temples. He had become a nervous man after Emily's accident and worried about things that wouldn't bother most parents. Emily guessed that her comment had triggered a small post-traumatic stress disorder (PTSD) reaction in her dad, bringing back memories of the accident.

Emily had always been an adventuresome person, and at age 11 her risk-taking nature changed her life and the lives of her family as well. After her physical recovery, Emily and her family participated in therapy sessions to help each of them heal, in their respective ways, from the incident. This included PTSD therapy for Emily and also for her father, who had been coming up the driveway as the accident happened. But her dad had never fully recovered, and while he wholeheartedly supported Emily in almost everything she did, he couldn't always hide his anxiety when subjects came up that might involve risk for Emily. The Ireland trip clearly fit into that category.

"I'm glad to hear that," said her dad, still a little tense, and the conversation came to a close. Emily felt terrible that her foolish behavior had so profoundly changed her father and hated to leave with him exhibiting these mild symptoms, but they had arrived at the airport.

Emily's father dropped her off at Terminal 5 at Kennedy, hugged her tightly, handed Emily her backpack, and told her to call if she needed him, no matter the time of day or night. Then he was gone, his car disappearing around a bend in the road.

Emily suddenly felt alone. A hollow feeling rose up in her gut. She didn't really want to go to Ireland, but she'd carved out the time for this trip and was hopeful it would result in a greater understanding of what her dreams meant. She drew in a deep breath, mustered some courage, and rolled her bag into the terminal.

Chapter 11

When the wheels of the Aer Lingus jet touched down at Dublin Airport five minutes ahead of schedule, the moderate bounce woke Emily from what felt like an all-too-short sleep. It was 4:55 a.m., Dublin time, on Sunday, June 6, meaning it was 11:55 p.m. on June 5 in the United States Eastern Standard Time Zone, from whence Emily had come. She was groggy, having just begun to sleep, but she had no choice but to get up and disembark from the plane.

Emily stood, pulled her backpack from the overhead bin, then filed out with the other passengers. She picked up her luggage in baggage claim, stopped at an ATM for some local currency, which was the euro, showed her passport in Immigration, and followed signs to ground transportation. It was only 5:45 a.m., meaning she had many hours to get where she'd been directed by the tour company to go.

The packet Emily received by mail explained that *this* tour was not a typical one for the Hill and Town Walking Tour company. In a usual *guided* tour, the company would send a van to the airport to pick up the people who had signed up for the tour. The van would drive the guests to the first B&B, and the walkers would operate out of that B&B for a period of days, making day hikes and circling back to the B&B until the time to change locations arrived. The van would then take the guests to the next B&B, and the process of day hikes would repeat itself. At the end of the tour, the van would return all the guests to Dublin Airport.

The literature explained that this guided tour would include some elements of a *self-guided* tour. In a self-guided tour, the tour participants would find their own transportation to the first B&B, using detailed instructions from the tour company. By definition, in a self-guided tour there was no tour guide, so the participants would walk on their own to each subsequent destination, using detailed maps and instructions provided by the tour operator. The six-day Wicklow Way tour was a hybrid in that there *would* be a guide, but he or she would meet the group at the train station in Rathdrum, then escort them to the nearby B&B where they would stay the first night. During the next four days, they would walk, accompanied by the guide, all the way back to Dublin, and on the morning of the final day, they would disperse to whatever activity or destination they had planned next.

The Hill and Town Walking Tour company was based in the western part of Ireland and did most of their guided tours in that region of the country. Apparently, they didn't have enough vans to spare for the eastern tours.

Emily was tired, so before she hailed a cab to take her

to the train station, as her instructions had explained, she wanted coffee. She found a coffee stand, purchased a large cup, and took a seat on a bench nearby. The coffee tasted quite good and was stronger than what she was used to. And *strong* was what she needed at that moment.

Emily sipped the coffee, then put the cup down on the bench and pulled out the instructions from the tour company. There was more than one way to get to Rathdrum, which was about 60 kilometers (37 miles) south of Dublin. Emily could hire a private taxi, but that option was costly, around 100 euros. A taxi to the Connolly train station in Dublin and the train fare itself would cost only around 40 euros. Emily was on a budget, so she'd opted for the less expensive, albeit less convenient, option.

Emily finished her coffee and walked across the street to a taxi queue. She noticed there was a light but steady drizzle coming down. She'd read that it rains a lot in Ireland, and her first encounter with the outdoors seemed to confirm that. It was also somewhat chilly, feeling as if the temperature was less than 60 degrees Fahrenheit.

Emily made her way up in the line, and when it was her turn, she stepped up beside a car that had a large yellow sign on top, with TAXI written in blue. She glanced down the line of taxis and noticed they were all different, the only common element being the large yellow sign on the top of the car. Emily was used to the more standardized yellow taxis in U.S. cities like New York, but her car seemed fine.

A man got out of the taxi from the right side of the vehicle, and Emily noticed that the steering wheel was on the right side as well.

"How ya doing this lovely morning?" asked the driver, reaching for Emily's rolling bag. "I'll just put this in the back for you."

"I can do it," said Emily, holding onto her bag.

"No trouble. I'll just have it then."

The man took the bag, popped the trunk, threw the bag in, then came back and opened the rear passenger door for Emily to get in. She removed her backpack, threw it onto the backseat, and ducked in. The man closed the door and got back into the driver's seat.

"Where can I take you?" asked the man. "Name's Murphy, by the way. Jack Murphy."

"Hi, I'm Emily," she said. "I'm going to Connolly Station."

"Oh, I see," said Jack. "You'll have a wee bit of a wait then."

"What do you mean?" asked Emily.

"Station doesn't open up till 10 on Sundays."

"Oh, my," she said. She looked at her phone and saw that it was not yet even 7 a.m. "Are there any cafes or restaurants near there where I can wait?"

"There's one or two might be open this time of day," he said. "We can have a look when we get closer."

"Okay, thank you, Mr. Murphy."

"Call me Jack, please."

"Very well, Jack. Are you from Dublin?"

"Lived here all m'life. How about you, miss? I take it you're a Yank?"

"Yes, I am," said Emily.

"Where abouts? I went to New York City once. Quite a

madhouse there, I'll tell ya."

"I'm from the state of Connecticut," she said. "Just north of New York City. Have you heard of it?"

"No, I've not heard of that. Sounds like a cat litter! How do you say it now? Connect a Cat, is it?" Jack smiled, as if he'd made a hilarious joke.

Emily saw him eyeing her through his rearview mirror, so she smiled. When he saw her grin, his eyes returned to the road. The taxi weaved its way out of the airport complex and merged onto a highway, traversing down the left side. Emily had been to England with her family and was familiar with cars driving on the left side of the road, but she hadn't really considered that might be the norm in Ireland as well.

The drive took less than half an hour, but Jack kept up the conversation the entire way, preventing Emily from getting the sleep she so desperately craved. He talked about sports she'd never heard of, like Gaelic football and hurling, politics, both international and local, and even his family. All in all, Jack seemed to be a very well-informed and friendly person, and Emily was grateful for that.

When they arrived in the area near Connolly Station, Emily noticed it was basically deserted, and not in the best condition. The buildings had a dark pallor to them, as if they had gone a long time without upkeep. Jack cruised past the station and then turned right up a small road. He pointed to a tiny restaurant on the left-hand side.

"Would you like to get out here?" Jack asked.

Emily looked at the place, which had the name "Tinley's" written on the side. She observed that Tinley's was fairly decrepit—and fairly empty.

"I don't think so," she said. "Maybe I'll just wait outside the station until it opens." She glanced at her watch and saw that it was only 7:20.

"Very will then," said Jack, getting the taxi moving again. He soon pulled up beside the station, got out of the car, removed her bag from the trunk, and set it on the sidewalk. "Best of luck to you!" he said, extending his right hand.

Emily reached out with her left hand and shook. She then gave him a 20 euro note to pay for the fare.

"Thank you, Jack. It was nice meeting you."

"And you as well! I hope your walk is just grand!" Jack got back into the taxi and drove away.

Chapter 12

Emily put on her backpack, pulled the hood of her jacket up, grabbed her rolling suitcase, and walked toward the entrance to Connolly Station. She tried the door and confirmed that it was locked. She noticed a couple sitting up against a wall, under the sheltering roof of a concrete overhang. The man and woman were about her age, dressed similarly to her, in jeans with rain-resistant jackets, with the hoods pulled up. She approached them.

"Good morning," she said. "Do you mind if I sit under here with you?"

"No problem," said the man, obviously an American, with a slight Southern accent.

Emily removed her backpack, slid down along the wall until she made contact with the concrete, then extended her legs out in front of her. "Where are you two from?"

"Richmond, Virginia," said the woman. "You?"

"Born and raised in Connecticut, but I've spent the past seven and a half years in Colorado."

"Oh, really," said the woman, seemingly intrigued. "My

name's Nancy, and this is Tim."

Emily wasn't close enough to shake hands.

"I'm Emily," she said. "Nice to meet you both."

"Where you headed?" asked Tim.

"Rathdrum. Going on a walking tour along the Wicklow Way."

"Well, that's a coincidence!" he said. "We're on that tour, too."

"Small world," said Emily.

"More like there are only so many ways to get to Rathdrum," said Nancy, rolling her eyes.

"Indeed," said Emily. "Were you on the Aer Lingus flight from New York?"

"No, we came in out of D.C. on United," said Tim.

"I see," she said. "Well, I suppose you're as exhausted as I am. What do you say we get some shut-eye? We'll have plenty of time to get to know each other over the next five or six days, right?"

"Good idea," said Nancy.

Emily set her phone alarm for 10 a.m. and tried to get comfortable. The next thing she remembered was her alarm going off. She woke up, stretched her arms, and looked over at Tim and Nancy. They were still sleeping soundly and apparently had not set their own alarms, nor had they heard hers. Emily got up and nudged them awake.

The three put on their backpacks and made their way into the station. They looked up at the big board, which listed the train departures and arrivals, and determined that the next train for Rathdrum left at 11:10 a.m. They bought one-way tickets, then spotted a café. Figuring they could get some food and coffee, they went in, sat down, and began to get to know each other as they ate and drank.

Emily noticed both Nancy and Tim furtively glancing at the end of the sleeve of her right jacket arm, at the spot where her right hand should be. This was something she was quite familiar with. Most people tried to avoid overtly staring and very rarely asked about her missing hand. Tim and Nancy fell into that category. But she didn't want anyone to be uncomfortable with her and was often proactive in helping people to overcome their anxieties surrounding her physical difference from them. So, Emily stood, removed her jacket, and unveiled her handless right arm, speaking as she sat back down.

"I lost my hand in an accident when I was 11," she said, giving them some time to process the information.

"Oh, my, I'm so sorry," said Nancy.

"Thank you," said Emily. "But there's no reason to be sorry. I've been able to live a normal life, and I do almost anything I want to do. I'm here, right? Just like you. A long way from home and getting ready for an adventure."

"Indeed, you are," said Tim. "I'm sorry if we were staring." Tim ran his hand through his tussled blond hair, starting to wake up a little.

"No worries," said Emily. "I'm used to it. The thing I hate most though is making people uncomfortable. I really hope you guys can come to know me as just a regular person and not worry about my missing hand."

"I'm there," said Tim. "I'm all good."

"Me, too," said Nancy, smiling.

"How did it happen?" asked Tim.

Emily winced. This was the *one* question she had difficulty answering. It sometimes set off PTSD episodes, which could range from a mild one, like what her father had experienced in the car ride to the airport, to very severe reactions that ended up with her fainting. Both Tim and Nancy noticed her reaction to the question.

"It's okay," said Nancy, her green eyes blazing at Tim, a frown on her face. "We don't need to talk about that."

"No," said Emily. "It's good for me to talk about it. I don't do it nearly enough. My accident happened outdoors, while I was climbing something I shouldn't have been climbing." Emily was afraid to say more because she didn't want to trigger a PTSD episode, but she also felt guilty that she'd been so forward in speaking about her injury and yet had not been able to provide all the details. "Is that enough of an explanation for now?" she asked, timidly.

"Definitely," said Tim, his face red with embarrassment. "I'm sorry to be so forward."

"No, no," said Emily. "It's what I prefer. I struggle with that *one* question, but thank you for asking. Like I said, it helps me to talk about it."

At 10:55, they boarded the train. It pulled away from the station around 11:15. Emily had traveled by train with her family throughout Germany, where they had vacationed a few times, and not once had a train departed late.

I suppose the Irish are a bit more casual than the Germans in regard to timeliness, she thought.

The train made its way out of Dublin and took a southerly route toward Rathdrum, making several stops along the way to deposit and pick up passengers. Every now and then, the train skirted along the Irish Sea, the body of water that separated Ireland and Northern Ireland from England, Scotland, and Wales.

The rainy mist had cleared, and the sun now shone brightly on the water. Emily took some shots with her phone, knowing they wouldn't adequately convey the beauty of the scene along the eastern shores of Ireland. She hoped the pictures would provide markers for her memory to re-create the feelings of excitement and anticipation that she was now feeling.

The train pulled to a stop at the tiny station in Rathdrum at around 12:45 in the afternoon. The three got off, and the train pulled away. There was a long metal building on the eastern side of the tracks that looked like a warehouse, and a square, three-story building that resembled a large house on the western side, but both looked closed. Emily, Nancy, and Tim walked up some stairs that led to an empty parking lot, as they had been directed by the tour company. The area was heavily forested in all directions, and Emily wondered what they would do if no one came for them.

"How do they know what time to pick us up?" she asked.

"Once we knew what train we'd be on, we texted our arrival time to the number they gave in the information packet," said Nancy. "They didn't respond, so I hope they got it."

"Me, too," said Emily, chastising herself for not being more proactive in arranging the pickup. She hadn't even seen the phone number when she scanned the packet, and this made her angry with herself.

The lot was empty, save for themselves. Suddenly, a small van appeared. It had "Hill and Town Walking Tours" printed on its side. Emily recognized it as the van from her second dream. Her heart beat faster. She began to get nervous, telling herself to calm down, that this was to be expected, but she was conflicted. Why would it be normal to *expect* to see a van that she'd only dreamed about?

The van pulled to a stop in the parking lot, and a man of about 30 years old got out. He had well-defined features and was very good looking. It was the man from the film. The man from her dreams. Emily kept telling herself this was inevitable, that it was why she'd come to Ireland: to see what her dreams led to. But seeing the man caused goosebumps to rise up on her skin, as if she were seeing a ghost. Her extremities began to tingle, and she felt the blood draining from her face.

Chapter 13

"Hello, I'm John O'Connor. I'm the owner of Hill and Town. Welcome to County Wicklow."

John reached out and shook the hand of the person closest to him, which was Tim.

"Tim Duncan," said Tim.

John then shook Nancy's hand.

"Nancy Deardorff," she said.

John then approached Emily, who'd been hanging back a bit, trying to calm down. John extended his hand to her. She tentatively reached out with her left hand, twisting it so it would make good contact with John's right hand. She spoke before her hand reached his.

"Emily Noland," she said, and then their hands touched. Emily felt a subtle vibration running up her arm, instantly spreading throughout her body. It wasn't painful, actually it was closer to euphoric, but nevertheless, it was disturbing. She pulled her hand back, perhaps a little more forcefully than she should have, and the surge abated. She recovered quickly, smiling at John and looking directly into his blue eyes. She noticed that his eyes were wide open, and the thought crossed her mind that he might have felt the same thing she'd just experienced.

"Well then," he said, clearly a little shaken. "The rest of your group is already at the inn, enjoying a few refreshments while they wait for the rooms to be made ready. Let me put your things in the back, and we'll be on our way to join them."

They all pitched in to load the van, then got in. The van was really a car that had a wide back for storage, with a squared-off hatchback door in the rear, two bucket seats up front, and a bench seat behind the front seats. Tim and Nancy got into the back and sat on the bench seat, which left the front passenger seat, on the left side of the vehicle, for Emily. She got in and buckled her seat belt, and John drove out of the station.

The van curled along on narrow country roads for around 15 minutes, then up ahead Emily saw a long, white building that looked familiar. Of course, it was the Glenmalure Lodge from her dream. She quietly shook her head, beginning to believe that Woha had been right about dreams being real. John pulled into the lot outside of the lodge.

Emily noticed there were several rectangular wooden tables with bench seats in front of the lodge, right beside the parking area. Most of the tables were full of smiling people of all ages. Children scurried about, playing tag or just skipping around playfully, and most of the adults nursed large glasses full of rich, golden ale or deep, brown stout.

The four got out of the van, and John spoke to them.

"You three must be exhausted. I'll move your things into the waiting area inside while you take a seat. I see an empty table for four right over there. I'll join ya soon."

While John unloaded their bags, the three made their way to the table, each collapsing onto the wooden benches. Emily was still sluggish and wanted more sleep, but she was also hungry and had a strong urge to try some of the golden ale the people around her were drinking. A woman came out of the pub, delivered some food and drink to another table, then came up to them. She put one menu on the table.

"Anythin' to drink while you check the menu?" asked the server, a pretty woman of about 40, dressed in jeans and a T-shirt that said *Glenmalure Lodge* on it.

Emily glanced at the next table and pointed to a glass of ale that a woman with very short, blonde hair was drinking. The glass was tall and wide, a full pint for sure, and it had an elegantly drawn "W" on its side, with the words "Wicklow Brewery" below the W and an illustration of what must have been hops below that. The beverage it contained was a golden brown, and it had a modest head of foam on it that looked good enough to eat.

"I'll have what she's having," said Emily, pointing at the woman's glass.

The woman at the other table noticed her pointing and heard what she'd said.

"Eeets fahn-tah-steek!" said the woman, her German accent obvious. She raised the glass and said "Prost," then took a large swig. Her two companions, both men, raised their glasses, repeated the word "Prost," and slugged their own ales down.

"I'll have that, too!" said Nancy.

"I'd like a Budweiser," said Tim.

"Forgive m'French lad," said the server, "but we doan serve tha' piss here. Sume pubs do, but naught this one."

Tim blushed, but he recovered quickly.

"Make it three of those then," he said, pointing at the woman's glass at the other table.

The server disappeared back into the pub just as John returned. He was carrying a glass of his own, a thick, dark stout in a tall pint glass that read *Guinness*.

"Our national beverage," he said, sitting down next to Emily.

Emily perked up at that point, remembering what had transpired between her and John when they first met. She became nervous and didn't know why, so she said nothing, simply smiling instead. John filled the void.

"I grew up not far from Glenmalure," he said. "The owners of this pub are close friends of m'family."

"Oh, wow," said Nancy. "Do you still live here?"

"Not anymore," said John. "I moved out west to start my own company about four years ago. I used to work in County Wicklow, for m'father and mother. They have an established tour company of their own, much larger than mine. But I wanted to be independent, so I went. Ireland is a small country, and all the tour companies offer walks all over the island. It was less than a four-hour drive for me to get here."

Emily was intrigued by John's independent streak,

which reminded her of her own need to be independent. He was about six feet tall, with broad shoulders, brownish red hair that came down over his ears and was a little bit long, a strong chin, high cheekbones, and those peaceful, ocean blue eyes. Even though she seemed to have something in common with John, she felt uncomfortable when she was near him. On the other hand, she felt foolish remaining mute, so she attempted to join the conversation as their drinks arrived.

"How did your parents feel about that?" she asked, sipping from her delicious ale.

"They were all for it," he said. "They have more business than they can 'andle. Fact of the matter is, some of the people on this walk are referrals from m'parents company."

"Where do you live in the west?" asked Emily.

"In the town of Dingle," said John. "It's a lively place, right on the north shore of Dingle Bay, which runs right out into the Atlantic. It's in the southwestern part of the country. Lots of good walking out that way. The West is the most beautiful part of Ireland, in my humble opinion."

John raised his glass.

"Now, for your first lesson in Irish."

The other three raised their glasses.

"Now repeat after me, 'Slawn-cha!'" he said, taking a long pull from his stout.

"Slawn-cha!" said the other three, in unison, drinking from their pints.

"Means *health*," he said. "And you doan want'a know how to spell it!"

They ordered food, continued to drink, and had a good

meal. The sun was shining, the ale was flowing, and the energy outside the Glenmalure Lodge in County Wicklow was pulsing on high. In spite of all this pure goodness, Emily was ready to pass out from exhaustion. She looked at her phone and saw that it was around 2:30 p.m.

"Any idea when our rooms will be ready?" she asked John.

"Oh, I'm sure they're ready b'now. You'll be wantin' a bit of a rest then?"

"Indeed," she said.

"Us, too," said Nancy.

"Well then, let's get you three inside and into your rooms."

They went inside, and the front desk manager gave them their keys. John warned them not to sleep too long, even if they were tired when they got up.

"Two hours at the most," he said. "If you do that, you'll have a chance of gettin' back to bed at a reasonable hour tonight."

Emily grabbed her suitcase and backpack, went upstairs, found her room, and didn't even bother to unpack. She set the alarm on her phone for 5 p.m. and fell into the bed, nearly asleep before her head hit the pillow.

Chapter 14

The alarm woke Emily out of a deep sleep. It took her a while to come out of it. And she didn't want to. She wanted more sleep. Much more. But she remembered other trips she'd taken to Europe with her family where she'd made the mistake John had warned them about, sleeping too much, and she knew intellectually that the best way to beat jet lag was to fight it early on. But it was still hard.

Emily forced herself up and out of the bed and made her way to the shower, stripping off her clothes on the way and jumping in. One of the things she'd found appealing about the tour was that all rooms were "en suite," meaning everyone got their own private bathroom. Without that, she probably wouldn't have come on the trip.

By the time Emily was soaking wet, she remembered that she hadn't unpacked her bags, so she got out, quickly dried off, darted over to her wheeled bag, and searched for her shampoo. Luckily, the room had been warmed by the afternoon sun, so she didn't get cold, even though she was naked and dripping wet. She found the shampoo, jumped back into the shower, and tried to wake up. Once clean, she exited the shower, feeling a little better, dried off, and applied a little makeup. She wasn't sure why she'd done that, but she speculated that it might have something to do with John. She was still quite wary of him because she wasn't sure if he was knowingly participating in some kind of bizarre plot in collaboration with the Projector Man, or if he was simply an unsuspecting party who was just doing his job. She felt from the brief time they'd been together that it was the latter, but she couldn't be sure.

The old man, Fred Watts, had seemed completely innocent as well, but why would he be so confident that she would want to return to see the projector again? Because that is exactly what she wanted to do—go back to Denver and get some answers!

Emily put on a clean pair of jeans and a white, short-sleeved collared shirt. Before she went downstairs, she took a moment to check on her phone to see if the hotel had Wi-Fi and found that it did. She found the password on a small paper card sitting on the bedstand beside the bed. From past experience, Emily had disabled the cellular data and roaming functions on her cell phone before the plane took off from Kennedy Airport. Otherwise, she could end up with a phone bill in the thousands of dollars when she returned home.

When the Wi-Fi connected, Emily checked her email, and a number of messages downloaded onto her phone. Most of them were spam, but she saw one from her father, asking if she'd arrived safely, which she responded to in the affirmative. She checked her Facebook profile and saw a private message from Woha asking for an update. She messaged him back, telling him that so far, her dreams were definitely playing out in the real world, but she skipped the details because she was in a rush to get downstairs. She grabbed her key and headed down to the pub. It was nearly 6 p.m.

When Emily entered the pub, she saw that it was quite crowded. She surveyed the surroundings and noticed that John was at a table with around 10 other people, presumably the group that would be walking the Wicklow Way together. She didn't see Nancy and Tim and assumed they were still sleeping, which would be a problem for them later.

The pub consisted of two connected rooms, and both were full. Emily looked behind the bar and saw a sign hanging from the back wall that read: ADVICE FOR MARRIED MEN. Never Laugh at Your Wife's Choices. You're ONE OF THEM. Emily smiled, beginning to get the feeling that the Irish had a unique sense of humor.

John had pushed three tables together to accommodate the entire group, and there were a few empty chairs at the far end of the table opposite from John. Emily took the seat at the end of the table, glad to have some distance from John. She noticed that everyone was staring at her right arm, except him. He was staring directly at her face. Their eyes locked, and another one of those mild electric surges pulsed through her body. John smiled at her and stood up.

"Well then, that was Emily who just sat down, from the States. I'll go round the table once more, and then we can order some food."

Emily noticed that most people already had drinks in front of them, indicating they'd been there for more than just a few minutes. John turned his head to his left to the person directly around the corner from him. It was the German woman with short hair, and beside her were the two men from her table that afternoon.

"This is Nadine, and beside her is her husband, Helmut. They're from Germany."

The couple smiled a greeting and raised their glasses, not in a toast, but as a way of saying "nice to meet you."

"Beside Helmut is Martin, from Austria."

Martin was about 30 years old with dark, unkempt hair. He smiled and lifted his glass a few inches off the table, nodding his head.

"Beside Martin are Babette and Paul, from France."

Babette had long, dark hair and was very pretty, about the same age as Emily. Paul looked a few years older and was tall, also with dark hair. The couple smiled, and John continued to move around the table.

"You just met Emily, and around the corner from her are Willem and Anna, from the Netherlands. They've done several tours with us in the past."

Willem and Anna looked to be in their mid-50s. Anna had short, blondish-gray hair, and Willem was completely bald. They both were very tanned, as if they'd just come from a vacation in the south, or else they spent a lot of time outside. They smiled and raised their glasses.

"And finally, we have Bev and Lee, from Australia."

Bev and Lee were women in their early 60s. Bev had short, gray hair, and Lee had mid-length, straight brown hair and a healthy complexion. They tipped their glasses and smiled.

John continued, "We're missing Nancy and Tim, from America, and I fear they will be up all night if they don't get out of bed soon! Now then, let's have a toast that the 13 of us have an enjoyable time over the next four days, walking the beautiful Wicklow Way!"

John raised his glass high and said, "Slawn-cha!" Emily had no glass to raise, but she would soon remedy that. She heard a few "Slawn-chas," a few "Prosts," and even a few "Cheers." John sat down just as the server came over and asked Emily if she'd like a drink. Emily asked for a glass of Sauvignon blanc and was pleased when the server turned away to fill the order rather than saying something like, "We doan serve that piss here." Her wine came quickly. She took a sip and found it delicious, with a burst of fruit flavor at the beginning and a smooth finish.

"Have you just arrived?" asked Anna, the Dutch woman.

"Earlier this morning, yes," said Emily. "And you?"

"We spent a few days in Dublin before coming down here," said Anna. Emily noticed that Anna spoke English with only a small hint of a foreign accent.

"How was that?" asked Emily.

"I think Willem enjoyed it more than I did. He loves history, so with things like the Book of Kells and Dublin Castle, he was in heaven. And he also loves Guinness Stout, so with the brewery tour there he got the absolute freshest stout you can buy."

Willem raised his glass of stout and said "Proost," similar to the German *Prost*, but not exactly the same.

"Vhat do you do for work?" asked Willem, his Dutch accent significantly more pronounced than Anna's.

"I've been a ski instructor and a bartender at Winter Park Resort in Colorado for the past four years," said Emily. "But I'm taking a new job in Denver when I get back."

"Vhat job is dat?" asked Willem.

"I'll be a client coordinator for the National Sports Center for the Disabled. I want to help people like myself."

"I don't understand," said Willem. "You do not seem disabled."

"Well, thank you," said Emily. She raised her right arm. "But I have a few challenges. Not as much as many people, but some."

"Yah," said Willem. "But you can use a walking pole. It vil help."

"You mean on the walk?" she asked, remembering seeing the people using the poles in the film and in her first dream. "Why do walking poles help so much?"

Anna said, "They're good for balance and rhythm, and sometimes, they help push you through difficult terrain. Most people use them on these tours. But Willem only uses one. If you would like to use his extra one, it would be fine."

"Why, thank you," said Emily. "Perhaps I will."

Anna turned to the French couple, Babette and Paul, and spoke to them in what appeared to be fluent French. The couple nodded. She then seamlessly switched to German and asked something of Martin, the Austrian. He nodded his head as well, then leaned toward Nadine and Helmut and said something in German, then looked back at Anna and nodded his head again.

"All the people on that side of the table use walking poles," said Anna. "My guess is that everyone here does."

"*We* certainly do," said Bev, one of the Australian women.

"I vil bring it for you in the morning," said Willem. "Othervize, I vould simply put it in my luggage." The luggage didn't come along on the walk. It would be transported by a service the tour company hired to move it to the next B&B.

"Thank you," said Emily. "That's very thoughtful of you. I'll give it a try."

Willem and Anna explained to Emily that they owned and operated a special kind of farm. All the workers at their farm were mentally challenged. The government paid most of the wages of the workers, and the couple explained that without that assistance, the farm would not make money. Emily was impressed and pleased that these two pleasant Dutch people made a living helping people less fortunate than themselves. Her desire to do the same thing created a bond between the three that would sustain itself for the entire trip—and beyond.

The group ordered dinner and continued to drink, heavily in some cases. There was still no sign of Tim and Nancy. Emily had baked salmon with citrus butter. Others had lamb, beef, chicken, or turkey, and Babette had vegetable spring rolls, the only non-meat dish on the menu. Martin from Austria had ham. The food was excellent, and very reasonably priced. As the meal came to a close, Nancy and Tim stumbled into the pub, looking very weary. John got up and guided them over to the table and introduced them to the group.

Around 8:30, the crowd began to thin. The older people, including the two Australian women and the Dutch couple, were the first to retire. Emily was very tired, but she knew she had to fight it as long as she could, so she hung in there. As time went by, the crowd thinned further until it was just her; the German couple, Nadine and Helmut, who both clearly liked to drink; and John, who was still nursing his first stout. The tables had been separated so other customers could get seats, and the four now sat around a single square table. Emily made a point of sitting directly across from John, staying as far away from him as she could. She was still very suspicious of him.

Nadine was an energetic, entertaining person, with a deep, melodious voice and a booming, engaging laugh that came at the end of her many hilarious stories. Nadine was only about 5 feet 2 inches tall and thin, but her voice and laugh were so deep and rich you would have thought they were coming from a much larger person. Helmut, a tall man with thinning dark hair, was more reserved, probably because his English was not nearly as good as Nadine's, but he kept up with her in the drinking category, as did Emily. She hadn't counted, but Emily figured she was on her sixth glass of wine, which meant she was into her second bottle. She could hold her alcohol, but considering the jet lag and the amount she'd imbibed, she was feeling a little tipsy, and she was worried she might embarrass herself.

In spite of Emily's heavy drinking, she was still uncomfortable with John. After one more drink, she excused herself and got up to leave. John looked her in the eye, as he always did, and she sensed a look of disappointment in his expression. She wondered why.

"We'll see you around 7:30 tomorrow morning then?" he asked.

"You bet," she replied. "Can't wait."

Emily left the room slowly, trying to remain steady on her feet and feeling more confused than ever. Even in her drunken state, she knew she'd have to overcome her fears and confront John as soon as possible. She couldn't confront the Projector Man until she returned to the States, so for the time being John was her best option for finding out what was going on.

Chapter 15

The exceptional amount of wine Emily had drunk the night before allowed her to sleep all the way until 6 a.m., which was an excellent result. The downside was a modest hangover. Emily was desperate for coffee, so she wandered down the stairs to the main floor of the B&B, saw that neither the pub nor the breakfast area was open, and reluctantly returned to her room. Back in her room, she spotted a note card that said, "Breakfast served at 7 a.m." She showered, removed her walking gear from her bag, and dressed for the day of walking. She was outfitted with light, water-resistant pants; two layers of T-shirts, one short-sleeved and the other long-sleeved; a light, water-proof jacket with a hood, and water-proof hiking boots. She would also have her backpack, which held a water bladder and other supplies.

Emily checked her phone and saw that more emails and texts had downloaded. She had a few minutes to kill before the breakfast area opened, so she responded to them, then went to her Facebook profile and private messaged Woha about meeting John at the train station, exactly as she'd seen in her dream, and telling him she intended to go back to the Projector Man as soon as she returned.

She packed her rolling bag, made sure the luggage tag provided by Hill and Town was attached to it, brought the bag down with her, and set it in the holding area just off the lobby, as she'd been instructed to do. It was only around 7:15, but several other suitcases were already there.

The breakfast area to the left of the small lobby was already full of people. Emily saw several members of their group, including John, who was holding court with the Australian women, Bev and Lee. Emily took a seat with Nadine and Helmut from Germany, just beside John and the Australian women's table. John smiled at her, and they exchanged "good mornings" as she sat. Emily resolved herself to stay calm when she was around John if she could. She breathed deeply and tried to relax.

"Guten morgen," said Nadine, smiling.

Helmut grinned and repeated the greeting.

"Good morning," said Emily. "Sleep well?"

"Like a log," said Nadine, her booming laugh welling up from inside her. Emily couldn't help but smile. Nadine's laugh was infectious.

"Me, too," said Emily. "The wine helped! What's for breakfast?"

"Full Irish breakfast, of course," said Nadine. "After all, vee *are* in Ireland, right?"

"What's a full Irish breakfast?" asked Emily.

"Bacon, sausage, tomato, egg, and somesing called black pudding," replied Nadine. "I'm not sure about dat one."

John heard Nadine's comment and leaned over from the adjacent table.

"It's blood sausage," he whispered. "Not for everyone."

The food arrived, looked very edible, and the three dug in, sipping coffee as they went along. Emily avoided the blood sausage, but Nadine and Helmut ate it, along with everything else on their plates.

After the group had finished eating their breakfast, John stood up and said a few words. "Make sure to leave your bags in the closet out near the lobby before we leave, with the luggage tag securely attached. And over there in the corner are the packed lunches. Be sure to take one. I believe you can choose a ham-and-cheese sandwich, an egg sandwich, and maybe a few other choices. They come with an apple and an energy bar. And bring a few liters of water as well. It will be a fairly long walk today. We'll meet outside at half past eight then, right?"

Everyone nodded, and John departed the breakfast area. Emily got up, made her way to the lobby, and went to find a place to fill the three-liter hydration bladder that was inside her pack. A hose came from the bladder with a valve on the end that Emily kept near her mouth, so she could drink without having to reach for a water bottle. Emily had purchased the bladder at the REI in West Hartford, Connecticut, and most of her other supplies as well, based on a packing list provided by Hill and Town.

Around 8:30, the 13 people gathered outside. It was overcast, with rain threatening, but according to some of the others, rain was always threatening, and while it came frequently, it did so in fits and starts. It would rain for five minutes, then not rain for half an hour, then rain for 10 minutes, in an ongoing, unpredictable cycle.

Emily noticed that Tim and Nancy were there, but their eyes were slits, from lack of sleep, no doubt. Willem from Holland approached Emily, holding out a walking pole.

"De pole," he said.

Emily reached out with her left hand and took the pole.

"Thank you," said Emily, an appreciative smile on her face.

"I adjust the height to make it fit you betta," said Willem. "Try it, and I vill tell you if it's good."

The top of the walking pole was similar to a ski pole. It had a molded grip at the top with indentations for each finger to wrap around and a leather strap to put a hand through. About halfway down the pole was a locking mechanism that allowed for height adjustment. For storage purposes, the bottom half could slide nearly all the way up into the upper half. A few inches from the bottom was a basket, which played a role in muddy conditions, Emily guessed. The very bottom was the tip, which Willem explained could be changed based on surface conditions. At the moment, there was a plastic cap with a flat bottom on the tip.

Emily held out her right arm and leaned the pole against it. She then slipped her left hand up through the strap and brought her hand down over the strap while securing her fingers around the grip. Her elbow was bent at more than a 90-degree angle, which seemed appropriate for walking.

"Perfect!" said Willem. "You are r-r-ready to go!"

"Awesome!" said Emily. "I really appreciate it, Willem."

Soon after that, John gave a quick speech to begin the walk.

"Well then. We now begin our trek on the Wicklow Way. As you probably know from our website and the packet you received from us, the Wicklow Way is the oldest waymarked trail in Ireland. It runs 132 kilometers, or 82 miles, for those of you not familiar with the metric system, from the town of Clonegal down south, all the way to Dublin proper. *Our* walk starts at around the halfway point, so we'll walk only around 70 kilometers, from here until we reach Dublin four days hence.

"By 'waymarked,' we mean that there are signs along the way that tell us where to go," John continued. "Now these are not large signs. They're quite small actually, and they take the form of what we call 'the little yellow man' and an arrow below him, pointing in the proper direction. It's quite easy to miss the little yellow man and get lost, so that's what I'm here for, mainly. For our self-guided tours, we provide you with detailed written instructions and maps to help you find your way. But if you don't pay close attention when you're self-guiding, it's fairly easy to miss a turn here and there. I'm sure some of you have done the self-guided tours before."

A few heads nodded, including the Dutch couple and the Australian women.

"Now then, today's walk is of medium length, around 17 kilometers or about 10½ miles. Just take your time, keep a steady pace, make sure to drink your fluids along the way, and let me know if you have any questions or need to stop for a rest. We've got all day to make this walk. It can be done in four to five hours, but we'll take our time and make it to Laragh in six or seven, depending on how much time we spend in Glendalough, which is a popular tourist site along the way. Any questions?"

No one said anything.

"Well then. Off we go."

Chapter 16

John strode out of the parking lot and onto the surfaced road, turned right, then turned right again at an intersection only 25 meters from the lodge. The road was still paved, but quite steep. People fell in behind John, staying mostly with their partners. Emily fell in alongside Martin, the only other "single" in the group.

"Hi," she said. "I don't know if you remember me, but I'm Emily."

"Martin," he said.

"You're from Austria, right?"

"Yes," he said, apparently not the most talkative sort.

"And what do you do back in Austria?" she asked.

"I'm a schoolteacher in a small village in the mountains."

"I see," she said. "So, you're used to walking the steep hills then."

"A bit," he said. "I've just come from the Camino Way in Spain."

"Oh, I've heard of that. It's quite long, isn't it?"

"Yes, about 800 kilometers long. I walked only for 10 days, so I didn't cover the entire distance." Emily noticed that Martin's English was excellent. He had a slight German accent, but not nearly as strong as Nadine's.

"What was it like?" she asked.

"A big party, mainly. Not nearly as civilized as this. You stay in hostels along the way. Pay five euros and sleep on the floor. Eat whatever food you come across. Drink like hell at night."

"Could be fun, in the right circumstances."

"It was good, but 10 days was all I could take. I'm not as young as I once was."

"How old *are* you?" she asked.

"Thirty-one," he said. "And you?"

"Twenty-five. Almost ready to start growing up."

"Yes, at some point we must. Sad, but true."

The conversation came to a close as the rain started. Martin threw up the hood of his rain jacket and continued on. Others had to stop to extract their rain hats from their packs. Emily had a rain hat, but she was wearing a rain jacket similar to Martin's, so she followed his lead and put up her hood. After five minutes, the rain stopped. Soon after that, the clouds blew off, and the sun broke through.

The group followed John and took a left off the paved road onto a gravel logging trail, still heading up hill. They traversed the logging trail for a mile or so, passing large stacks of felled timber along the way. Then John suddenly stopped in the middle of the road.

"We're lucky that it's cleared up right at the moment," he said. "It's not likely to last, but the timing is perfect."

John raised his left pole in the air and pointed to the south. "Over there, you will see the Glenmalure waterfall."

Emily looked in the direction John was pointing. She saw the valley down below. Flowing down from the top of the ridge on the other side of the valley was a thin, white sliver of water, flowing against a narrow gray background of rock, stretching all the way from the top of the ridge and cascading down and down toward the lush, green valley floor. A few people took out their phones and took pictures.

John turned and began walking up the trail again, and they all followed. After another mile or so, he stopped again.

"You'll notice the little yellow man up ahead is telling us to turn right," he said.

Emily peered ahead and caught a glimpse of the little yellow man sign. The sign was about 8 inches tall and 4 inches wide. It was mounted on the top of a black 4-inch-by-4-inch post that was around 3½ feet tall. Emily could see how the tiny sign would be easy to miss if you were daydreaming or in a conversation. In this case, the arrow below the man was pointing to the right.

John turned right at the sign, leaving the logging trail and walking up a very steep rock-laden path. The group followed, forming a single-file line because the rough, stone stairway was quite narrow. For the first time, Emily experienced the usefulness of the walking pole, using it to help push herself up the steep incline and to keep her balance. She could see how two poles would be even better, but that wasn't an option for her, so she remained content to have at least one pole.

When John reached the top of the steep rock path, he turned left, making room for all of the walkers to get themselves up onto the narrow, dirt trail he was standing on. He gave them all a minute to rest because many of them were struggling to get their breath. He maneuvered the valve of the hose from his water bladder to his mouth, pressed the valve, and drew deeply from it. The others noticed him doing this, and most of them made sure to get their own water, be it from a bladder or a bottle. Emily found that manipulating her own hose and valve was difficult with the pole in her hand, so she took her hand out of the pole and leaned it against her outstretched right arm, freeing her hand to get the water flowing into her mouth. She then put the pole back on. No one seemed to notice that it was more difficult for her to take water than people with two hands, and she was glad to avoid the sympathetic stares that often accompanied such small inconveniences.

Emily scanned the group and determined that the people who seemed to be suffering the most were Nadine and Helmut and Nancy and Tim. They were all bending over, drawing in ragged breaths. Emily felt fine. She was in tremendous shape, and her years at high altitude in Colorado were paying off in what was a relatively low altitude environment for her, but not for the others.

John started the human train moving again. The trail meandered along the slope of Mullacor Mountain, slowly weaving further up the hill. The composition of the trail soon changed from dirt to two side-by-side railroad ties, which John called a "boardwalk." The boardwalk continued up, passing through boggy fields that would have been difficult, if not impossible, to traverse without the man-made path of railroad ties they were on. Emily and the others had to concentrate to avoid stepping off the boardwalk, which might lead to a sprained ankle or another injury. An accident that limited a person's ability to walk would be highly inconvenient at this point because they were many miles in either direction from the civilized world.

Eventually, the boardwalk ended, and they arrived at the proverbial fork in the road, two paths that both led downward into the forest.

"We have a choice of taking the Red Route down, or staying on the Wicklow Way," said John. "Both trails end at Glendalough, which is the tourist site I mentioned earlier. The views from the Red Route are better, but the forests along the Wicklow Way have their own inherent beauty, and the trail is smooth and not quite as rigorous as the Red Route. A few of us seem a wee bit tired already, so we'll stay on the Wicklow Way. The good news is that we'll be heading downhill for quite a stretch now."

John forged ahead, staying on the Wicklow Way. The path they were on was actually a gravel road that traveled through a dense, evergreen forest, the trees brushing up tightly against the sides of the path. A little lower down, they entered the forest, which was generously adorned with bubbling brooks and clear pools, nestled below banks abundant with beautiful ferns. The trail became soft, padded with the brown pine needles that had fallen onto it. The forest was quiet, as still as the woods on a snowy evening in a Robert Frost poem, the only sounds the walkers' breathing and muffled footfalls. As they walked, all of them instinctively refrained from conversation, reveling instead in the silent beauty of the forest. Emily relaxed as if meditating, leaving all thoughts behind, just being. The calming presence of the forest merged with the beating hearts of the human beings, each of whom was emanating the same peaceful energy that Emily was feeling. *This is magical*, she thought. *I could live my life doing this.* And then the moment passed.

Eventually, the winding path flattened out, and they arrived at the floor of the Glendalough Valley. The further along they went, the more people they saw. Eventually, they came to a field of mowed, very green grass and saw signs for a visitors center. John stepped onto the field, walked about 50 meters into it, then came to a stop.

"For those of you who need the restrooms, they're just about 100 meters that way," said John, pointing with his pole. "We'll use this spot as our base of operations, have some lunch, wander around and take a look at the lakes and such, then regroup."

Emily removed her pack and laid it on the ground, then accompanied the people who needed the restrooms, noticing some tour buses parked in a lot not far away. She took care of business, then returned to the spot where she had left her backpack, where John and the others were gathered. She sat by her pack, fished out her lunch, and quickly munched it down. John had a few more things to say.

"There are two glacial lakes down here," he said. "Feel free to roam around, check out the lakes, and go into the visitors center, which includes a shop for gifts and mementos. We'll go as a group down to the Monastic City, which is along the trail we'll take to Laragh. Why don't we meet here around 1300, about an hour from now?"

The group dispersed, and soon only Emily and John were left sitting on the grass. The same uncomfortable feeling Emily seemed to always experience when she was close to John crept into her being, but she was determined to overcome it.

"So, you do these guided tours all year long?" she asked.

"Not really," he said. "We sometimes do custom tours for people in the winter months, but the vast majority of our tours take place in July and August, when people are on holiday. June and September are also good, but by late October, we're essentially shut down."

"I see," said Emily. "Well, it certainly is beautiful. But I'm not a fan of touristy places like this."

"Nor am I," he said. "And you won't be disappointed the rest of the way. The next tourist place we'll come upon is Enniskerry, and it's actually quite small and pleasant. It won't be until we reach Dublin itself that we'll come upon tourists again in these numbers. There's some tough hiking the day after tomorrow and the next. Tomorrow is a relatively easy day, although we'll spend more time on surfaced roads than what is ideal." John seemed to be rambling on and on, as if he was as nervous as her.

"Great!" she said, running out of things to say or ask while she tried to come up with a plan that might get her some answers. But John relieved her of that responsibility.

"Can I ask you something?" he asked. He was looking directly into her eyes, as he always did. She had yet to catch him staring at her right arm, and she'd gotten pretty good at spotting that over the years. John always locked his eyes firmly onto hers. His gaze was peaceful but layered with an intensity of emotion that seemed to linger just under the surface.

"Sure," she said, turning her head and pretending to watch something happening in the distance. She was nervous to hear his question.

"When we met, you seemed to recognize me. And you were surprised to see me. Am I right?"

"Well, I think I saw your picture on your website," she lied, stalling for time while deciding how to handle this subject. Her heart rate was increasing, and she tried to settle it down by breathing more slowly and deeply.

"It seemed more than that," he said. "It truly did."

Emily told herself there was no reason to hold back. After all, she was here to find the connection between the film and her dreams. John was the main character in the film *and* in her dreams, so it made sense to at least engage him in some way on the subject.

"It's true," she said. "This might seem odd, but I saw you in a film clip that I watched in Denver."

"Well, now! I'm a motion picture star then!" John said. He was smiling, acting as if what she said was a joke.

"I'm serious," she said. "Were you ever filmed, maybe as some kind of news show, or to help promote your business?"

"Never," he said, a look of confusion crossing over his face. "It's a strange thing."

"Sure is," she said. "I was completely stunned when you got out of that van in Rathdrum."

"I could see that," he said. "And as I said, the look on your face was that of someone who'd seen me before, and not just in a picture on a website."

Emily was uncertain what to say next. She was uncomfortable revealing her dreams to John at this point, so she had no basis for further discussion, other than the electricity between them when they shook hands, but that seemed too personal to bring up. As she pondered this, she noticed a few of the tour members coming back toward them, so she tried to bring the conversation to a close.

"Anyway, it *is* all a bit strange," she said. "Maybe we can talk about it again at some point."

"I hope we can," he said. "My view is there's more to be said."

Chapter 17

They made their way out of the park at Glendalough, stopping at the Monastic settlement along the way. This ancient site had been originally built in the sixth century by Saint Kevin, and several of the stone structures still remained. The most impressive was a circular stone tower that was about 100 feet tall.

According to John, the site had been developed into a full Monastic City during the 600-plus years it had operated, in spite of periodic raids by Vikings, many of which resulted in the deaths of the monks who lived there. The settlement was finally destroyed by the Normans in the year 1214 A.D., leaving only the scattered buildings behind.

Emily was left with the impression that Ireland was a much more ancient culture than she had first thought, far older than the United States. She wondered if the people of Ireland were wise because of all this history, hoping especially that John was a wise and honest man, which is what he appeared to be, although she was still confused regarding his role in her perplexing situation.

The group moved on, and after a few hours of walking in less pristine surroundings compared to what they'd experienced on the way to Glendalough, they arrived at Laragh. They would stay in two different B&Bs, neither of which was large enough to hold the entire group.

Both B&Bs were the homes of the owners, and neither had a pub or a dining hall, so all of the walkers met for dinner at a local restaurant, then most of them retired early, worn out from the first day of walking. Even Nadine and Helmut, the biggest partiers from the previous night, went to bed early. Only John and Emily remained at the restaurant, neither showing any sign of fatigue from the 17-kilometer walk that day. They moved over to the bar, ostensibly to continue the conversation they'd begun at lunch.

Emily ordered another glass of wine while John nursed the stout he'd ordered when they'd arrived. Emily was becoming a little more comfortable with John. He'd shown absolutely no signs of knowing anything about the film, and he hadn't become anxious at all when she brought it up. Emily could sense that he *was* interested in what she had to say, but she now realized it made no sense to withhold information from him, because there seemed to be nothing to lose. What harm would there be to discuss it with him, regardless of whether or not he had prior knowledge?

Emily noticed that even though they were sitting side by side at the bar, her heart rate hadn't increased noticeably, and she was breathing steadily. She wasn't nearly as nervous around him as she had been initially, and she hoped it was because she was intuitively sensing that he *really* was the honest, sensitive, caring man that he appeared to be.

"How old are you, John?" she asked.

"I'm 29," he said.

Emily was surprised that he didn't follow up with the obvious question, which would be to ask her how old she was.

"And you've lived in this Dingle place for four years?"

He nodded.

"Dingle's a funny name," she said. "What's it like?"

"It's become a big tourist town, but fishing is still an important part of the economy. We've got a famous dolphin that lives in Dingle Bay that the tourists want to see. His name's Fungie, and he's been hanging around for over 20 years now. He's very friendly and unafraid of people and boats."

"That's cute," she said, relaxing a little more. "And you say it's more beautiful in the West than here?"

"I think most would agree that's true, although by no means all. The West is rugged country. The walking trails are generally more challenging than what we're doing this week. The Kerry Way, for example, can be quite a challenge, depending on the weather."

"I'd like to try that one day," she said, surprised that she honestly felt that way at the moment.

John smiled.

"It would be a privilege to show you," he said. He paused and coughed once, clearing his throat. "I'm hopin' we can continue our conversation from earlier today, if you're willing."

Emily was prepared for this. She nodded her head, but she didn't say anything, wanting him to take the first stab at it. He readily complied.

"Well then, so when we left off, you were telling me that you'd seen me in some kind of film, back in Denver, I believe you said."

She nodded.

"And how did you come upon this film then?"

"I was looking at an old projector that was for sale. I studied cinema in college, and I find the old machines that made and showed the first movies fascinating. Anyway, the guy who owned the projector, a strange old man, showed me a short film that he claimed to have randomly selected from a big assortment of films he owned. And *you* were in the film."

"What was I doin' in the film?"

Emily was relieved that John was no longer resisting the idea that the film was real, so she plowed ahead.

"You were guiding a group through the mountains, at first. Then you and the group were in a busy little town, maybe it was Dingle, and I saw a big van with the name *Hill and Town Walking Tours* on it."

"And that's how you found us?"

"Yes, but there was more." Emily saw no reason to hold anything back at this point because she was anxious to figure things out, and John seemed to be genuinely unaware of what was going on, at least so far.

"Oh, was there now?" he asked.

"Yes. That night, I had a dream about the film, and the next night, I dreamed that we met at a train station, probably Rathdrum, and then I dreamed we went to Glenmalure Lodge."

"And you'd never seen nor heard of Rathdrum or Glenmalure before?"

"No. I never knew anything about *Ireland* before! When I Googled it, I found that your company is a real company and the Glenmalure Lodge is a real place in the Wicklow Mountains."

"So ya signed up for the Wicklow Way six-day tour then?"

"Yes. A friend, a person I trust, encouraged me to do it. So, I did."

"And here we are."

"Do you believe me, John? This afternoon you seemed, well, skeptical."

"What I believe is that you're an honest person, Emily. So, at the very least, I can say I believe that *you* believe what you're saying."

"But you think I'm crazy," she said.

"Not at all. I'm just saying that I was never filmed, to my knowledge, but you say you saw me in a film, so it's what we might call a leap of faith for me to say I completely believe in this film you saw. The dreams are another matter altogether."

"I understand," she said. "But you could have been filmed and not have been aware of it. Maybe someone from one of your groups filmed you and gave the reel to the man I met in Denver."

John scrunched his lips and briefly placed his right hand on his chin.

"Well, now, that *could* be," he said. "People in my group often take short videos with their phones. And I pay them no mind, so your point is well taken."

"Well, that's *something* then. But the projector that played the film was an antique. It played cellulose film on a reel. I know there are ways to digitize cellulose film, but I don't know how or why someone would convert a digital video into cellulose film."

"That's a subject for another day perhaps," said John. "But there's another subject, which is more personal, that we should probably discuss."

Emily stiffened. She had an idea of what was coming but didn't really want it to happen.

"Are you okay?" asked John.

"Yes, I'm fine," said Emily, obviously not completely fine.

"Look," said John. "We're just two people here, trying to make our way in the world as best we can. If there's a connection between us, then so be it. I'm not saying we should pursue it, mind you. What I'm trying to find out is if I'm crazy or not, mainly."

Emily was nervous about the direction the conversation was taking, but she was also intrigued. She wanted to know what John was feeling, but she was simply too shy to bring it up herself.

"Why would you say there's a connection between us?" she probed.

"Well, now, this film of yours connects us. And you say your dreams connect us. And then, our handshake at the station connected us, didn't it, or was that just me?"

Emily was silent. It was a moment of truth for her. Her entire adult life she had resisted any kind of physical intimacy, even something as minor as the "electric handshake" she and John had experienced. It was a barrier she had yet to break through, mostly because she'd been unwilling to try.

Emily's failure to speak caused John to react.

"I've gone too far with that," said John. "I apologize. I'll not speak of it again."

"No," said Emily. "I want to talk about it. It's just hard for me."

"Are you sure?" asked John. "Because I'm not at all comfortable speaking about it either. I've just never experienced anythin' like that."

"Me neither," she said.

"Well, then, that's a relief!" exclaimed John. "Now I know *I'm* not crazy."

"But you think I might be, right? Because of the story about the film and my dreams?"

"Not at all," he said. He put his glass to his mouth and drained the remaining stout from it. "But I *can* say that our discussion tonight merits another pint! Can I get you another wine?"

"Sure," she said, emptying what remained in her glass into her mouth.

Emily was relieved—not about the mystery surrounding the film, which continued to be unresolved, but because for the first time in her life she'd admitted to another human being that she'd experienced a physical connection with them. For *her*, this was progress—progress in an area she'd been stagnant in for her entire adult life. After they returned to their B&B, Emily laid in bed thinking. She wondered if an opportunity to build upon this progress would present itself, and if it did, what her response would be.

Chapter 18

"Today, we'll walk from Laragh to Roundwood," said John. "This walk will be our shortest day. Only 12 kilometers. About 7½ miles."

It was 10 a.m., and the group had gathered together in the center of the village of Laragh at the Glendalough Green. John had suggested they all get some extra rest that morning or just relax and enjoy the countryside, because the walk that day would be a short one.

"Much of the walk today will be on narrow, surfaced country roads," he continued. "Not all, but a good portion of it. So please remember to walk single file and give the alerts we discussed previously when vehicles are approaching. Now then, if there are no questions, we'll be off."

Led by John, they marched onto the surfaced road and walked north out of town. As instructed, they filed into a single line. The walking poles clicking on the pavement provided rhythm to the beginning of their day. People in the back yelled, "Car back!" when a vehicle approached from the rear, and people in the front yelled, "Car front!" when one approached from ahead.

After about a kilometer, they turned right and entered the forest, rejoining the Wicklow Way. The path took them gradually up, and after another kilometer, it leveled off and came out of the forest into an area that had been stripped of its trees by loggers. Ahead, Emily spotted something she hoped they wouldn't need to climb, but as they got closer, it became obvious that her hopes would be dashed.

John stopped at the structure, which crossed over a stone wall.

"This contraption is known as a *stile*. It allows us to cross over walls and fences without opening a gate, which most farmers keep chained shut."

The stile was essentially a ladder that rose to a small platform. On the other side of the platform was another ladder. You climbed up the ladder on one side, went across the platform, and went down the ladder on the other side. It was a simple procedure, except Emily had no intention of climbing the ladder, even though it was only four rungs up to the platform. Her heart rate was increasing rapidly, and she began sweating. Her mind slipped back, and she saw herself when she was 11, lying on the ground at the base of the rock ledge, the ladder on its side beside her. She began to panic, worried that if she didn't do something quickly, this could turn into a full-fledged PTSD episode.

Emily devised a plan and executed it quickly. While John was climbing the stile, she moved off the path and made her way to a section of the stone wall to the left of the stile. She hoisted herself up onto the wall, which was less than four feet tall, rolled over it, and dropped to the ground on the other side. She looked up and saw John standing on the path, looking at her with a perplexed expression on his face. As other members of the group came over the stile and onto the path on the other side, they also stared at Emily, wondering why she had climbed the wall rather than going up over the stile. Emily made her way back to the trail and walked up to John, putting her mouth up close to his ear.

"I'll explain later," she whispered.

John nodded his head, then started walking, swiveling his head around to speak to the group as he advanced forward.

"We'll encounter quite a few stiles in the coming days," he said. "Most of them are a bit taller than this one, and the next one is just up there. That will be the last one of the day, but there will be many others tomorrow and the next day."

Emily suspected John had made these comments specifically to give her advance notice that she would need to take further evasive actions. He raised his pole and pointed ahead at the stile, which crossed over a stone wall similar to the first one. He continued forward until he reached the stile and made his way over, glancing at Emily, who once again left the path and quickly scrambled over the stone wall. Once over the wall, her feet planted firmly on the other side, she felt relief, knowing that she wouldn't be seeing another stile that day. Her symptoms dissipated, and she casually rejoined the group, which had begun reassembling on the other side of the stile. They proceeded forward behind John and took a right on a laneway, which then joined with another surfaced road.

"Well then," said John. "This next section will be our

longest of the trip on a surfaced road. About 3.7 kilometers I'm afraid. It gets very narrow in some sections, so stay alert and keep each other informed about approaching vehicles."

Emily was relieved that the group was once again walking single file because this prevented any questions or conversations about her strange behavior crossing the stiles. She listened to the rhythmic clicking of all the walking poles making contact with the road surface, trying to relax her mind. This reminded her of the technique her hypnotist had employed when she worked with Emily on her fear of ladders. The hypnotist used to play a recording that made a ticking sound like a large clock, clicking away the seconds. The hypnotism never solved her problem, fear of ladders, but it was always relaxing to her to hear the tick-tock, tick-tock, tick-tock sound of the clock that the hypnotist always played during their sessions. She let the tapping of the poles flow into her ears and faded away into a zone no one but her could occupy.

An hour or so later, after emerging from a short jaunt in the forest and joining with yet another surfaced road, they came to one of the little yellow man signs. This one marked a right turn onto a path, with a sign beside it that said "Wicklow Way." John had a few things to say.

"This is where we'll rejoin the Wicklow Way tomorrow morning," he said. "When we do that, we'll have a lot of tough walking in the forests, hills, and fields. But unfortunately, that's tomorrow. Today, we have another three clicks on this surfaced road before we reach Roundwood. I suggest we stop here for lunch, then carry on to Roundwood. For those of you who want more walking, there's a nice 8-kilometer loop around the reservoir lake once we arrive in town."

John found a grassy area not far in from the entrance to Wicklow Way and settled down to eat his packed lunch. The rest of them did the same. Emily removed her pack, sat down, and grabbed her sandwich. She laid the sandwich on the ground in front of her and carefully unwrapped the foil with her left hand, then snagged the sandwich and took a big bite. While she was chewing, she glanced over at John, who was staring at her with a questioning look on his face. There was no opportunity to speak privately, but Emily knew she would have to reveal her secret to John in the near future.

After the quick meal, the walkers resumed their trek. They arrived in Roundwood around 2 p.m. They were staying at the Coach House, a B&B right in the center of town that had its own pub and restaurant. Surprisingly, the French couple, Babette and Paul, and the Australian women, Bev and Lee, decided to make the 8-kilometer walk around the lake. They departed immediately after checking in.

But first, John informed the group that the food and drink at the Coach House were excellent, and he also mentioned the Roundwood Inn across the street as a good alternative. He told them to meet at 8 a.m. the next morning for the long walk to Enniskerry, implying that everyone would be on their own that evening. He also mentioned that the Coach House did not provide packed lunches for the next day, but those were available for purchase at the convenience store on the other side of the main road, catty-corner to the Coach House. As people dispersed, John came up to Emily and whispered in her ear.

"Meet me up the road for dinner at Byrne and Woods, will you please?"

Emily didn't hesitate.

"Of course. What time?"

"Is half past five too early?" he asked. "I'm famished."

"No, that's fine," she said. "What was the name of the place?"

"Byrne and Woods."

"See you at 5:30 then," she said and left for her room.

Chapter 19

Byrne and Woods was about a five-minute walk from the Coach House. Emily got directions from the B&B front desk attendant. She walked up the main road, looking for the road sign for the R764 and a hardware store, where the attendant had told her to turn left. She thought she might have missed it, so she turned back to get her bearings and saw Anna and Willem a few hundred feet behind her. They appeared to be following her, but when they saw her looking, they came to an abrupt stop. Anna took Willem by the hand, and they crossed the road and went into the convenience store. Emily shrugged it off and turned back around, looking for the hardware store that was her landmark for turning left. She saw it up ahead and then the road sign appeared. She turned left onto the R764.

After a few hundred more feet, the restaurant was on her left. It was a pleasant stone building with a big sign out front. There were two entrances, one to the pub and the other to the restaurant. Emily peeked into the pub and didn't see John, so she went back out and then entered the restaurant. She saw him sitting at a table in the rear. While the pub had been crowded, the restaurant was nearly empty. As Emily approached the table, John stood up.

"I took the liberty of ordering you a Sauvignon blanc," he said, glancing down at the wine glass sitting on the table.

"Why, thank you," she said, taking a seat. John waited for her to be seated, then sat back down himself. She noticed that John had already begun drinking from his pint of stout. It appeared to be nearly half gone.

"Have you been here long?" she asked.

"About half an hour. Started over at the pub, then made m'way over here."

"I would've come earlier if that's what you preferred," she said.

"No, this is fine. I needed to relax a bit by m'self. Don't get much of that during these tours."

Emily recalled that when John was telling them about places they might eat, he hadn't mentioned Byrne and Woods. She wondered if he'd done that on purpose, so he could be alone, or more to the point, so he could be alone with her.

"I'm sure that's true," she said. "And here *I* am, adding more stress to your day."

"Now that's a good kind of stress, or so I'd like to believe."

"Until you find out why I don't like ladders, right?" she said.

"Depends on why you don't like them, I suppose. If it's because you once pushed a person off a ladder and killed them, then I might feel some stress. But if you fell off a ladder and badly hurt yourself, then I'd be fine, although I'd feel sadness for you."

"It's the second scenario," she said. "That's how I lost my hand."

"Well, then," he said. "I can work with that!"

He raised his glass in the air.

"Slawn-cha!"

Emily tipped her glass and repeated the word, then took a healthy sip of wine.

"So, you have a fear of ladders," said John. "I think we can fix that."

"I'm sorry to disappoint you," she said. "But everyone in the past who's tried to work with me on my fear of ladders has failed. Even a hypnotist failed, and she tried for years."

"I'll take that as a challenge then!" John smiled at her, gazing directly into her eyes.

"Why do you never look at my right arm?" she asked. "You're the only person I've ever met who I've never caught staring at the empty space there, where my hand should be."

"That's easy," he said. "Nothing there to see!"

Emily laughed, and John laughed along with her. Her intellectual side cautioned her to be careful, but it was impossible for her emotional side to deny that she was feeling much more at ease with John O'Connor, born and raised in Wicklow, now living in Dingle, in the beautiful little country called Ireland. In spite of her growing affection for John, she couldn't find any words that might help the two of them further explore the feelings between them, so she kept to more practical matters.

"So, you said there are going to be more of these stiles along the way, right?" she asked.

"Yes. Quite a few more. And not all of them will come with an easy alternative for getting to the other side, as was the case today. We're going to have to come up with a plan, Emily."

"Any ideas?" she asked.

"Is there a possibility you could simply climb over the stiles?"

"Anything is possible. But you might not want to deal with the consequences if I do."

"What would happen?"

"I have a thing called PTSD," explained Emily. "Post-traumatic stress disorder."

"Yes, I know of it. Many of the lads who come back from war have it."

"Yes, yes," she said, somewhat impatiently. "Everyone knows about them. But war veterans are only a small percentage of PTSD victims. Not to dimmish their service or their sacrifice, because what they've done is noble and the ones who have PTSD have it really bad in some cases, but many other victims of PTSD aren't treated with the same deference given to military veterans. Think of all the survivors of fires, floods, hurricanes, tornadoes, domestic abuse, sexual abuse, car crashes, and concussions from falls or athletic competitions. And think of all the first responders who become involved in all of those tragedies—the firefighters, police, EMTs, emergency department staff, and more. Not all people who experience trauma develop PTSD, but many more do than most people think. And each one of us has our own set of uncontrollable physiological reactions to our triggers. Our brains have been rewired and can never be fully wired back to the way they were before our trauma. When we experience a trigger, which for me is ladders, our bodies go out of control."

"I had no idea," he said. "I feel extremely uninformed on the subject. What kind of physiological reactions do you have when you see ladders?"

"My breathing rate and heart rate increase dramatically. I start sweating profusely. I feel unbearable fear. And then I faint."

"I'm glad that didn't happen today," he said. "But what about tomorrow?"

"I don't know," she said. "If you're saying there's no way other than the ladders to get to the other side of some of the fences, I just don't know what to do."

"But Emily, a stile is *not* a ladder."

"How do you mean?" she asked.

"First of all, a stile has steps, not rungs."

"Oh really? They certainly looked like rungs to me."

"Might that be because you were seeing something in your mind, rather than what was actually there?"

"Possibly," she said.

"I promise you; a stile does not have rungs. It has steps. A stile is a stairway: first, because it has steps. But also, because it's fixed in place. It's not meant to be moved like a ladder."

"Okay, I'll buy that. I'm sold, intellectually."

John finished his stout. Emily wondered if he was

drinking more quickly because of her, and what that meant if it were true. Was it a good thing or a bad thing?

"So, there we have it," said John. "Intellectually, you agree. Now we have to get you to *actually* agree."

"How do we do that?" she asked.

"Let's get some dinner, and then I'll show you," he said.

The two ate a fine meal. Emily had roast chicken with vegetables, and John had beef and potatoes. They talked mostly about Emily's experiences in the mountains of Colorado. John knew of the mountains, of course, but he'd never met anyone who'd actually lived high up in the Rockies. He said he'd very much like to go there one day, and Emily promised to take him.

Emily noticed that John had stopped drinking after he finished his first stout, and she wondered why. She was on her third glass of wine by the time they finished the meal.

"So, now are you going to tell me how you're attempting to get my full agreement that a stile is not a ladder?" she asked.

"Indeed, I am, m'lady," John said, as he paid the bill and then stood up.

"Thank you for dinner," she said. "I'll get the next one."

"I will look forward to that," he said. "Now, let's go back to the Coach House. I need to borrow a car."

"What? Why?"

"I'll explain on the way back."

Chapter 20

On the walk back to the Coach House, John explained that Ireland is much further north than even the most northerly parts of the continental United States. At a latitude of 53 degrees, it's as far up as the northern part of Newfoundland in Canada. This meant that during the summer months, it stayed light in Ireland much longer than it did in the continental U.S. During early June, it would remain light until around 11 p.m. He said this was relevant because it would give them time to go inspect a stile. He also disclosed that he knew the owners of the Coach House well and was certain they would loan him a car, which turned out to be the case. He told Emily she didn't need to change into her walking gear because the stile they were going to was only 250 meters off the road. While they were driving, John explained more.

"Do you remember when we passed by the little yellow man that I said was the marker to take us back to the Wicklow Way tomorrow morning?"

"Yes," she said.

"That's where we're going. And if you remember, it's only about 3 kilometers from here."

"Yes, I remember," she said, feeling a hollow spot in her stomach. While she had intellectually accepted that a stile was not a ladder, the reality of facing one soon was not a comforting thought.

They arrived at the point of entry to the Wicklow Way around 9 p.m. There seemed to be as much light in the sky as there was in the afternoon, but the light was somehow softer, quieter than it was earlier in the day. John drove the car into a small pull-off on the side of the road. They got out. John looked her straight in the eye.

"I know you've only known me a few days, Emily," he said. "But you seem like a perceptive sort, and I hope you would classify me as a trustworthy person. Am I right?"

"I want to trust you, John. And you *do* seem to be an honest person. But with the film and my dreams, I'm very confused."

"I can see that. So, let's just narrow the concept of trust to one thing. The stiles. You understand that I'm trying to help you with the stiles, don't you?"

"Of course," she said. "I'm just not sure you fully understand what you're dealing with."

"Indeed, I don't," he said. "But sometimes, a basic understanding is better than a detailed understanding."

"Possibly."

They walked the 250 meters, and Emily could see the stile in the distance. This one was a little taller than the two they'd passed over before, with five rungs to the platform instead of four. Her heart rate increased dramatically.

"They're not rungs, Emily. They're steps. Seriously."

Emily didn't respond, frozen in place, fear in her eyes.

"Let's walk back away from the stile, all right," said John.

John took her by the arm and walked with her back toward the road. When they'd reached a point where the stile could no longer be seen, he stopped, still holding her arm, and turned to face her. He was going to say something, but Emily put her hand to his lips to quiet him. With all the courage she had ever summoned, she stepped toward him, put her arms around him, and squeezed tightly. She pushed forward, pressed up against him, and kissed him, closing her eyes and trying not to remember that this was the first *real* kiss of her life. John hesitated.

"No, I want this," she whispered, pulling him to her.

"I do, too," he said. "But."

Again, she stopped him from talking, this time by pressing her lips to his. His will faltered, and he gave in, pushing back strongly, embracing her fully with his powerful arms. The mild electric surge from their first meeting became a strong current pulsing through her body. The kiss lasted a long time. They finally released each other, and the surge abated. Emily's mind cleared a little. She looked at John and saw that his head was down, and he had a frown on his face.

"I should not have done that," he said, slowly shaking his head from side to side.

"Why?" she asked, squeezing her eyes open and shut to continue waking up from the kiss.

"There's a strict, well-defined line that's not to be crossed with customers. I learned that from my parents.

They drilled it into me actually, me being young and single when I worked for them. Having a few pints and a few laughs is all fine; it's expected actually. But there's absolutely no intimate relations allowed with the customers, for any reason. None. And now here I am, still relatively young, and still single, and what do I do? I break the rule. My parents would not approve of what I've just done. And neither do I. It's not right for someone in a position of authority to take advantage of a person he is responsible for. I apologize."

"You're not the guilty one here, John. I initiated it, and I'm glad I did."

"All the same, I should not have reciprocated. It was wrong of me."

"It doesn't seem wrong to *me*," she said. "In fact, it seems as if we had no choice. That's what bothers *me*."

"How do you mean?" he asked.

"It's like I was sent here, by someone, or some*thing*, some *force* that decided I should be with you. And I had no choice in the matter."

"I don't know about that," he said. "After all, *you* made the booking with us, and *you* bought the plane ticket. And even though it was very wrong what I did, I hope it was your choice to kiss me. It was, wasn't it?"

"I hope so," she said. "I'm glad it happened, no matter what caused it."

Emily was conflicted. She was relieved that she'd had the courage to kiss John, but she was suspicious of where that courage had come from. Was it all *her*, or was some other influence dictating her actions? John interrupted her deliberations.

"Well, no matter how it happened, we can't take it back. And I want you to know that if we weren't on this tour, I'd have no hesitation whatsoever. I'm attracted to you, Emily. I want more, and I hope we have the chance to spend some time together when I'm free of my responsibilities. And speaking of responsibilities, we came here with a task to do, and we haven't fulfilled that yet. Will you walk with me now and go over that stile?" John asked.

"I'll try," she said, uncertain.

They walked slowly to the stile.

"I'll stand beside the steps and hold onto your right arm," he said. "You can use your left hand to hold onto the side. Okay?"

"Okay," she said, noticing that her heart rate was steady, and she wasn't experiencing any other symptoms that were precursors of an episode.

John took Emily's right arm, and she approached the stile. Suddenly, she felt wide awake. She was staring directly at the stile. It was obvious to her that the stile was more like a ladder than a stairway, but she didn't care. And at that moment, she realized something had changed. Like the flick of a switch, her life had gone from point A to point B. Time had somehow shifted, and she was in a place that didn't include her fear of ladders. And that place was the present, in the beautiful Irish countryside, the light soft and gentle, with a man she felt safe with. The stile was no longer part of her past. She was completely calm as she faced what used to be the greatest fear of her life.

"Here we go," said John. "Now put your right foot up

on the first step."

Emily placed her right foot on the first step, with John waiting on the ground, still holding onto her right arm. Emily stepped up to the second step, then the third. John released her arm and came around to begin coming up the stile behind her. Emily stepped up onto the fourth step, then the fifth, then onto the platform at the top of the stile.

"Now go on down the stairs to the other side," he said.

Emily shuffled her feet and turned around to face the steps. She readied herself to descend, but then another sudden shift occurred in her mind. She proceeded downward, but with each step she took, her mind veered further away from the miracle that had just transpired. The stark reality of yet another previously unattainable ambition took hold of her thoughts. Her mind filled with new possibilities— possibilities of what a future with John might hold.

Suddenly, instead of being afraid of the stile, she was dismayed that this strange trip would end in just three days, and she would return to the U.S. to her dream job, and the dream of Ireland that had become real would return to being just a dream.

Emily reached the bottom, turned, and walked aimlessly down the path. John caught up with her and put his hand on the end of her right arm as if he were reaching for her hand. He held tightly to the end of her arm, turning her around and pointing her back toward the stile.

"Let's go back to the stile now," he said.

They walked side by side back to the stile.

"Go ahead on up," he said. "I don't need to hold onto you."

Emily climbed robotically up the stairs of the stile and stood on the platform, feeling numb, but not at all concerned that she'd just climbed a ladder and was getting ready to go down another one.

"Go on down the other side," he said. "I'm on my way up."

As Emily went down the steps, her mind began to clear. John followed her, and when he caught up with her on the other side, he congratulated her enthusiastically for her accomplishment.

Emily vaguely remembered thanking him, but her mind was already whirling in another direction. As they walked together toward the car, Emily fell deep into her own mind, processing all that had just happened. She was thinking clearly now, almost analytically, and while her lethargic outward actions must have seemed strange to John, she was putting it all together internally. She acknowledged that in a span of about 10 minutes she'd overcome, at least temporarily, the two most enduring fears of her life. She recognized that John had been a part of that and also that she was attracted to him and wanted to find a way for their relationship to go further than the simple kiss that *she* had initiated.

On the other hand, she was more certain than ever that something had entered her life that was pushing her in a direction that wasn't what she'd planned. She desperately needed to learn just what it was.

Before Emily was completely finished with her internal cataloging of thoughts, John brought her out of her head and back to the present reality.

"Tell me this," he said. "Knowing what you do now, would you still choose to come on this trip?"

Emily didn't hesitate.

"Without question. Yes, I would. But I need to get some answers back in Denver. I need to find the *why* behind all of this."

"Not yet," he said. "Please don't go yet."

Chapter 21

The third day of walking, Roundwood to Enniskerry, was the longest day, but it was also the best day. The sun was shining as they gathered outside of the Coach House at 8 a.m. Everyone looked well rested, except for Tim and Nancy, who were presumably still not adjusted to the time zone.

John gave the instructions on how far they'd be walking (22 kilometers/13.7 miles) and how long it would take (around 7 hours). They set off on the surfaced road, beginning the 3-kilometer walk that John and Emily had driven last night, the symphony of their walking poles clicking rhythmically on the surface of the road.

Emily was anxious about the life-changing events from the previous evening, worried that her fear of ladders would return, nervous about what might or might not happen next with John, and determined to confront the Projector Man as soon as she got back Denver. To keep her mind off things she couldn't control, Emily decided to get to know some of the people on the tour she hadn't spent much time with. She fell in beside the French couple, Babette and Paul.

"Bonjour," she said to them.

"Bonjour," came their reply in unison.

"Parlez-vous Francais?" asked Paul.

"Un petite peu," she replied. "But I think it would be better if we spoke in English, if you don't mind."

"Bien!" said Babette. "Eet will give us some practeess."

"Where in France are you from?" asked Emily.

"We are from a village called Arques," said Paul. "It's about 3 hours north of Paris, on the way to Calais, where the famous Chunnel is located." Paul was referring to the tunnel that had been built under the English Channel, connecting France and England.

"What do you do there in Arques?" asked Emily.

"We are both glass makers," said Babette. "Most adults in Arques do zat."

Paul explained further.

"We work for the largest glass maker in the world, Arc International."

"Wow," said Emily. "That sounds cool."

"Eet *sounds* cool," said Babette. "But in zee end, it's just a job. In Franz, people do not live to work. We work to live. It is our life outside of work that means more to us."

"What do you do outside of work?" asked Emily.

"We are musicians," said Paul. "We have our own band and play on weekends at the local bars."

"What instruments do you play?" asked Emily.

"I play ze keyboard piano," said Babette. "And Paul plays ze guitar."

Emily was noticing that Paul's English was less accented than Babette's, but both of them seemed quite comfortable with English, much more comfortable than Emily's seven years of classroom French had made *her* with their language.

"Wow, amazing," she said. "Making glassware. Making music. And you look so young!"

"We *are* young," said Paul. "But we love life. We try to do all we can while we are here."

"I'm jealous," she said. "I'm still figuring out what I want to do."

"Do you have some ideas?" asked Babette.

"Yes, I think I want to help people like me have better lives."

"What do you mean, like you?" asked Babette.

Emily held up her right arm. Babette and Paul both smiled, but they stiffened ever so slightly.

"I want to help people who have physical challenges, like I do. Mine is nothing compared to many others, but it's enough to challenge me in some ways. For example, all the things both of *you* do, making glassware, playing musical instruments. I'm not sure how I would do those things."

"It's not impossible," said Paul. "We work with a woman who has one arm, and she does similar work to us."

"That's good to know. It makes me happy to hear that."

They arrived at the turn onto the Wicklow Way marked by the little yellow man, turned in, and quickly traversed the 250 meters to the first stile. People lined up and went over one at a time. Emily fell in behind Babette and Paul, and when it was her turn, she took a deep breath, went up the steps and down the other side. She looked ahead and saw John watching her, a huge grin on his face. This caused Emily to tear up a little, but she held it together, relishing the fact that she and John had silently shared something that none of the others had any idea about. It was a special moment for her, and for him, too.

They slowly ascended, and eventually they could see the village of Roundwood and the reservoirs around it. John explained that the reservoirs had been built in the 1860s and still supplied water to south Dublin. Emily was surprised that the mention of Dublin caused her heart to skip a beat. In one way, it was coming too soon, and in another, not soon enough.

Further up, John told them the names of two beautiful lakes, Lough Tay and Lough Dan, on the left side of a green valley. He pointed at a huge building in the top right of the valley and told them it was the Guinness family summer residence, which was built in the 18th century and was still owned by a family member. John explained that the movie *Braveheart* was filmed in this area. He also suggested they stop for an early lunch because this was such a beautiful site. People pulled off their backpacks and took out their packed lunches.

The Dutch couple, Anna and Willem, sat beside Emily.

"De pole is good for you?" asked Willem.

"Fantastic," said Emily. "The walking would be challenging in some places without it. Thank you, Willem."

"It is my pleasure," he said. "I would like you to keep it, please."

"I couldn't do that," said Emily. "Then you would have only one pole."

"Which is all I need. And what I prefer."

"Take it, please," said Anna. "Otherwise, he'll become depressed. He wants you to have it."

"Thank you, Willem," she said, the feeling of having made new friends enveloping her in a cocoon of happiness.

"So," said Anna, speaking almost in a whisper. "We saw you at Byrne and Woods last night. Alone with John." Anna raised her eyebrows. "Inquiring minds want to know," she said, grinning mischievously.

Emily blushed.

"I didn't see you," she said, trying to recover. "Well, I *did* see you behind me while I was on the way there, but then you went into the convenience store. I didn't realize you'd be coming there later. Why didn't you join us?"

Anna hesitated ever so slightly before responding, and Emily wondered why.

"We didn't realize either," she said. "We asked at the convenience store about the best restaurant in town, and they sent us to Byrne and Woods. We were in the pub and having a good time, and I saw you when I went to the toilet. You and John seemed to be getting on well, so we decided to leave you alone. Why should two old farts ruin a good time!"

Emily was looking closely at Anna and Willem's expressions during the conversation. Anna was hard to get a read on, but Willem seemed somber. She didn't understand why, but she figured it could be anything. Maybe he wasn't feeling well that day.

"Well, it would have been fine," she said. "I really enjoy your company."

"Perhaps tonight we all eat together," said Willem, brightening a little.

"Let's make a point of it," said Emily.

They finished lunch and got back on the trail. Emily worked her way over to the two Australian women and spent some of the walk chatting with them. She discovered they'd been a couple for 40 years, since their early 20s.

They're pioneers of a sort, thought Emily.

It made her proud to know these two women had never hidden their true selves from the world, living the lives they wanted to live. The two were cooks at a mine in western Australia, in a very remote section of the country. They worked eight-week shifts, then got four weeks off, so they made trips like this all the time. They had walked all over Europe, including many times in Ireland. They normally didn't do guided tours, but they wanted to take it easy this time and let someone else figure out the route, where to eat, and where to buy the packed lunches. Emily thoroughly enjoyed their company.

During her time walking with the Australians, the group ascended high into the mountains, temporarily entering the clouds. They crossed over several stiles on the way up, and Emily went right over them with no difficulty. She was pleased that after so many years of futility, she'd finally made progress with her fear of ladders. They walked single file down narrow paths that were mostly used by sheep, which they could hear from time to time, bleating in the distance, hidden by the fog.

At one point, the walkers came up on a line of sheep ahead of them on the path. The sheep bleated randomly, picked up speed, and eventually scurried off the trail and disappeared into the mist. They soon came out of the clouds and went down a long, gradual descent. They then climbed straight up a very steep rise and turned right, traversing the side of the hill until they reached a bridge, which led them to a surfaced road. They turned onto the road and made their way into Enniskerry.

Enniskerry was a charming, busy, little village, population 2,000, according to John, with shops, pubs, and restaurants all over the place. They were staying at the Enniskerry Inn, a B&B in the center of town that featured a wonderful restaurant and pub. They gathered in the restaurant around 6 p.m. and had a fantastic meal together. At 7:30, a traditional Irish band came on the stage at the end of the room and entertained the crowd with a number of beautiful Irish folk songs and ballads. A fiddle, flute, banjo, and uilleann pipes, which were Irish bagpipes, combined to make music that Emily truly enjoyed. And all of the band members were great singers as well.

It was a festive evening, and everyone drank heavily, with the exception of John, as usual. But people were very tired from the long day's walk, and many retired early. In the end, it was Nadine and Helmut, John and Emily, and Martin from Austria holding down the fort.

Emily was drinking Sauvignon blanc, and was working on number seven when a wave of fatigue swept over her. She had hoped to speak with John privately, but considering how she felt, she decided against waiting for that opportunity, said her goodnights, and retired to her room. Tomorrow was Thursday, and they would walk to the outskirts of Dublin. On Friday morning, it would all be over, and Emily would go to the airport and fly back to America. At least that's what her trip itinerary indicated.

Chapter 22

The final day of walking was from Enniskerry to Marlay Park in Dublin. At breakfast, they all took note of the heavy rain and wind outside. It would be a long day if that kept up. Nadine told John she'd developed blisters and that she and Helmut would spend the morning and early afternoon in Enniskerry, then try to take a taxi to the B&B in Dublin. John told them he knew a taxi service in Enniskerry that would do that and offered to call them for Nadine and Helmut. Tim and Nancy, still struggling to get a full night's rest, overheard the conversation and asked if they could join the German couple in the taxi. Nadine and Helmut agreed.

After breakfast, John gathered everyone together in the hotel lobby and explained a few things to them.

"Grab your rain gear if you're not wearing it already," John said. "The weather forecast for today is not promising, at least in terms of the sun shining during our last day of walking. But that's Ireland. It rains here a lot. Most of the time, the rain is light, but some days it's heavy and windy. Today will be one of those days, or so it seems. A few people have decided already to spend some time here in Enniskerry and take a taxi to the Lansdowne Hotel in Dublin. I've arranged the taxi for them and can do that for any others who wish to follow suit. I won't lie to you. It's going to be a hard day, but there is one thing we can do to lessen our burden.

"The total distance for today's walk is 20 kilometers, about 12½ miles. But the first 7K is walking on the surfaced roads to get back to the Wicklow Way. If I'm honest, I will tell you that the surfaced road portion of the walk will not present us with any noteworthy sites or monuments, and it will be quite tedious in the rain. Therefore, I recommend we hire a few taxis to take us the 7K to the spot where we join back up with the Wicklow Way."

John's proposal was readily agreed to by the eight others who wanted to walk. After a brief wait, they said their goodbyes to the other four and made their way out to the two taxis that were waiting for them. Emily noticed that the taxis weren't real taxis. They were just cars, owned and driven by local people who needed to make a little extra cash. John explained that the Irish people had been doing this long before Uber came around, which had just begun operations in 2009.

The taxis curled along two-lane roads and dropped the walkers at a car park that was at the base of a tall mountain. They got out, put on their backpacks, and worked their way into the forest. The rain and wind were less severe in the woods, but they were all still getting wet. Emily already felt water in her hiking boots and wondered why the manufacturer marketed them as waterproof.

John led them slowly up the side of a mountain, much of which was deforested, leaving them fully exposed to the elements. The further up they got, the stronger the wind became. Emily noticed several group members tightening the straps that held on their rainhats. Emily had a rainhat in her pack, but she chose instead to pull the drawstring of her hood tight. It made a small circular opening on her face, barely allowing her eyes to see.

Eventually, they made it to the top of the mountain. John stopped briefly, telling them that on a clear day they would have great views of the Irish Sea and the coastline along the Wicklow and Dublin shores. He didn't stop long, however, because the wind was strong, and a forest up ahead beckoned them to enter. They entered the forest, crossing a small stream that had become swollen with rain and was flowing rapidly. John explained that they had left the Wicklow Mountains and were now in Glencullen Forest, having now joined up with the Dublin Mountains.

The forest trail headed downward and eventually led them to a road where vehicles sped by at high speed. John warned them to be careful on this short stretch of road. He crossed the road and turned left, facing traffic, and waited for the others to make their way across. The spray from the wheels of passing vehicles pelted them with water, and they learned to turn their heads away from the road when cars approached.

After walking for around 10 minutes on the road, they turned back into the forest and began a steep climb, which was their last ascent of the trip. When they got to the top,

John pointed out that on a clear day they would see Dublin down below, but that was not to be the case today.

They descended out of the mountains, came into a forest for a short way, and then reached the surfaced roads of Dublin. Emily was disappointed to see litter along the sides of the road, but she had no bag to put it in. It was still raining hard, so she carried on. Before long, they reached Marlay Park, a beautiful, semi-rural park that would have been a nice place to rest if the weather was more pleasant. Emily realized they hadn't stopped for lunch. She fished her phone from her pocket and saw that it was 1 p.m., past lunchtime, but she was glad they hadn't taken a break to eat. The walk had been unpleasant, and she was relieved that it was over.

John hailed taxis for half of them and sent them on their way to the Lansdowne Hotel, then got another for the final members, which included him and Emily. John got in the front seat, and Emily, Willem, and Anna got in the rear. John turned around and spoke to them.

"Hungry?" he asked.

"Yes," said Anna. "But it was the right thing to keep moving. The weather was horrible."

They were all soaked. Emily's boots were so wet that they squeaked when she walked.

John said, "When we get to the hotel, I'll ask them for some newspapers. They work well to dry out the inside of hiking boots. You just scrunch it up and stuff it in. In a few hours, the boots will be 90 percent dry on the inside."

After 20 minutes, they reached the hotel. The Lansdowne was a family-owned establishment, not far from the center of Dublin. It had its own pub and restaurant. The rooms were small, but clean, although they had no air-conditioning. That wasn't an issue in early June, however, because temperatures rarely exceeded 70 degrees Fahrenheit.

The luggage was waiting for them when they arrived, and they all checked in and went to their rooms. Emily removed her wet clothing and hung it up to dry. She showered, then dressed and went down for lunch in the pub. She was surprised that she didn't see anyone from her group in there. After she ate, she returned to her room, laid down on the bed, and thought. She needed to figure out a plan for her last night in Ireland. Her entire being told her this was an important moment in her life. She wasn't completely sure why, but she had time to think it through. And then she fell asleep and dreamed.

Chapter 23

Emily slept until 6 p.m. She woke up refreshed, but also knowing that it might be a long time before she was able to go back to sleep. She showered again and dressed for dinner, putting on a little makeup and wearing some flattering jeans and a white, stretchy top. She felt a chill coming from the open window, so she slipped on a light-blue cardigan, but left it unbuttoned. She'd carefully shopped for this cardigan because she needed one she could easily button with her left hand. Instead of slits in the fabric to receive the buttons, this sweater had large loops running down the edge of the right side, so she could easily fasten the buttons.

When Emily woke, she had vividly remembered one of her dreams from that afternoon, and it both excited and burdened her. She sat on the bed and listened to the rain through the open window, falling lightly on the windowsill and the cobblestone alley below, not nearly as heavy as it had been during their walk. The wind had also died down. It had disappeared actually. It was a peaceful moment, yet

Emily was troubled.

The dream was the first she'd had of a potential future event since her last days in Colorado more than a month ago. Between then and now, she'd remembered none of her dreams, which was preferable to her because the dreams she *did* remember seemed to push her into things that weren't part of her plan. She had no regrets, so far, but *this* dream might truly complicate her life if it came true.

Emily pushed herself up off the bed and left the room, entering the narrow hallway. She weaved her way to the pub and restaurant, which was on the lowest floor of the hotel, a half-basement with a short stairway that led out to the street. The entire gang was there. Nadine greeted her with her thunderous voice.

"Our American friend has finally arrived!" she roared.

"Hey, what are we, chopped liver?" asked Tim, grinning.

"I love chopped leever!" yelled Nadine, then her booming laugh came out, drawing chuckles from almost everyone.

"Hi, everybody," said Emily, raising her left hand and giving a slight wave.

"Proost," said Willem, raising his glass of stout in the air.

"Slawn-cha," said John, his eyes gazing directly into hers, as always.

Emily sat down at the large table that held all 13 of them. She ended up with Babette on one side and Anna on the other. John was on the other side of the table at the opposite end from her, so she prepared herself to wait. Babette leaned over to her.

"You look so beautiful tonight," she said.

"Indeed, she does," said Anna. "Our new friend could be a movie star."

"Oh, stop," said Emily. "You two are the most beautiful in this room, without question!"

Everyone had dressed up for their final night together, at least as much as they could considering all their belongings had to fit in the small rolling suitcase permitted by Hill and Town.

Emily ordered a glass of wine, chatted with Babette and Anna, and they all ordered their meals. The food was solidly dependable and reasonably priced, as all the food along the way had been. There was tremendous energy in the room, and the mood was festive, but for Emily it was torturous. Something reminded her that tonight was important, a turning point, perhaps. Anna leaned over and whispered in her ear.

"What will happen between you and John?" she asked.

Emily feigned ignorance.

"I don't know what you're talking about."

Anna smiled, but she didn't relent.

"My dear, Emily," she said. "I've been on this Earth for 54 years, more than double your time here. And I know when two people are attracted to one another."

Emily scrunched her lips, giving her face the look of someone who'd been found out.

"Okay," she said. "There *is* something there. I just don't know how to pursue it. He's bound by some rules about relations with his customers. And I'm bound by some rules of my own, which I don't always agree with, but which are there nonetheless." Emily felt a little guilty referring to her inhibitions about intimacy as "rules," but she'd never spoken about this issue with anyone and wasn't going to start now. But at the moment, Anna was more focused on John's rules.

"It's *his* company for goodness' sakes!" said Anna, in a harsh whisper. "He can break the rules if he chooses to!"

"I suppose he can," said Emily, "which means it's up to me to break my rules, I guess."

An Irish band had set up on the stage in the front of the room and started playing, relieving Emily of the need to explain her "rules" to Anna and drowning out conversations that needed to be handled in whispers. Anna winked at her, mouthing the words *go for it*, a broad smile on her face.

Emily ordered another wine, only her second of the evening. She wanted to be buzzed, but not drunk, this time. She needed to have her wits together, but she also wanted to relax a little, and the wine helped with that.

The evening dragged on for her, which was frustrating because she couldn't even speak with John. Eventually, people began to say their goodbyes, exchanging phone numbers and Facebook profiles with the people they'd become close to. Anna and Willem departed, both hugging her tightly. Willem looked her in the eye and told her he expected to see her in Holland soon, as a guest at their farm. She promised she would come, and she meant it.

The remaining guests tightened up their seating arrangement. Nadine and Helmut were in fine form, full of energy, having skipped the walk that day. Tim and Nancy were hanging in there as well, also the beneficiaries of a rest day from the trail. Babette and Paul stayed for a while longer, then said their goodbyes, inviting Emily to come visit them in Arques and promising a tour of the glass plant. Martin was also there, and he seemed to have intentions regarding Emily, but she led him in another direction by buttoning up her cardigan and frowning when she caught him staring at her. Rebuked, Martin soon said his goodbyes and departed.

As the crowd thinned, it struck Emily that the tour was over. She'd made some great friends, met John, and overcome some huge barriers in her life. All in all, the trip had been far more rewarding than she could have ever imagined. But her remembered dream from earlier would not let her rest. It clung to her conscious mind, refusing to bury itself in the recesses of her subconscious from whence it came. She began to feel anxious, her breaths coming faster and her heart rate increasing. Emily understood that what the dream was telling her to do and what she wanted to do were the same thing.

So, where's the conflict? she asked herself.

Then she realized, there *was* no conflict. She wanted to be with John, and her dream had told her she would. *But how to accomplish that?*

She realized that she and John would never outlast Nadine and Helmut, meaning there would be no private moments between them here at the pub. She formulated a plan, gulped her fourth glass of wine for courage, slipped her hand into her pocket, and found the key to her room.

She discreetly handed the key to John, keeping her hand below table level. John looked down at the key, raised his eyebrows, then gave her a slight nod, seemingly indicating he understood. Emily stood up and said goodnight to the three. John got up from his seat and shook her hand. Emily felt their secret connection tingling up her arm.

Nadine and Helmut each gave Emily a big hug. Nadine told her she was welcome anytime at their home in Germany, which was on the border with the Netherlands. She suggested Emily could see them as well as Anna and Willem during the same trip because it was only a few hours' drive between the two. Emily promised she would try, said her final goodbyes, and left the pub.

Emily made her way up the stairs from the pub to the front desk of the hotel, explaining to them that she'd locked her key in her room and needed a spare. They asked to see her passport, which she pulled from the left pocket of her jeans, and she was presented with a new room key. Key in hand, she negotiated her way through the maze of narrow stairs and hallways and found her room. When she arrived, she removed her cardigan and sat on the bed. And waited.

Around 20 minutes later, the phone in her room rang. She picked up the receiver.

"Hello?" she said.

"Hi, it's John."

"Where are you?"

"In m'room."

"But I gave you my key!"

"I know. And I want to use that key, Emily. I truly do. But it's not right for me to come to your room while the tour is still in progress."

"But the tour's *over*! Everyone is going their separate ways tomorrow morning."

"That's right. Tomorrow morning. Anyway, listen. I have an idea."

"What?"

"When I was turning in your key at the front desk, I checked to see if they could keep you in your room for one more night, and they said they could. I've already got my room for one more night, so I thought we could spend the day together tomorrow. We could have a really good time in Dublin. What do you think?"

"I don't know, John. I've got a lot to do when I get back home."

"I understand, but will a day make a difference?"

"Not really," she admitted. "But I don't know if the airline will be able to change my flight."

Emily was feeling rebuked by John, and while his proposal was enticing, her anger prevented her from readily agreeing to it.

"You're on Aer Lingus, right?" asked John.

"Yes."

"They have the lowest change fees in the industry. Last I saw it was only 30 euros to change a flight on Aer Lingus. I'm happy to pay the fee."

"The fee is no problem. But I would have to call and find out if they could change it. It seems like a lot of hassle for just one day."

"Please, Emily. I've felt so trapped by the rules this week. I couldn't be the real me. It's just a day. But it's a day we both deserve, don't you think?"

John's persistence and honesty were breaking down Emily's prideful anger. Her resistance softened, but she wasn't quite there yet.

"I don't know, John. I don't even know how to get in touch with Aer Lingus."

"Just our luck, I've got Aer Lingus on speed dial, which makes it easier to check on customers' flights while I'm driving. Let me read the number to you."

The moment of truth had arrived. The last vestiges of resistance crumbled, and Emily capitulated.

"Okay," she said, reaching for a pad and pencil by the phone. "Go ahead."

John gave her the number, and she wrote it down.

"Call me back and let me know what they say, all right?"

Emily made the call to Aer Lingus and changed her flight to Saturday. She called John and let him know, and he said he'd make the arrangement with the front desk to extend her room for one more night. He said goodnight and told her he'd see her at breakfast tomorrow.

Emily logged onto the hotel Wi-Fi, emailed her parents to tell them she would be coming home on Saturday rather than Friday, and hoped it was okay. The plan *had* been for her father to come directly from the city to JFK on Friday afternoon, then drive back to Connecticut. Now he'd have to drive all the way back down on Saturday, and she felt a little guilty about that.

Emily was also frustrated and embarrassed that she'd given a man the key to her room, and he refused to use it. She understood why, and she respected John for his professionalism, but it hurt, nonetheless. She'd finally worked up the courage to cast her inhibitions aside and take another step toward being a normal human being, which is all she'd really wanted to be since her accident. She understood that tomorrow would bring another opportunity, but she had no idea how she would feel then, nor did she have any idea how John would feel. He certainly hadn't been banging down her door tonight. Eventually, she fell asleep in her clothes, with more questions than ever floating through her mind.

Chapter 24

On Friday morning, after a hearty breakfast and more goodbyes to their friends from the walk, John and Emily left the hotel and walked toward the center of Dublin. They started their day at Trinity College, the oldest university in Ireland, founded in 1592. Their primary destination at Trinity College was the Long Room, which housed 200,000 of the oldest books in Ireland, some of the oldest books in the world.

John explained that *The Book of Kells* was the most famous book in the Long Room. Created in the 800s, it was a beautifully illustrated manuscript that contained the four gospels of the New Testament in Latin and was composed of extraordinarily detailed and colorful illustrations and text, all etched onto its vellum pages.

The Long Room itself, as its name implied, was long and narrow, an atrium of sorts, with a ceiling high up above the floor and chambers of books on two levels. Each chamber had its own arched ceiling, all of which were perpendicular to the arched ceiling of the atrium, which ran the full length of the room. Emily felt the Long Room very closely resembled the library in the Harry Potter movies, and the Jedi Archives in one of the Star Wars movies, but John explained that neither movie was filmed there and had simply "borrowed" from the Long Room design and created computer-generated versions.

From Trinity College, they strolled through the Temple Bar area, the biggest partying scene in Dublin, but John said he preferred a less touristy area for lunch. They crossed over the River Liffey and weaved through narrow streets to a quieter locale. John stopped in front of a small shop with no sign on the window. He entered, and Emily saw that it was actually a small pub, with half a dozen tables for four, only three of which were occupied. A portly, older gentleman with a full head of gray hair rushed up to John.

"Well bless me soul, 'tis John O'Connor!" he said. "What brings you north from the country, lad?"

"I'm showing my friend Emily around town, Mr. Doyle."

"Well then, hello m'lady," said Mr. Doyle, extending his hand. Emily reached out with her left hand and shook.

"And by the way, John. I know I'm as old as your da, but now you're a grown man yourself, so let's be friends, eh? No need to call me Mr. Doyle any longer!" Liam Doyle let out a long, hearty laugh.

"Very well, Liam," said John, chuckling. "What's on the menu today?"

"First off, you'll need a pint of Guinness. And for the lady?"

"Can I try a half pint of Guinness, please?"

"Indeed, you can, m'lady. I'll be right back."

Liam went behind the bar and began the process of pouring the stout, which took some time. The proper way to fill a Guinness is to tilt the glass at a 45-degree angle, fill the glass about three-quarters full, then let it settle for a minute or so, the contents cascading from top to bottom in a show of heartiness. The glass is then returned to the tap, this time at a 90-degree angle, for the remaining fill. The whole process took Liam about two minutes. He performed the fill with a pint glass and a half-pint glass, then brought them over to John and Emily. Both of them left their glasses on the table while Liam spoke.

"Today we have fish and chips," said Liam. "Will that do ya?"

John looked at Emily, and she nodded.

"Indeed, it will, Liam. Thank you."

While Liam wandered off to prepare their food, John explained to Emily that Liam served only one kind of beverage, Guinness, and one meal recipe per day. If you didn't like either of these, Liam didn't hesitate to remind you that there were plenty of other restaurants to choose from. Liam had made a lot of money running a proper pub in the Temple Bar area, but he'd sold that to have a more leisurely lifestyle now that he was older. His limited menu approach meant that the small pub was rarely full, and because there was no sign out front, only locals came there to drink and dine.

John further explained that his father and Liam had grown up together in County Wicklow. As a young adult, Liam had left to make his fortune in the big city, while John's father had stayed, starting his own tour company when he was just 24 years old. But they kept in touch, and Liam had known John since he was a little boy.

While they waited for the food, John raised his glass of stout.

"Slawn-cha," he said.

"Slawn-cha," she replied, and the two of them drank.

"How do you like it?" asked John.

"It's different," she said. "Tasty, but heavy."

"It 'tis," said John. "But we'll do a test. Later we'll go over to the Guinness tour, which includes a fresh stout. My guess is you'll like what they serve over there a little more. Liam is a loyal Guinness customer, but he doesn't get the stout right from the brewing vat, like they do over there."

"I'll let you know," she said.

Liam brought the food, and they enjoyed it thoroughly, said their goodbyes to Liam, and continued on with their day. They spent some time at Dublin Castle, which has a rich and varied history and continues to serve as an active facility for the Irish government, then meandered over to the Guinness tour.

As John had predicted, the fresh stout had a completely different taste than the slightly older stout at Liam's. It seemed lighter in some way and was easier to drink. After that, John took Emily to a wonderful French restaurant in another part of town. They had a fabulous meal, and she drank with less caution than she had the night before. Eventually, they returned to the hotel. John walked Emily to her room, and she invited him in. This time, he didn't refuse.

When they got into the room, Emily sat down on her bed. John grabbed one of the small chairs near the window and moved it beside the bed, then sat down and faced Emily. She was nervous, but she had no intention of backing down. She wanted the life of a normal person, and this was part of it. John was the first person she'd ever met who made her feel comfortable enough to try.

"John, I need to be honest with you right now," she said. She was blushing, and her jaw was shaking a little. John reached out and took her hand in his.

"It's fine," he said. "All will be well."

His touch calmed her, so she pressed forward.

"What I want to tell you … is that … I've never been with another person … uh … intimately."

John took the information in and didn't seem shocked.

"I understand," he said. "I'll follow your lead, then." He remained as calm as ever, continuing to hold her hand gently.

Emily pulled him toward her and glanced down at the bed, encouraging him to join her there. He got up and sat on the bed beside her. He brushed his hand lightly across her cheek. Then his hand found its way to the back of her neck, and he pulled her gently toward him and kissed her, and she kissed back. Her head began to swoon, and she didn't really register all that happened next. But things *did* happen, and then the two of them were under the covers, their clothes strewn haphazardly on the floor. John was gentle, slow, and passionate. The last thing Emily thought before she was taken away into realms heretofore unknown to her was that dreams were dreams, and life was life, but dreams could never be a substitute for the real thing.

Chapter 25

Emily woke up Saturday morning with mixed emotions. She was at peace with what had happened and glad she'd finally gotten over another of the barriers that had plagued her life before this trip, but she was unclear about what she should do regarding John. He obviously cared for her, even though they'd known each other for only seven days, and she also had strong feelings for him. He was a gentle, caring soul, very mature and wise for his years. But she had a life back home that was worth pursuing, and she fully intended to do that.

So, what do I do about John? she asked herself.

As if John had read her mind, he reached over and put his arm around her.

"Sleep well?" he asked.

"Yes, very well," she said. "You?"

John looked at his watch.

"Quite well," he said. "I haven't slept this late in ages."

"What time is it?" she asked.

"Half past nine. Shall we go down for breakfast?"

"I'm not sure we have time. My flight's at 1 p.m., and I need to shower and pack. I should arrive at least two hours before the flight, right?"

"True. Well then, I'll go to my room and shower and pack, then I'll fetch my van. The people from Glenmalure Lodge were kind enough to drive it up for me. I'll be outside the hotel, on the street waiting for you, at what, quarter past ten?"

"Sounds good. See you then."

Emily showered and packed her bags. She was happy to see that the walking pole Willem had given her fit easily into her suitcase, once fully retracted. She left the room and went down to check out, then went outside and saw John parked right in front of the hotel. He got out and helped her put her bags in the back, then they got in the van and drove away. It was 10:20 a.m.

On the way to the airport, John and Emily discussed the future. Emily opened up the conversation.

"Can we start working on a plan to stay in touch, going forward? Maybe see each other every now and then?"

"Certainly," he said. "My proposal is for you to come here and become a guide for Hill and Town—a guide who specializes in tours for the disabled, but who can also take people out on the regular tours, too. I think you're the perfect person to expand the reach of tour companies like mine to people who might think the tours are not for them."

Emily was shocked by John's proposal. They'd only known each other for seven days, and he already had her coming to live in Ireland, maybe even with him. It was an intriguing possibility, but for later, certainly not in the near future. She was reluctant to hurt him, however, so she chose her words carefully.

"Interesting," she said. "But I think that would have to be down the line. I really *do* have to go back, and while I'm not saying it couldn't happen, I'm pretty certain it can't happen any time soon. You understand that, right?"

"Of course," he said. "I just wanted you to know where *my* head is at this moment. I never expected you to come back right away. And I suppose it would be good for both of us to see how we feel, once we're separated. Right now, I feel extremely close to you, Emily. I want to spend time with you. Maybe that will change when you go, but I doubt it."

"Maybe," she said, not at all sure how she would feel after she returned home. She definitely had a connection with John, and she felt very close to him after their intimacy the night before, but she was also strongly committed to the job at NSCD, and she wanted to confront the Projector Man to try to learn more about what had been happening to her since she viewed the film clip at his house in Edgewater.

Once they arrived at the airport, John brought the van to a stop at the side of the roadway in the departures area. They got out, and John pulled Emily's bags from the back of the van. He placed the rolling suitcase beside her on the sidewalk and handed her the backpack. She quickly put it on.

"You won't forget me, will you?" he asked, his voice hopeful.

"I don't think I could if I tried," she said, working hard to control her emotions.

"I know you have a lot going on back home," he said. "But I hope you'll give some thought to my offer for you to come work here, and if not that, I hope we can visit one another often."

"I promise all of the above," she said, leaning forward into his arms and hugging him tightly. They kissed for a long time, but she finally pushed herself away, turned around, and walked somberly into the terminal. She turned back and peered through the glass. John was still standing where she'd left him, wiping a tear from his eye, trying to see her through the glare on the floor-to-ceiling window. Suddenly, a wave of despair rolled over her. She realized that once again, she was leaving a place, and a person, that meant a lot to her to pursue other ambitions. It frustrated Emily that no matter how right something seemed, a force inside her inexorably drove her away from it. And this, inevitably, led to her being alone. But as always, even with a heavy heart, Emily summoned the strength to carry on, turning away from the glass and stepping tentatively toward an uncertain future.

Chapter 26
Late June 2010

On the morning of June 21, 2010, Emily slipped into her car at the Courtyard by Marriott in Lakewood, Colorado, and drove north on Wadsworth Boulevard. It took her almost 15 minutes to reach Edgewater, and another 5 minutes to reach 22 Maple Street. She had a 10 a.m. appointment with Fred Watts, the man she sometimes referred to as the Projector Man.

He'd seemed excited to hear from her when she called, but he also couldn't help reminding her that he'd told her she *would* call, even though she'd insisted she'd never speak to him again while hastily exiting after their first encounter. Emily remained friendly while he gloated, even as anger boiled up inside her, because she very much needed to speak with the old man to clear up the mystery of all the strange occurrences in her life since her original visit. He'd agreed to the meeting only if she would watch another film, which wasn't a priority for her, but she played along to make the meeting happen.

Upon Emily's return from Ireland on June 12, she'd

spent almost a week with her family, then drove her old Jeep Cherokee back to Denver. She'd booked a 10-day stay at the Marriott to search for a place to live before she started her job on July 1. But her first priority upon her return to Colorado was to see the person she held responsible for her strange dreams, and her confusing, yet richly rewarding trip to Ireland. During her seven days in Ireland, Emily had made some great new friends, overcome two of her most enduring and frustrating vulnerabilities—her fear of ladders and her struggle with intimacy—and met a person with whom she had a connection that was unlike anything she'd ever experienced before. In spite of this, she was convinced that her apparent good fortune had not happened naturally and was directly influenced by the film she'd seen at the Projector Man's house.

Emily had heard from John nearly every day since her return. They'd friended each other on Facebook and could keep up with their respective day-to-day lives and share private messages through that medium. But John reserved most of his more intimate writings for his emails, and there had been plenty of them. He had expressed several times that his feelings for Emily had not abated since she left and that the emptiness he felt could only be filled by her.

Emily was somewhat overwhelmed by the intensity of his writings, and while she still felt strongly toward John, her other pressing priorities caused her replies to be less saturated with profound love than his. She explained that her feelings for him were still strong and that she fully intended to stay in touch and would try to find a way to see him again soon. But she also pointed out that she had responsibilities at home that she was obligated to fulfill. Emily felt guilty to be so dispassionate with John, but she didn't feel it was fair to lead him on when she could foresee no imminent reunion on the horizon.

Emily parked her car in front of the tiny, rundown house at 22 Maple Street, noting that the dilapidated "Projector for Sale" sign was still up, still tilting precariously to one side. She got out and strode up the walkway, then quickly climbed the steps. Just as she was about to knock, the door opened, and Fred appeared.

"Well, hello, Emily," he said.

"Hello Mr. Watts," she replied.

"Call me Fred, please. I know I'm old, but it makes me feel younger when people call me by my first name."

Emily noticed that Fred had a significantly more friendly demeanor than during their first visit.

"Okay, Fred."

"Come on in. Let's go take a look at what's playing today."

Emily entered the house, but she had a few things to say as Fred hurried through the living room on his way to the projector in the dining room.

"Say, Fred, do you think we could speak for a while before we watch another film?"

Fred stopped in his tracks and turned his head back toward her.

"What about?" he asked.

"About some of the things that happened to me after I left here last time. Would that be okay?" Emily noticed that Fred seemed to brighten at her request.

"Sure," he said. "Why don't we sit here in the living room? Can I get you something to drink? Water? Coffee?"

"Coffee would be great," she said.

"How do you take it?"

"Black is fine, thanks."

"Have a seat over there on the sofa," Fred said, gesturing to the couch. "I'll be right back."

Emily sat down and waited. She looked around and noticed once again that there was no television in the room. She wondered what the old man did all day long without a TV. Fred returned with the coffee and placed it on the ragged old coffee table in front of the couch, then sat in the lounge chair across from it.

"Now, then, what can I do you for?" he asked, as casual as casual could be.

Emily sipped her coffee, which seemed quite old and strong, then placed the cup back on the table. She wouldn't be drinking *that*.

"Fred, have you ever had people come here to see a film, and then come back and tell you they've had dreams about the film you showed them?"

Fred cupped his chin in his hand and pressed his lips together, presumably straining to try to think of a situation that fit the description of Emily's question.

"Well, now that you mention it, there have been one or two who have said that," he said.

"Don't you think that's a bit strange, Fred?"

"Not really," he said. "I watch films all the time that I have dreams about later. Most people *do*, I think."

Emily realized that she would have to explain more if

she was to have any chance of learning anything important during this meeting.

"Have you ever had anyone tell you that not only did they dream about the film you showed them, but they also dreamed things about people and places that *weren't* shown in the film, and even dreamed they were part of what was going on?"

Fred seemed excited and didn't hesitate.

"Are you telling me that's what happened to you?"

"Yes. The first night, my dream was similar to what was in the film, but the scenery was different, and the B&B was different. And in the second dream, the next night, it was a whole different sequence of events, but with a lot more detail than the first one. So, I went to Ireland, and the man from the film was there, in exactly the same van and at exactly the same train station that was in my dreams. How can you explain that, Fred?"

Fred fidgeted, literally on the edge of his seat, but his words did not convey enthusiasm.

"Now, young lady, I can't explain anything. I don't know nothin' bout that kind of dream. I imagine people dream stuff that's similar to things from real life all the time."

Emily maintained her composure, even though Fred was beginning to strain her patience.

"Maybe," she said. "But do people then go on to actually live the things they dreamed?"

"I couldn't say," said Fred, but Emily sensed growing excitement inside him.

She persisted, repeating the things she'd told Fred about her dreams and how subsequent actual events had mirrored the dreams. She watched Fred closely while she conveyed this information. He continued to squirm around in his seat, scrunched his lips, put his hand to his chin, but then said very little when it was his turn to speak, stringing her out but giving her nothing in return.

"So, you're saying you had this dream, then you went and lived this dream out, with the actual people and places from the dream?"

"It's more than that, Fred!" screamed Emily, frustrated. "I saw the film first, *then* I started remembering my dreams, which I've *never* done before, by the way. And the dreams were not same as the film. The second dream had only one common element to the original film and that was the presence of John, uh, the man from the film. And he met me at the train station from my dream! The dream became real in the *future*, Fred!"

"Well, that's either one heck of a big coincidence, or else, well, I don't know what else," he said.

"But you can't tell me anything about *why* it happened?" she asked, exasperated.

"I can't."

"Or you won't?" she asked, pressing him to give her something.

"I can't," he said. "But I can offer you the chance to see if you can do it again."

"What are you saying?"

"By watching another film!" he said. "If you watch another one, and nothin' happens, then the first time was probably just a fluke. But if this same kind of stuff happens, then we'll know you've got some kind of special ability or somethin'. And then we'll…well…I don't know what we'll do then, but we'll have to do something."

Emily was irritated. Fred seemed extremely interested in what had happened to her, but at the same time he expressed a sense of surprise at everything she'd told him. His rant about her having some kind of special ability was just a rambling fantasy from a lonely old man, and she gave it no credence whatsoever. But she *was* interested in learning if watching another film produced dreams that she could remember. She hadn't remembered any of her dreams since she'd left Ireland. She felt that if it happened again, she'd have at least one more data point that linked the films to her ability to remember dreams. She wouldn't make the mistake this time of following the dreams, but if it happened again, at least she would have some solid information to show an expert in dreams, or *some* kind of expert. She really wasn't sure what she would do next, in part because she didn't know what would happen after she watched the next film.

"Fine," she said. "Let's watch another film."

Emily stood up, prompting Fred to get up, and they moved across the room, went through the kitchen and entered the dining room, which looked exactly the same as it had two months previously.

"How should we decide what film to put in the projector?" asked Emily.

"I don't think we *should* decide," said the old man. "Let's just use the one that's in there already, make it kind of random?"

"What's in there?" she asked.

"It's the film I showed to the last guy who was here. But I probably shouldn't tell you, 'cause the first time you were here I didn't say nothin' and why would we want to change that, right?"

"I suppose," said Emily, moving up and taking the same seat she'd taken last time, on the front left side of the room. She sat down and folded her arms, a little impatient, but the comfortable chair helped her to relax a little.

"Ready?" asked Fred.

"Fine," said Emily.

Fred dimmed the lights and started up the projector. Once again, the film was in black and white and had no sound. It was grainy like before, poor quality. The backs of two men in suits appeared. Both men had their arms behind their backs, each with his hands clasped together. They were strolling along a wide stone pathway. In the distance, she could see that the pathway was at the top of a massive stone wall that curled for what seemed miles into the distance, climbing over hills and into valleys. The wall was divided into sections by taller towers at intervals along the way.

"Is that the Great Wall of China?" she asked.

"I think so," said the old man.

The two men were small and thin, with short dark hair. She couldn't see their faces, but she assumed they were Chinese. Then the scene changed. The two men were now inside a large room. Inside the room were different items: a treadmill, an elliptical trainer, a stationary bike, and other kinds of exercise equipment. A balcony ran around all four sides of the room, and Emily could see other products up there that were similar to the ones on the main floor.

Now Emily could see the faces of the two men. Both were Chinese, and they were showing two other men, who were Caucasian, the various products in the room, obviously a showroom. The two Chinese businessmen were clearly trying to sell their products to the two Caucasian businessmen.

The film ran out, lapping against the bottom reel as it continued to rotate. Fred reached over and switched off the projector, then turned up the lights.

"What do you think?" he asked.

"I'm not sure what to think," she replied. "But I don't see going to China in my future plans, under any circumstances. So, this is probably a dead end."

"Oh, well," he said. "At least we tried."

Emily got up to leave.

"I'd like to say thank you, Fred, but I don't feel like I'm getting much help from you."

"I'm sorry," he said. "I don't know what I can do."

"Is the price of the projector still $1 million?"

"Yes, it is. Minus the $10,000 discount I offered you last time."

"Okay," she said, a bit disgusted by this whole confusing charade.

Emily left the room, and Fred called out to her.

"You've still got my number, right?"

"Yes, I have it," she said. *But I hope I never use it again*, she thought to herself.

And with that, Emily departed from 22 Maple Street, resigned that she would never uncover the mystery of what had happened to her and resolved to pursuing the life she had planned for herself, as opposed to a life born of inexplicable films and dreams.

Chapter 27

Emily purchased a *Denver Post* on the way back to the hotel, grabbed some lunch from the bistro in the lobby, and sat down at a table, eating and checking for apartments in the Denver area. She circled a few, made some calls, and set up appointments for later in the afternoon. Before the day was over, she signed a one-year lease for a nice apartment in downtown Denver, walking distance from many of the popular shops and restaurants in the area. She dined at one of those restaurants, then went back to the hotel and called Woha to bring him up to date.

"That's good news," he said, after she told him about the apartment. "Anything else new?"

"Well, I went to see the Projector Man this morning."

"I see," said Woha. "Was he able to give you any insight into what's going on?"

"Nada," she said. "The guy was as surprised as I was by the whole thing, or so he said."

"Hmmm. Anything else?"

"He showed me another film."

"Oh? What was it about?"

"It was about two guys walking on the Great Wall of China and then trying to sell fitness products to some Western guys."

"Hmmm. That's a strange one."

"Yes, and before you get any ideas, please allow me to state the obvious. I'm not going to China!"

"So you say," he said. "But then again, you haven't gone to sleep yet."

"Doesn't matter if I dream about the film or not. I've signed a one-year lease, and my dream *job* starts in 10 days, so I'm *not* going to China."

"Fine," he said. "But will you keep me updated?"

"Of course. How are things with you?"

"Well, I've started working now. It's an internship with the Secretary of Natural Resources for the Cherokee Nation. So far, I find it quite interesting."

"Awesome," said Emily. "And the no drinking is going well?"

"Yeah, it's fine," he said. "The rehab place was really good, and I'm fully convinced that I just can't drink anymore. And I don't really want to, because I'm happy with the direction I'm taking professionally, and it's great to be back with my family and my people."

"I'm so happy to hear that, dude! But I miss you. A lot."

"I miss you, too. I'm glad you're back in the West. Now you're only 10 hours away by car, so that's not too bad. We should be able to get together every now and then, right?"

"For sure," she said. "Okay, it's my bedtime. I guess we'll find out what happens next."

"Indeed," said Woha. "Sleep well."

"You, too," she said. "Goodnight, buddy."

"Later, Em. Be well."

Emily ended the call, got ready for bed, and turned on the television to help her get sleepy. Before long, she pushed the off button on the remote and fell into a sound sleep, not worrying at all about what might happen during the night.

Chapter 28

Inevitably, the dream came, and she remembered it in the morning. There was no new information in the dream, just a rehash of what had happened in the film. The two men were walking along the Great Wall, and then they were in their showroom, trying to sell products to the guys from the West. It frustrated Emily that this had happened, but she went on with her day as if it hadn't. The apartment she'd rented was furnished, so she didn't need to do much shopping to prepare for moving in when the lease started on July 1. That left her with literally no responsibilities for the next nine days. Emily knew herself well enough to conclude that this wasn't going to work.

Emily considered calling Woha to arrange a visit with him in Oklahoma, but she decided the timing wasn't right for that. She'd *had* the dream he predicted she'd have, and she didn't want him telling her to follow that dream and make it a reality.

Emily emailed John, updating him on her status, and he replied almost immediately, asking her how much vacation time came with the job. This further dampened her mood because she didn't have the emotional energy to think about seeing John at that moment. She went for a run, showered, then drove downtown to get to know the area she'd be living in a little better. She wandered around all day, going into shops and purchasing a few things like sheets, towels, and lamps. She had dinner downtown and made her way back to the hotel, drank a few glasses of wine at the bistro, then went to her room and watched television.

Emily was completely, absolutely bored, and she knew without question that she could never make it another eight days like this. She resolved that tomorrow she would go up into the mountains for a long, refreshing hike, so she set her alarm for 6 a.m. And finally, she went to sleep.

The next morning, Emily was awoken before the alarm by her rapidly beating heart. She was struggling for breath, on the verge of having a PTSD episode. She wanted to go to the sink and splash water on her face, but she was afraid to leave the bed, fearing she might pass out and injure herself. She concentrated on bringing herself out of the panic attack. First, she slowed her breathing and tried to relax. Then she used the grounding techniques her therapist had taught her, feeling her body lying against the mattress, rubbing her fingers on the edges of the blankets, counting backwards by 7 from 100. *100, 93, 86, 79, 72 ...* And then she began to calm down.

The reason behind Emily's unexpected, alarming attack was something she remembered from her dreams. A ladder. She'd been in the showroom of the two Chinese men. She asked them a question, the details of which remained blurry, and the two men had pointed at a ladder that went up from the main floor of the showroom to the balcony that surrounded it. The men explained that the showroom was new, and they still needed to build a proper set of stairs to access the balcony, but it wasn't urgent because the products up on there were all discontinued and of no immediate interest to most customers. But apparently, she'd asked them about a product, and they had said that yes, they had one of those, but it was up on the balcony. One of the men went up the ladder, and Emily approached it, grabbed onto it, and felt fine.

But now, in real life, visualizing that ladder, Emily was terrified. It was as if her dream was taunting her, telling her that all she had to do was to pursue it and she would be fine, but if she refused, she would once again be burdened with her fear of ladders.

After a few minutes, Emily's heart rate settled back to normal, and she felt better, relieved to have avoided a more serious incident, so she got up and prepared to leave for her hike. The previous evening she'd brought in most of the gear she would need for the hike, including her hiking boots, her daypack, and the water bladder she'd used on the Ireland trip. She filled the bladder at the sink, finished packing, and left the room. On the way out, she grabbed a breakfast sandwich from the bistro and bought two ham sandwiches and several energy bars for later. She stuffed the food into her pack and walked out to the car.

When Emily got there, she removed the breakfast sandwich from the pack, threw it on the passenger seat, then put the pack in the backseat. After she navigated her way to the highway, she put her right arm on the wheel to steer and reached for the breakfast sandwich. She munched the sandwich down quickly, not wanting to rely on her right arm for steering for an extended period of time.

Emily had decided to attempt the Longs Peak hike, something she hadn't done since her college days. The Longs Peak trailhead was up near Estes Park, about an hour and a half drive north from Denver. She arrived at 8 a.m., which was later than what was recommended as a start time for most hikers trying to reach the summit of Longs. The most fit hikers, a group that Emily felt included her, would take around 10 hours to complete the trip up and back. Some people took up to 15 hours to make it, and about half of the people who tried the climb turned back before reaching the summit.

Longs Peak was a 14,259-foot-tall mountain, and the Keyhole route that Emily would be taking climbed 5,000 feet in elevation from the trailhead to the summit and was more than 15 miles roundtrip, so about 7½ miles each way. The first 5 miles were easy going, mostly class 2 hiking, with a few steep sections and one or two boulder fields, but it was mostly quite manageable. The last 2½ miles to the summit were class 3 scrambling, meaning it was very steep and required the use of your hands to help pull yourself up through the boulder fields. Emily wasn't intimidated by this, in spite of having only one hand, because she'd reached the summit of Longs Peak several times during her days living and studying in Boulder.

Emily parked her car, noticing that the lot was quite full. She got out her pack, put it on her shoulders, snapped the waist belt and cinched it tight, then headed up the trail.

She hadn't seen any hikers yet and assumed most of them were well ahead of her on the way up into the high peaks of the Colorado Rockies. The air was crisp and clean, the sky was blue, and all of this merged with her steady exertions to put her into a new, more positive frame of mind. She put the valve of her water hose to her mouth and took a long drink, enjoying the fact that she didn't have to stop to take off her walking pole to drink because she'd left the pole behind. When Emily got into the steep boulder fields up above, the pole would be more of a hindrance than an asset.

As Emily ascended, the hike continued to have its desired effect, calming and relaxing her. Her thoughts began to drift, and before she knew it, she was daydreaming, not really knowing what thought would come next. Without notice, her mind floated to the one place she didn't want it to go. She was back in the showroom in China, approaching the ladder. Her heart rate increased, she started sweating, and a slight shaking took hold of her body. Suddenly, her thoughts shifted, and she was in a different time and place altogether.

Emily was 11 years old, back at her childhood home in Connecticut. It was around five in the afternoon on a beautiful spring day in May. Emily had just ridden her bike back from soccer practice at a nearby field. Her brother was at his own practice, which was further away, so her mom had driven him over. She assumed her dad was still at work, although he usually got home around this time, not wanting Emily to be by herself for an extended period. But for the moment, she was alone.

The Nolands lived in a very rural area in the northwest corner of Connecticut. Most homes sat on lots of five acres or more, and the Noland home rested on a beautiful park-like plot of land that spanned 11 acres. At various spots throughout the property, stunning glacially made rock formations rose up from the ground, several of them climbing more than 20 feet into the air. When they'd built their home, the Nolands placed it so that one of these formations sat just behind the parking area where the driveway met up with the garage. People pulling into the drive or the garage enjoyed a great view of this spectacular formation.

As Emily rode up the driveway and parked her bike, she glanced up at the rocks, noticing a baby bird that was perched on a ledge near the top of the steep side of the formation. The baby bird was chirping furiously, obviously stranded. Emily looked up at the tree that grew in front of the rocks and saw a bird's nest up there, filled with other chirping baby birds. She wanted to help the baby bird get back to its family, especially because she knew that snakes lived in the rocks and could easily capture and eat the little bird.

The snakes weren't poisonous, and Emily rarely saw them, but they were there. Her father told her there were two kinds of snakes living in the rocks: milk snakes and garter snakes, neither of which could harm a person. But they could harm a baby bird, and Emily wanted to help it. Suddenly, she had an idea.

Emily ran to the front of the house and went under the deck, which was so tall that you could walk under it. She knew her dad kept a ladder there, and she wanted to use it to help the baby bird. She found the ladder and dragged it around to the back area where the rocks were located. The ladder wasn't heavy because it was made of aluminum. Her dad had told her it was a 16-foot ladder, and he'd showed her how to make it taller by pushing one piece over top of the other piece and then letting the latches catch on the rungs so the ladder would stay that way.

Emily extended the ladder and made sure the latches were secure, then she raised the ladder up and placed it against the rocks, as close to the bird as she could get it. The ladder settled onto a big boulder. She checked the ladder, and it moved just a little bit, but not so much that it worried her. She remembered her dad had once said to stay away from that big boulder because it wasn't completely secure. He'd told her that one day he was going to go up there and push the boulder down so he didn't have to worry about it anymore. He never got around to it though. And the ladder seemed fine. Emily wasn't worried.

Emily scaled the ladder quickly. It didn't reach all the way up to where the baby bird was, but if she stretched her left arm up, she could reach the bird with her hand. Her plan was to catch the baby bird, put it in a box, then move the ladder over to the tree branch where the nest was located and put the baby bird back in its nest.

Emily got all the way up the ladder. Her feet were on the third rung from the top. She held onto the top rung of the ladder with her right hand and reached out for the bird with her left. Her fingers were only a few inches away from it. The bird didn't seem to know she was there, so it wasn't trying to get away from her. If she could only stretch a few more inches, she could get it.

Emily lurched her body upward, and the jerking motion caused the ladder to pull on the boulder. The boulder very slowly began to move, and the ladder lost its purchase.

Emily and the ladder tumbled down. She hit the ground with enough force to knock the wind out of her, and she didn't realize that the boulder was still rolling. She was splayed out on the ground below the cliff, her arms extended and flush with the ground. The ladder was on its side, leaning up against the rocks. The boulder rolled left then slipped off the edge of the cliff and fell straight down. It nearly missed her completely, but then it slammed down with a thud, landing directly on Emily's right hand. The thud was accompanied by an audible splat as her hand was mashed by the boulder. The pain was so severe that Emily nearly fainted. She tried to pull her hand out from under the boulder, but this just caused the horrific pain to escalate further. She tried to scream for help, but her lungs were still recovering from having the air knocked out of them.

Luckily, Emily's father had been pulling up the driveway when the accident occurred. He saw the entire incident as it unfolded. As Bill Noland jerked his car to a stop and leaped from it, running toward Emily, he had called 911. Within 10 minutes, the ambulance and first responders were there. Emily was in terrible pain, but she was alive. Unfortunately, her hand had been crushed so severely that she was rushed by helicopter from the local hospital to a surgical center in New Haven. Tragically, the pulverized hand could not be saved and required immediate amputation, changing Emily's life forever.

From that point forward, *ladders* had been the trigger that sent her back to relive that horrible day. Her father would also never fully recover from the shock of watching it all happen, and the guilt of having failed to deal with that loose boulder.

Emily felt someone pushing on her shoulder. She heard voices, but they were dull and distant. As she regained consciousness, she finally could understand what they were saying.

"Miss, are you alright? Can you hear me?"

"Yes, I can hear you," she said, still groggy. "Where am I?"

"You're on the trail to Longs Peak. We were on the way up and found you lying here. Are you alright? Are you injured?"

"I'm fine," she said, pushing herself up into a sitting position.

"Why don't you drink some water," said the man beside her.

Emily pushed the water valve up to her mouth, released the valve, and took a deep draft of water. It felt good and revived her further.

"I think I'm going to be fine," she said, getting unsteadily to her feet.

"It's a few miles back to the parking area, miss. We're happy to walk down with you."

"No, thank you," said Emily. "I'm fine. I'll just go down on my own."

"Are you sure?" asked the man. "It's no trouble."

"I'm fine, thank you, really!" said Emily, anxious to get

away and humiliated about what had happened. "I see a few groups up above making their way down, so if I have any more trouble, I'm sure they can help me. Please, go ahead and continue your ascent. I apologize for having slowed you down."

"No trouble," said the man. "Take your time, okay?"

"I will," said Emily. "Thank you."

Emily took a few slow steps down the hill, then picked up her speed, not wanting the people to think she couldn't make it on her own. She eventually made it down the trail to the lot, put her pack into the backseat, got into the front, and turned on the engine. She ran the air-conditioning to help her wake up, in no hurry to drive back to Denver because her day had already been shortened. This gave her time to consider what was happening to her.

The one thing that was abundantly clear was that her PTSD trigger had reasserted itself, more strongly than ever. She was having episodes now based on dreams and daydreams of ladders when it previously took the physical presence of a ladder to thrust her into an episode. She remembered the *shift* her mind had experienced when she first overcame her fear of going over the stile in Ireland. At that time, her mind had been totally immersed in the present moment, safe with John in the beautiful Irish countryside, and the stile no longer represented something from her past. It was part of a serene, peaceful present. She understood that her mind had now shifted back, and the trigger had returned—more of a hair trigger than ever. The greatest fear of her life was back in force, and she could think of only one thing that might enable her to once again free herself from her past. The future. The future from her dreams.

Chapter 29

The next morning, Emily awoke remembering a new dream she'd had the night before. The dream started in the showroom in China. One of the men was coming down the ladder, carrying what looked to be a set of walking poles. He showed them to Emily, demonstrating how they worked. She remembered very distinctly that seeing the ladder had not frightened her in the least. The dream then shifted to another scene. Emily was walking around a farm, apparently being given a tour by Anna and Willem. Another shift occurred, and she was in Ireland, walking down a busy village street with John. Was that Dingle?

Emily couldn't piece it all together at that point, but it was becoming increasingly evident to her that she was entangled in something that wasn't going to go away. Her mind was taking her places that she didn't want to go. But the most awful and depressing concern was that her PTSD had returned with a vengeance.

Someone who hadn't experienced PTSD wouldn't understand the pure joy and sense of freedom she'd felt when she'd rid herself of her fear of ladders. The prospect of never again being catapulted back to relive the most horrible moment of her life had been exhilarating, but now that the trigger had returned and was capable of thrusting her back like a helpless rag doll, she was frantic. She became desperate to reclaim the freedom from her past tragedy that she'd so briefly experienced. Since her episode at Longs Peak, she'd developed a very clear, albeit unwelcome, sense of what it would take to regain control of her PTSD, and her latest dream confirmed that her hypothesis was probably correct.

After going down to the bistro for coffee and breakfast, Emily returned to her room and went online, investigating what was needed to make a trip to China. She could get a round trip plane ticket to Beijing, the closest major city to the Great Wall, for less than $1,000, but she would need a visa, and in order to get the visa, she had to provide evidence that she'd purchased a ticket *and* had a hotel reservation. The website of the visa service she was looking at explained that she could expedite her China visa application and have it in less than a week. It was June 23, so if she left for China on June 30, she'd arrive in China on July 1, which was her start day for the job at NSCD. She looked at the calendar on her phone and saw that July 4 fell on a Sunday that year, meaning that Monday, July 5, would be a national holiday. July 1 was a Thursday, so if she could arrange with NSCD to start on Tuesday, July 6, she'd only be delaying her start by two business days.

She called the NSCD office and told her contact she'd secured an apartment in Denver and was excited to begin the job, but needed two extra days to handle a personal matter. Her contact didn't seem bothered at all about the slight delay, telling her it was a slow time of year for them anyway. When Emily hung up the phone, she purchased a ticket on United Airlines that would depart from Denver on June 30 and fly to San Francisco. In San Francisco, she would board another plane that would fly to Beijing. Her return date was Monday, July 5.

Emily then found a very reasonably priced hotel in Beijing and made a reservation. Next, she filled out the application for a tourist visa to China, which was a somewhat tedious process because she was a one-finger typist. When she used to type class papers, she could type reasonably fast, but an application like this, which had blank space after blank space that needed to be filled in, took more time. But she got it done, then sent it by FedEx to the visa expediting service, along with her passport.

On Tuesday, June 29, Emily's passport arrived back at the hotel. Inside the passport, a tourist visa allowing her to enter China was stamped on one of the pages. On Wednesday, June 30, Emily boarded the early morning flight in Denver, flew to San Francisco, then made her way to the International Terminal and waited to board the flight to Beijing.

While she waited, Emily texted Woha to tell him she was on her way to China and would brief him upon her return early next week. She emailed John and told him the same thing, explaining that her trip was part of her effort to learn more about the films and her dreams. She also emailed her itinerary to each of her parents, then called her dad and explained that she had the opportunity to go to China before her job started and wanted to see the Great Wall and Tiananmen Square. Her dad was confused regarding her sudden interest in China, but both of her parents had resigned themselves long ago to accept and encourage their only daughter's independence. They supported her in nearly everything she tried, no matter how outlandish. Her father extended his good wishes for her safe travels, and she said goodbye and pushed the off button on her phone.

The San Francisco flight departed at 11:30 a.m. Pacific Standard Time on June 30, and it arrived in Beijing at 2:40 p.m. on July 1, China time. It had been a 12-hour flight, but China time was 15 hours ahead of U.S. Pacific Time, so it felt like she'd lost a day of her life somehow.

Emily felt extremely tired and sluggish. But she'd arranged for the hotel shuttle service to meet her as soon as she came out of immigration. She was told she just needed to look for her name on a sign that a hotel employee would be holding. The difficulty came when she emerged from immigration and saw hundreds of Chinese people lined up behind the barrier, all of them holding up signs! Eventually, she spotted a sign with the hotel name on it, Marriott, followed by several other names, one of which was hers. Emily waited with the person holding the sign, who spoke *some* English, until the others on the list were all assembled. The group of six hotel guests then followed the driver out to a van, dodging what seemed liked thousands of people bustling through the radically busy airport.

Emily noticed that the air smelled different here. It had a heavy scent, not completely pleasant. She'd read that for the 2008 Olympics, which were held in Beijing, the Chinese government had gone to great lengths to clean up the air, which had traditionally been quite polluted. As Emily looked at the sky, she saw a little blue, so she wondered if what she was smelling was pollution or simply that China smelled a little different from the West. Regardless, the odor wasn't overwhelming, and she quickly adjusted, not even registering the scent after a while.

What Emily *couldn't* ignore was the heat. It felt as if it were 95 degrees Fahrenheit and humid. She began sweating almost immediately, but that came to a quick halt when she entered the shuttle, which was extremely cold. Nevertheless, it was preferable to the heat.

Emily had booked the Marriott through Priceline and had gotten a really good deal. She'd paid only $60 per night for the hotel. When she arrived at the hotel around 30 minutes later, the lobby was immaculately clean and luxurious, the floors and walls made of black granite. When she entered her room, she found it to be of the same high quality as the lobby, and also quite spacious. Her first order of business was to get some sleep, but not too much. The time adjustment in China would be even more difficult than it had been in Ireland.

Two hours later, the alarm woke Emily up. It was 6 p.m. in Beijing, but only 2 a.m. in Denver. Emily was tired, but needed to wake up, so she showered, dressed, and went to find something to eat. The hotel had five restaurants, and she found the one that specialized in Western food. She ordered bottled water and a burger and fries. When the food arrived, she discovered that the burgers in China tasted nothing like the burgers in America. The beef was tough and gritty, and it was heavily seasoned. She spit the contents of her mouth into a napkin, then washed her mouth out with the bottled water. She ate all of the fries, which were fine, and decided that next time she would try a non-meat dish such as cheese pizza and see what happened.

Emily had time to kill, so she stopped by the concierge desk and asked for a map. She also asked how far the hotel was from Tiananmen Square and found that it was a 4-kilometer (2½-mile) walk. She decided to take a taxi, but before she went outside, she stopped at the front desk and exchanged $100 for some Chinese currency, which the young woman behind the desk called "RMB" when she counted the bills out for Emily. She departed the lobby, and a man dressed in an elaborate uniform asked her if she needed a taxi. She nodded her head. He blew a whistle, and a taxi appeared. He asked her where she was going, and she told him. He spoke Chinese to the driver as he opened the rear door for Emily. She got in, and the taxi took off.

On the way to Tiananmen Square, they passed by a Ferrari dealership, then surpassed that when they passed a Lamborghini dealership. It was after 7 p.m. on a Thursday evening, but the streets were still crowded with traffic, and the sidewalks were packed with people. The taxi dropped her off at Tiananmen Square, which was *incredibly* crowded. It was still hot and humid, although not nearly as bad as it had been when she arrived.

Emily walked from the street out onto the expansive square. She didn't really know what she was looking at, but it was common knowledge outside of China that

Tiananmen Square was the site of the 1989 massacre of hundreds of student-led protesters by the Chinese military. No memorial of this event is present on the square, but there were many huge buildings that memorialized heroes of the Chinese Communist movement, including Mao himself, and other cultural and governmental centers.

To the north of the square, across a wide, busy roadway, was the Forbidden City, the ancient palace-complex that was the home of the Emperors of China since the early 1400s. It was closed for the day, so Emily couldn't gain entrance. She wandered aimlessly around Tiananmen Square, impressed with the majesty of the place but also constantly dodging the throngs of people. There were people flying kites, and vendors selling kites, watches, and other assorted items. When the vendors spotted her, several of them approached and began trying to sell their products to her. It became a competition between them, and their voices became louder, spewing clipped and heavily accented English at her.

Emily heard a voice screaming, "Rolex watch only figh dollah!" The man who was selling watches stretched out his arms toward her. They were covered with Rolex watch look-a-likes from the elbows down. As the cacophony of voices escalated, she became uncomfortable and tried to escape, but she was literally surrounded at that point. Suddenly, she noticed two men in suits approaching.

At first, Emily thought they were some kind of security people, but as they came closer, she recognized them as the two men from the film she'd seen in Fred Watts's dining room only 10 days previously!

How can this be? she asked herself. *How can they simply appear out of nowhere?*

But then Emily realized that the men didn't just appear out of nowhere. They had appeared in her dreams, and by following her dreams, she had validated a newfound power: the ability to predict the future.

Chapter 30

One of the men from the film aggressively yelled something in Chinese at the mob of vendors surrounding Emily, waving his arm as if to shoo them away. The vendors slowly backed off, with angry looks on their faces and some aggressive words of their own yelled back at the men in the suits.

After the vendors were gone, one of the men addressed Emily in English. "We so very sorry for your trouble, miss."

"Thank you," said Emily. "I wasn't sure what to do."

"We understand," said the other man. "But why you here by yourself? China very safe country, but not always easy for foreigners to understand the ways of our people."

Emily noticed that both men were exactly the same height and stature. They were shorter than her, slender, with neatly combed, short black hair, and looked to be around 40 years old. Their dark suits and thin gray ties were also identical. She wondered if they were twins or, at the very least, brothers.

"I recognize both of you," she said. "I have seen you

before."

"How is this possible?" asked one of the men.

"I saw you both in a film. You were walking on the Great Wall, and then you were in your showroom."

"Don't know about film," said the man, "but our show-room not far from here. We on our way home from there now. It is our honor to walk through this great square two time each day. Many hero from our country's past and present can be found here."

"I see," she said, extending her left hand. "My name is Emily."

One at a time, each man bowed slightly and shook her hand.

"My English name is Thomas," said the man on the left. "This my twin brother, who in English is called Wilson. We are honored to meet you, Miss Emily, and we are very sorry for your confusion."

"I don't know what you mean," she said.

"You must confuse us with others," said Thomas. "We are humble businessmen. We have never been in any film. We are not famous like many of our countrymen who serve in the Great Hall of the People." He turned his head, gazing at a massive structure in the distance.

Emily wasn't surprised to hear the men knew nothing about the film, especially because the same thing had happened with John. She made up her mind not to force her story on these men, but at the same time she didn't want to lose contact with them.

"I understand," said Emily. "I must be confused. But you have been so kind to me by helping me out of a difficult situation. Please allow me to take you to dinner."

"This very kind of you," said Wilson. "But no need. We give some small help to a person who new to this place. You will learn to travel with companion when you visit spots like this in future. You need to be with people who know how to handle vendors."

Emily took this small opening and tried to use it to her advantage.

"But I have no companions," she said. "I am here by myself. I only have a few days before I must leave, and I would like to see the famous places. Can you help me?"

The two men spoke to each other quietly in Chinese. Then they turned back to look at her.

"We must work tomorrow and for a half day on Saturday," said Thomas. "But we invite you to visit us in our showroom any time."

"May I come there tomorrow morning?" she asked.

"Yes, of course," said Thomas. "Are you business person?"

Emily paused, thinking.

"Uh, yes," she said. "I have just started my own business. I want to import products from China." She felt guilty lying to the two kind gentlemen, but she was desperate to maintain contact.

"What kind of product you import?" asked Thomas.

"Uh, well, sporting equipment," she stammered.

"I see," said Thomas, a smile forming on his lips. "That is our specialty!"

"Yes, maybe you know us after all!" Wilson said. "We happy to have you as guest in our showroom!"

Wilson removed a card from his shirt pocket and handed it to Emily.

"Please come to address on card. We at showroom all day tomorrow."

"Thank you," said Emily, extending her left arm and shaking hands once again with both men. "I will see you tomorrow then."

Both men bowed.

"We will see you tomorrow," said Thomas. "Nice to meet you, Miss Emily."

The two men turned and walked away. Emily shook her head, but she was relieved to have met the two men from the film—and from her dreams. They were undoubtedly the key to unlocking the secrets of her future, especially the secret to controlling her PTSD trigger, but she was concerned that the price of pursuing these ambitions would be steep.

Chapter 31

Emily arrived at the address on Wilson's business card at 9:05 a.m. The building that housed the showroom was actually a multi-tenant office building. She looked at the sign in the lobby of the building for the name T.W. Athletic Equipment Company and found that it was on the first floor. After wandering around on the ground floor and not finding it, Emily suspected she knew what was going on. She went to the elevator, pushed the button, and the doors opened. As she'd thought, the elevator buttons included a "G," which stood for ground floor, meaning floor number 1 would be what is considered the second floor in U.S. buildings. The Chinese obviously used the European system of floor numbering.

Emily pushed the number "1" button. The elevator doors closed, and the elevator rose, the doors opening again on the first floor. She went out and quickly located the door to the showroom. She opened the door and entered the room. Memories from the film and her dreams flooded her consciousness.

The showroom had the shape of a shortened cube. It was about 40 feet wide by 40 feet long, and the ceiling seemed to be about 20 feet high. The floor of the balcony was about 10 feet off the ground, with a railing on the edges for safety, but each side had an opening in the railing that was about 4 feet wide, and this allowed a rolling ladder to access all four sides of the balcony. The ladder in question was currently resting against the balcony on the rear wall of the room.

Emily remained calm when she glanced at the ladder, the same ladder that had caused her great troubles back in Colorado, less than two weeks previously. She suspected that by coming here and pursuing the future she'd seen in her dreams, she was exorcising her fear of ladders once again. She certainly hoped that was true.

About 10 feet from the entrance to the showroom sat two side-by-side desks, twins of each other, and sitting behind them were the twins from the film, her dreams, and the previous evening. Thomas was on the left, and Wilson was on the right. They both stood up quickly and bowed to Emily, with big smiles on their faces.

"Please come in," said Wilson, waving his outstretched arm into the room.

"Thank you," said Emily. "I'm glad I found you. Your showroom is so beautiful!"

In reality, the room was somewhat mundane. Off to the left, in the front corner, were four desks, occupied by office people who didn't look up and acknowledge her. The floor of the entire room was vinyl, the walls were painted white, and the balcony was supported by round metal beams that rose up from the floor to the bottom of the wooden balcony floor, also painted white. The main floor was filled with fitness equipment—treadmills, elliptical trainers, stationary bikes, and a variety of weight-lifting apparatus.

The balcony contained a variety of smaller machines, plus numerous accessories, such as exercise balls and exercise mats of all different sizes, many of which were rolled up and leaning against the wall. Emily didn't see the walking poles from her dream, but she planned on asking about those when the moment seemed right.

"Thank you for your compliment," said Thomas. "Please, Miss Emily, may we offer you tea? Or coffee?"

"No, thank you," said Emily. "I've been drinking coffee since three this morning!"

"Oh, my," said Wilson. "Seems you have the jet lag."

"I suppose I do," said Emily. "But right now, I'm fine, and I'm so happy to be here!"

Emily *was* genuinely excited to be there with the twins, and she was surprised at this emotion. But she was a long way from home, and it was always good to meet friendly people in such circumstances, even if these were the very same people she had already "met" in the film and in her dreams.

"Would you like to see the products in our showroom?" asked Wilson. "Maybe you see something you like to buy for your new company!"

"Yes, of course," said Emily.

The two escorted her around the room, explaining who the main buyers were for each of their products. She passed by the ladder and noted that once again, she remained calm.

As they toured the showroom, Wilson explained that most of the sales of T.W. Athletic Equipment Company went to Europe and the Middle East.

"Do you sell some products to the U.S. market?" she asked.

"Not yet," said Wilson. "But we hope that can change soon!"

"Yes," said Thomas. "Perhaps you will become our first customer in the USA! Do you see something that is good product for you?"

"Not yet," she said, feeling somewhat guilty about her deception, but knowing the time wasn't right to confess the truth to the twins. On the other hand, the opening she'd been waiting for had clearly arrived.

"Do you make walking poles?" she asked.

The two brothers both tilted their heads slightly, then turned to each other and spoke in rapid Chinese. Suddenly, both started nodding, then turned to her.

"You mean *trekking* poles?" asked Thomas.

"Why yes," said Emily. "I suppose that is the more common name for them."

"We have that product up on balcony!" said Wilson. "Please, wait a moment. I will get for you!"

While Wilson scurried off for the rolling ladder, Thomas took the opportunity to explain more about the trekking poles.

"We made these poles for a company in Europe, but they go bankrupt and do not make entire payment. They pay deposit, but did not pay balance, so we have full container load of these products, but no customer."

Wilson went up the ladder. Emily dared to move closer to the ladder, probing to see if she had a reaction. Nothing. She reached out with her left hand, grasping the rail of the ladder. Still fine. She had no fear of the ladder. She believed she could have climbed it with no problem. She moved out of the way for Wilson to descend the ladder. Wilson came down the ladder and handed the poles to Emily. She looked them over and noticed they were virtually the same design as the pole that Willem had gifted to her back in Ireland. There was a molded grip and strap at the top, a basket and tip at the bottom, and the pole was retractable, with a locking mechanism near the center. She also noticed that it had a brand name printed on it that circled the top of the metal shaft, just below the finger grip. It said "Wanderer." Thomas saw Emily looking at the brand name and explained its origin.

"'Wanderer' is the German word for 'trekker.' This the brand name the bankrupt company use for their products."

"I see," said Emily. "But I don't think we could use that name, right?"

"Not sure," said Thomas. "But we can change name. It's just a label. Can be replaced by new label. What is name of your brand?"

"Uh, we haven't decided on that yet," she stammered.

"I see," said Thomas, a slight frown on his face. Emily felt she needed to keep the ruse going, sensing a deflation of interest from the Chinese twins, so she improvised.

"We have several names we're considering," said Emily. "But my favorite is 'Hill and Town.'"

"Hmmm," said Thomas.

"Why this name?" asked Wilson.

"Well, uh, you can use the poles in the mountains, but also in the streets. Many people can benefit from that, right?"

"Perhaps," said Thomas. "You know market better than us."

"What price do you charge for these poles?" asked Emily.

"Normally, we charge 20 U.S. dollar for each set," said Thomas. "But since first container load already made, and half money already paid to us, we charge only 10 dollar per set for first container load."

Emily had received a minor in business administration at CU. Her father had wanted her to major in business, but Emily had her own ideas. She'd always loved movies, and she wanted to learn the nuts and bolts of how they were made, so she majored in cinema studies. But it was really no trouble to obtain a minor in business, which amounted to nothing more than taking five classes in economics/business, two of which were required courses anyway. She'd especially enjoyed the course she took on international business, and she'd learned enough to know how distribution channels worked.

Emily didn't know the retail price of walking poles, but she imagined it must be around $100, based on what she knew about ski poles. If the normal factory price in China was $20, and the additional costs of shipping and duties to the U.S. were $5, then the delivered price was $25. If the importer then sold the product to retailers for $50, the retailers would double the price, so the $100 retail selling price made sense.

"How many sets of walking poles did you make for the bankrupt customer?" she asked.

"We make 7,000 sets," said Thomas. "This the quantity which fit 40-foot-high cube container."

"So, that means you want to be paid $70,000 for the first container load?"

"Yes," said Thomas. "Normally the container load would cost $140,000, but we give special deal in this case."

Without knowing why, Emily found herself negotiating.

"We don't want to spend that much for our first order," she said. "What can be done to make the cost less?"

"You can take 20-foot container load for first order," said Thomas. "Twenty-foot container only half as long as 40-foot and not as tall, so hold only 2,900 sets of poles. This make your first order cost total only $29,000."

Emily made some calculations, concluding that she could sell the poles to retailers for $40, which would lead to a retail price of $80, which would result in a price advantage versus the competition of around 20 percent.

"That's more reasonable," she said. "But we would want you to hold the balance of the goods for our second order, and to hold the $10 price for that order."

"Of course," said Thomas. "Can do."

"So, you will make the order?" asked Wilson.

This question brought Emily to her senses. She'd momentarily forgotten that the Chinese men were serious about selling the poles to her. They were used to making sales to the people who visited their showroom. She wasn't sure what to do, although she *had* become intrigued with the possibilities. If she was able to actually sell the first container of poles, she'd earn approximately $75,000 in profit. She could then easily afford to purchase and deliver the second 20-foot container, and when she sold that, she'd have more than enough money earned to afford 20-foot loads at the full China price.

Emily was *actually* excited about the opportunity, and she had an idea that would enable her to pay for the first container load if she pursued it. While she wasn't at all sure how she would sell the poles, she had some ideas about that as well. However, she'd made a commitment to NSCD back in Denver, to do a job that would help others as opposed to just helping herself, and this weighed heavily on her. She needed to buy time to think this through.

"I cannot commit to making the order today," said Emily. "I need to think about it, and I need to discuss it with my partners."

"Very well," said Thomas. "Will you be visiting other suppliers of trekking poles here in China?"

"I don't see the need for that," said Emily. "I feel very comfortable that I have already found the best supplier."

Thomas and Wilson both bowed deeply.

"Perhaps you join us for dinner tonight," said Wilson. "We take you to best Peking duck restaurant in all of China!"

Emily thought about the food in the hotel and concluded quickly how she would answer this invitation.

"I would be honored," she replied.

"We will meet you outside your hotel at 7 p.m., if that is okay," said Thomas.

"That's great," she said. "I'm staying at the Marriott Hotel Beijing Central."

"Okay, good," said Thomas. "We know this hotel."

"I'll be ready!" she said, hoping that Thomas and Wilson would not be disappointed if she decided not to purchase the poles. But as she rode back to the hotel in the taxi, her mind began to whirl with possibilities about the poles, so she decided to remain open-minded before completely ruling them out.

Chapter 32

Emily returned to her hotel just before noon, had lunch in the lobby restaurant, then went to her room and took a long nap. She awoke at 5 p.m., and this gave her some time to kill before dinner. She powered up her laptop and went online to do some research on trekking poles. She found that the retail prices were highly variable. A set could be priced as low as $50 or as high as $200, and she wondered what the difference between them was.

When Emily looked closer, she found that the expensive ones usually promoted that they were "made in the USA," whereas the less expensive ones didn't advertise where they were manufactured, which probably meant they were imported from China. The materials the poles were constructed from also made a difference. The aluminum ones were less expensive, and the carbon fiber ones were more expensive. Based upon her research, she formulated some additional questions for Thomas and Wilson, and then she closed her laptop. She showered and dressed, then went down to the lobby to wait for the twins.

She went outside, and soon a very nice Mercedes sedan approached the hotel. It turned in and came to a stop beside her. The rear door opened, and Wilson stepped out, bowed, and swept his right arm toward the door, beckoning Emily to get in. She smiled at Wilson, stepped toward the car and saw Thomas on the far side of the backseat. She slid into the middle of the seat, and Wilson got in beside her. When the door closed, the driver of the Mercedes pulled slowly away.

"Good evening, Miss Emily," said Thomas. "I hope you are hungry."

"Very hungry," she said. "The hotel food is not so good."

"Ahhh, yes," he said. "We know many Westerners struggle with the food in China. Tonight, we hope to relieve you of this burden."

The sedan turned out of the hotel and made its way through streets densely packed with cars and people. After about 10 minutes, they stopped in front of a building that looked to be at least seven stories high. A sign on the building had Chinese characters on it, but it also had English words, "Quanjude Roast Duck Restaurant."

After the car stopped, Wilson got out and extended his hand to help Emily. She waved him off and exited the car. Thomas slid out, and the three of them made their way into the restaurant.

Inside, the racket of voices was nearly deafening. Emily saw hundreds of people eating, drinking, talking, and laughing. Thomas and Wilson spoke to a hostess, and the three were led to an elevator. The hostess pushed the number "6" on the elevator control panel, which Emily assumed was the seventh floor, using the European numbering system. The elevator ascended, and the doors soon opened. The hostess rushed out. They followed her to a doorway down the hall, and she bowed and spread her arm out, inviting them to go in.

The room was small and had a medium-sized table for eight inside. There was no one else in the room.

"Please, take seat," said Wilson. "We make arrangement for private room for our V-I-P guest."

"Thank you," said Emily.

The three sat at the table, with Thomas on the end, Emily around the corner to his left, and Wilson around the corner to his right. The hostess left menus for them and departed. At the same time that she left the room, a female server entered and spoke in Chinese to Thomas and Wilson.

"Would you like some drink?" asked Wilson.

"Do you think they have Sauvignon blanc?" asked Emily.

"Something quite similar, I believe," said Thomas. He then spoke in Chinese to the waitress, and she left. Wilson addressed Emily.

"Quanjude the oldest and most famous Peking duck restaurant in Beijing," said Wilson. "Now have eight locations throughout city. This one not original, but it most popular with government official. Can seat 2,000 people at one time and serve 5,000 meals in one day."

"And the food is excellent!" said Thomas.

"I suppose you recommend the roast duck?" she asked.

"Of course," said Thomas. "Already ordered. I hope you don't mind."

"Not at all," said Emily. "I eat meat, and I've had duck a few times, so I'm looking forward to it."

The waitress returned with the drinks. Emily noticed that both Wilson and Thomas had received a glass of clear liquid. Wilson saw her looking at their drinks.

"This called baijiu," said Wilson. "Means white wine."

"But not like the white wine you are drinking," interjected Thomas. "A little bit stronger."

Thomas raised his glass, and Wilson followed him. Emily raised her glass.

"Gon-bay," said Thomas. He and Wilson put their glasses to their mouths and drained them.

Emily took a healthy sip of her wine and found it to be cold and sweet, not completely unlike Sauvignon blanc, but it would take some getting used to.

"What does Gon-bay mean?" she asked.

"Means 'dry cup,'" said Wilson.

"Am I supposed to empty my glass like you did?" she asked.

"Technically, yes," said Thomas, "but we make exception for foreigners who drink Western-style white wine. We realize *that* not meant for dry cup." He smiled but had more to say. "Tell me, Miss Emily, you say you saw us in film. We wonder where you saw this film?"

"I saw it in Denver, Colorado," she replied.

"What we do in this film?" asked Wilson.

"You were walking along the Great Wall. And then you were in your showroom with two Western customers."

"We sometimes take our customers to the Great Wall," said Thomas. "And most of them are Western people."

"Do you remember any of them taking a film of you?"

"Wilson and I have discussed this possibility," said Thomas. "And we remember two men who brought wives with them. One of the wives take a lot of videos. It is possible this film came from her."

"Where were they from?" asked Emily.

"They say they live in California," said Thomas. "I don't remember which city."

"Do you still have their contact information?" asked Emily.

"Yes," said Thomas. "We can give to you."

"Thank you," said Emily. "I appreciate that."

"Why did film make you want to come to China?" asked Wilson.

"Well, it wasn't really the film," she said. "It was the dreams I had after seeing the film."

"Ohhhh-awwh," groaned Wilson, who seemed intrigued by her comment.

"Dreams very important in Chinese culture," said Thomas. "Tell us your dream, and we interpret for you."

Emily explained that at first, she had just dreamed what the film had shown, but then she had extended the film to make dreams of her own. She had been in the showroom. She explained that she had seen the ladder that went up to the balcony but did not go into the effect the ladder had on her. She said that in the final dream she had about China, Wilson was showing her the walking poles.

"Ah, so that is why you come to China," said Thomas. "But how did you know you would find us? Was our company name or address in your dream?"

"No, it wasn't," she said. "I thought I would find you at the Great Wall. But you found me instead, at Tiananmen Square."

"Hmmm," said Thomas. "I see." He seemed very interested in what she was saying, as did Wilson.

"What are you thinking?" she asked.

"I will explain," said Thomas. "As I say, dreams very important in Chinese culture. Ancient Chinese believe that when you dream, your soul leaves your body and travels to dream world. In dream world, there is no time. No past, no present, no future. When you remember dreams, it is very important to interpret those dreams because dreams you remember are very important to your future.

"Your case different than normal because your dreams have already come true. You have lived them in the real world. Most times, dreams not so clear. They must be analyzed based on things you saw in the dream: the people, the animals, the weather, the objects. These things are signs about what will happen next, but we never know of someone who dreams exactly what will happen. So, in your case, no analysis necessary. Your dreams tell you directly what your future will be."

"It's that simple?" she asked.

"Seems so," said Thomas.

"But why am I having these dreams?" she asked. "Before I saw the films, I never had them."

"Films?" asked Thomas. "I thought you saw only one film."

"I saw another film a few months before the film of you two. In that one, I saw a man walking in the mountains in

Ireland. Then I dreamed that I met him at a train station. I went to Ireland and met this man, at the train station from my dream. I had never seen or known this man before."

"Ohhhh-awwh," groaned Wilson.

"Hmmmm," said Thomas.

"What?" she asked. "What does it all mean?"

"Don't know," said Thomas. "But it's quite clear you can dream your future."

"So it seems," said Emily.

"Did man walking in mountains in Ireland have trekking poles?" asked Wilson.

"Why, yes, he did," said Emily. "Does that mean anything?"

"It connect Ireland dream to China dream!" said Wilson, very excited.

"Yes," said Thomas. "This strong signal you must buy the trekking poles."

Emily laughed.

"Well, that's quite convenient," she said. "For you!"

Thomas wasn't smiling.

"Also, for you," said Thomas. "Dreams must be taken very seriously."

"I understand," she said. "It just seems like you two might be more interested in selling the poles than in interpreting my dream. Am I wrong about that?"

"Chinese people are merchants," said Thomas. "We love to sell. Love to make money. So, yes, we want to sell the poles. But it will make very little difference to our life if we don't. Wilson and I have made a lot of money already in our business. Now we look to experience more with our lives than just make money. So, when we meet a person like yourself, we become interested. We want to know more about you, especially about your dreams, which seem special."

"Okay," she said. "But before we talk more about the dreams, can I ask you one question about the trekking poles?"

"Yes, of course," said Thomas.

"What material is the shaft made from?" she asked.

"Carbon fiber," said Thomas. "The best material in the world for trekking poles."

Emily was impressed by this. A retail price of $80 for carbon fiber trekking poles was exceptionally low. This opportunity was beginning to become *very* intriguing. But before she could ask any more questions, Thomas directed the conversation back to her dreams.

"Was there more China dreams than what you tell us so far?" asked Thomas.

"I'm not sure," said Emily. "The last dream I remembered was a few weeks ago. That was the one where Wilson showed me the trekking poles. But then the dream shifted, and I was in the Netherlands, meeting with a couple I met in Ireland, and then I was back in Ireland, meeting with the man from the film that I had met there."

"You making business with them!" cried Wilson. "You sell them trekking poles!"

"I don't know that," said Emily. "It was unclear why I was there."

"I think Wilson make good prediction of why you there," said Thomas. "But I have another idea that might help you understand better. You must take trip to temple at top of mountain."

"What? Why? Are you serious?"

"In China, the monks at Buddhist temple the best people to predict the future. They can do this for you. Tomorrow morning, Wilson will take you. I will stay in showroom."

"Where is this temple?"

"There are many temples throughout China. The one we send you to is west of the city, in the mountains."

"But I was hoping to go to the Great Wall before I leave. My flight is on Monday."

"Wilson and I will take you to the Great Wall on Sunday. Okay?"

"Okay," she said, intrigued by the conversation but disappointed she had achieved no final clarity regarding whether or not to pursue the walking pole project.

The meal arrived, and it was delicious. For the first time since Emily had arrived, she felt satiated, at least her stomach did. Her mind, on the other hand, was still starving for understanding, for something to explain the strange circumstances that had enveloped her life.

Chapter 33

Wilson opened the door to the Mercedes sedan for Emily at 9 a.m. on Saturday morning, July 3. She got in, and the car smoothly worked its way out of the city, heading west, toward the mountains. After about one hour, the driver pulled into a parking area beside a steep, tall hill. To Emily, it looked as if the vertical rise from the parking lot to the summit was about 1,500 feet. She'd brought her backpack and water bladder on the trip, although she'd thought she'd be using it at places like the Great Wall, not for mountain climbing. But the vertical rise wasn't intimidating to her, especially because she'd been doing a lot of walking in the mountains lately.

She noticed that Wilson was no longer dressed in his suit, clothed instead in khaki pants and a polo shirt and wearing running shoes. He had a bottle of water in his hand.

"Now we go up mountain, okay, Miss Emily?" he asked.

"Sure!" she said, with genuine excitement in her voice. She hadn't expected this, and she hoped it would be an experience she would remember.

At a ticket stand near the entrance to the hill, Wilson bought two tickets and handed one to Emily. She put it in the pocket of her shorts. Emily noticed a few people looking at her right arm. This was the first time she'd seen people staring at her arm since she'd been in China. Perhaps her focusing on all that was new and different here had mitigated her tendency to make subtle observations of the gazes of others, but what she preferred to believe was that the Chinese people might be less judgmental than other cultures.

Although the hill they were climbing was steep, the path up wasn't. It was a series of many switchbacks that allowed them to slowly climb the hill. The distance they were covering was substantial, and Emily was glad she had plenty of water. She glanced at Wilson and noticed he was sweating profusely and had consumed more than half of his water already. Emily hoped they sold water at the top for poor Wilson.

After an hour of climbing, they reached the summit. It was a relatively clear day, and Emily could see the outskirts of Beijing in the east. The top of the summit was flat. She saw the temple itself off to one side. A line of people waited to gain entrance. On the other side of the summit, she observed another line of people and ascertained they were waiting to have their fortunes told. She saw wooden privacy fences that had been constructed to form five stalls of a sort, inside of which the monks were located, looking busy.

Wilson stopped at a stand and bought a stick of incense and a lighter, and also a bottle of water.

"You will need this," he said, handing Emily the incense and lighter. "When you go in, light it and place it where monk show you."

It took about 20 minutes for Emily to be motioned forward by one of the monastery employees. Before she went in, Wilson took her arm.

"Give donation, and monk will tell fortune," he said.

"How much should I give?" she asked.

"The more you give, the better the fortune!" he said, laughing afterward.

"Okay," she said, a little disappointed. She was actually hoping for a legitimate fortune telling, but now it appeared this was just a way for the monks to raise money for the temple.

Emily moved forward and made her way into the next open stall. Wilson followed her, ostensibly to serve as a translator. Inside, a monk sat cross-legged. He was bald, and his orange robe looked faded. Emily saw sticks of incense burning in small bottles throughout the stall. The monk reached forward with an empty bottle and held it out to her. She lit the incense and placed it into the bottle. The monk withdrew the bottle and placed it on a flat rock to his left. He looked up at her, and she remembered she was supposed to give him money. She withdrew a 100 RMB note from her pocket and gave it to him. He nodded his head, placed the money aside, then rotated his palm toward the sky and extended his arm, inviting her to sit on the cushion that was directly in front of him. She sat on the cushion, then crossed her legs. Wilson remained standing behind her.

The monk reached over and took hold of the incense bottle that he'd placed on the rock. He brought the bottle close to his face, observing the smoke wafting up from the incense stick. He drew in some of the smoke through his nose, then bowed his head and closed his eyes, seemingly in deep concentration. After about one minute, he raised his head and opened his eyes wide, a look of awe on his face. He reached over and grabbed the 100 RMB note, then handed it back to Emily. She turned around and looked to Wilson for guidance.

Wilson spoke in Chinese to the monk. The monk spoke back to him.

"He say he tell your fortune for no money," explained Wilson.

"Why?" she asked.

"I don't know, but I think it something important. Let us hear what he has to say."

Emily turned her attention back to the monk. After a few seconds, he began to speak. He spoke for about 30 seconds. Emily turned back to Wilson for a translation.

"He say you very powerful person. He say you will be successful in business and then become very powerful person in your country. He say you can become most powerful person in the world if you choose."

Even though Wilson's demeanor was profoundly serious, Emily had to resist the urge to laugh. But then she remembered the monk had accepted no money to tell this fortune. This presumably would allow him to be truthful in the telling of her fortune, so she was confused as to why he'd made up such a ridiculous story for her. The part about being successful in business she could buy, but the rest of it, especially becoming the most powerful person in the world, was ludicrous.

Emily looked into the monk's eyes. He continued to stare at her, the look of awe and reverence still on his face. She stood to leave, and the monk stood up as well. He bowed deeply, holding the bow until she exited the stall.

As Wilson and Emily walked away from the fortune-telling area, Wilson addressed her.

"I never see fortune-telling monk stand and bow before. *Never* see that."

"Why do you think he did that?"

"I don't know," said Wilson. "I will ask Thomas."

It had become clear to Emily during the brief time she'd known Wilson and Thomas that even though the two were twins, Thomas was the senior member of their partnership. Thomas always spoke during important moments, and now Thomas would be consulted regarding the events at the Buddhist temple. Emily was anxious to hear his take on it, but in her mind, she was already chalking it up as a waste of time. At least that is what she was trying to do.

Chapter 34

On the morning of Sunday, July 4, Emily woke with vivid memories of a dream from the night. The details of her visit to see Anna and Willem had fleshed themselves out in the dream. They picked Emily up at a big airport, drove to their farm, and helped her unload. In addition to her suitcase and backpack, Emily had brought a large cardboard box as part of her luggage. When they got inside, they opened the box, and Emily withdrew a set of trekking poles from it. There were obviously more sets inside the box. Emily noticed the words "Hill and Town" circling the top of the metal shaft below the grip of the pole.

The scene shifted to them driving on a highway. She saw the word "Venlo" on a highway sign. Then they parked the car and went into a large building and were escorted to a conference room. A meeting took place with people apparently from that company. After they got up, they all shook hands and departed. The dream ended.

Emily made coffee with the machine in her room. It was around 8 a.m. She showered, dressed, and used the bottled water she'd bought the night before in the shop in the lobby to partially fill her water bladder. She made sure she had what she needed for the trip to the Great Wall, picked up her backpack, and went downstairs for a quick breakfast. At 9 a.m., she went outside, and within one minute the Mercedes sedan pulled up, Wilson popped out, she got into the car, and off they went. She sat in the middle again, between Thomas and Wilson. She noticed they were both wearing their business suits and wondered why.

On the drive to the Great Wall, Emily shared her latest dream with Thomas and Wilson. Thomas told her that Wilson had discussed their visit to the temple with him, and now with this new information from her dream, it was obvious that she needed to go to Europe to set up distribution of the trekking poles. He said they would have a box with six samples prepared for her and made a call on his cell phone to arrange it. He then told her that T.W. Athletic Equipment Company would make all the arrangements and pay all her travel expenses to go to Europe, then to Ireland, and then to whatever destination she wanted to go to after that.

Emily felt overwhelmed, but she didn't resist. The power of what was going on had subdued her desire to pursue anything except what was foretold by her dreams. She started making a mental list of all the emails she'd need to write later that day.

The trip to the Great Wall was interesting. The driver let them off in a vast parking lot at the foot of the wall. They climbed a long set of stairs, alongside of which were many small shops where merchandise, food, and beverages were sold. Throngs of tourists were packed into them. Many stalls sold Great Wall T-shirts, and Emily told the twins she wanted to buy one. Thomas stopped and gave her some advice.

"I tell you the way to negotiate with Chinese vendors," he said. "Ask them the price, and no matter what number they give you, offer 5 RMB for the shirt. They will complain and pretend to walk away, so then *you* turn to walk away. They will rush over to you, screaming out a new price, acting as if it kill them to give you this price. Then you raise your price to 10 RMB. The process will repeat, but don't go higher than 15 RMB. They will sell you the shirt for that price. Also, tell them from the beginning that you want the shirt they are holding. No other shirt than that."

"Can't you just buy the shirt for me?" she asked.

"No, it won't work that way," said Thomas. "They won't negotiate with a Chinese if they know we are with you. They want to sell the shirt at inflated price to unsuspecting tourists. We will wait here for you. Go."

Emily walked into the area that had dozens of stalls selling T-shirts. Several of the vendors saw her and started holding up beautiful Great Wall T-shirts, yelling "Best price! Best quality!" and urging her to come look at their shirts. Emily chose a stall and approached. An old man was holding up a black shirt with printed images in white and lettering in red. The shirt had a picture of the Great Wall across the center and the words "I climbed the Great Wall" printed across the top.

"Besta quality! Lowest price!" screamed the old man.

"How much?" asked Emily.

The man looked at her, tilted his head and then spoke.

"For you, special price. Only 100 RMB!"

"I want *this* shirt," said Emily, grabbing hold of the shirt. "No other shirt. This one, okay?"

"Okay," said the old man, a suspicious look on his face.

"I will give you 5 RMB," she said.

"Ohhh!" screamed the old man, frowning and making a half turn as if he were going to walk away. Emily turned and began to walk away herself.

"Wait!" yelled the old man, running after her. "Fifty RMB!" he screamed.

Emily stopped and turned back toward him. The man retreated back to his stall, and Emily took the few steps back to it as well.

"Ten RMB," she said.

"Ohhh!" moaned the old man, turning again, pretending to walk away.

Emily turned and walked away. The old man ran back to her.

"Twenty-figh RMB," he yelled. "I make no money, but I do for you."

"Fifteen RMB," she said.

"Cannot do," said the old man. "I lose money."

"Very well," said Emily. "I am sorry we could not come to an agreement." She turned and walked briskly and resolutely away.

"Okay!" yelled the old man, frowning and shaking his head, speaking words to himself as if he'd been robbed.

They returned the few steps to the stall, and the old man hurried to the back, where he kept boxes of shirts. At that point, Thomas appeared, yelling at the old man in Chinese. The old man turned around and yelled back. Thomas said something else, and the old man's expression changed to one of fear and reverence. He bowed and brought the original shirt forward, handing it to Emily. Emily gave him the money, and they turned around to leave. The old man continued bowing, up and down, saying what appeared to be kind words to them.

Emily was pleased at the result of the negotiation. She felt she'd learned something about business in general from the small transaction, and she also proved something to herself: that she could do it! She had the confidence to make a deal that was good for her in spite of the seemingly incongruent actions of her opponent. Yes, Thomas had given her the guidance she needed, but she'd done it perfectly and was proud of herself. Yet at the end, Thomas had intervened, and she wasn't completely sure why.

"What did you say to him?" she asked Thomas.

"He was going to get a cheap shirt out of the box and give it to you. The first thing I said was that you had negotiated for the nice shirt that he'd been holding."

"But that didn't work, did it?"

"No."

"So, what else did you tell him?"

"I told him that I am member of the Party," said Thomas.

"The Communist Party?" she asked.

"Yes," said Thomas.

"And *are* you a member?" she asked.

"Yes," said Thomas.

"Is Wilson a member?"

"No."

"The man seemed scared," she said.

"He was. And he should be. There are 1.4 billion people in China, but less than 100 million in the Party. I never say this to foreigner before, but you are special, Miss Emily. Party member have power. Power to make things happen that not always pleasant for people."

"I see," said Emily, hoping Thomas would continue to view her as someone he should help, not hurt.

Chapter 35

The trip to the Great Wall had been fun and educational. At one point, when they'd climbed all the way up to the wall and were walking down the wide stone pathway, Emily had stopped to look at the view. Thomas and Wilson had continued on, and when Emily turned to catch up with them, she saw that they were walking side by side, their arms folded behind their backs, hands clasped. It was the image from the film and her first dream about China. She removed her cell phone from her pocket and took a picture of the two. She wasn't sure why, but it was a memory she wanted to keep.

When Emily got back to the hotel, she had a lot to do. She tackled the most difficult email first, which was to inform NSCD that due to her unresolved personal matters, she would not be able to begin working at NSCD on July 6. She apologized profusely and asked them not to keep the job open for her because they had extended themselves more than she deserved already.

The second email was to her father. She explained the

business opportunity she'd stumbled upon in China, and her confidence that she had the right contacts in Europe to sell out the first container load quickly. She then asked him for a $50,000 loan, to cover the cost of purchasing and delivering the first container load, plus some additional money to cover travel and marketing expenses. She proposed that she pay back the loan with interest, after the second container load was sold. She also proposed that in the event the business venture failed, a 10-year amortization schedule be developed for her to pay back the loan out of her future earnings at whatever job she ended up with.

Next, she emailed Anna to tell her she would be flying into Schiphol Airport in Amsterdam in the coming days. Thomas had told her the name of the destination airport for the commencement of her Europe trip on the way back from the Great Wall and informed her that her entire itinerary would be completed by that evening. Emily explained to Anna that she would very much like to see her and Willem, and also get some guidance on a new business venture she was pursuing that had great potential in the European market. She explained that she would follow up in a matter of hours with the timing of her flight arrival.

Finally, she emailed John, telling him that she was coming to Europe and would be in Ireland sometime late that week and hoped to see him. She apologized for the short notice and told him she had secured the rights to a product made in China that might be a big opportunity for Hill and Town Walking Tours. She promised to email again soon with the details of her trip.

After finishing all the emails, Emily laid down for a

nap, hoping she would have no further dreams because her plate was already full from the dreams she'd remembered so far. She woke at 5 p.m., showered and dressed, then went down to meet Thomas and Wilson for one last dinner engagement before she left.

The twins took her to a small but elegant Chinese restaurant, explaining that the food was very high quality and perfectly safe for Westerners to eat. They ordered steamed pork dumplings, chicken and vegetables, and vegetable fried rice. The food came in stages and was served to them on a lazy Susan turntable that sat on the top of the round table at which they were sitting. There were several other dishes on the turntable, and Wilson explained that people could take from any dish they wanted to try. Chopsticks were provided. With Wilson's help showing Emily the proper way to use them, she easily managed to eat her food. Because of her sole reliance on her left hand, her fingers had become quite nimble. Using chopsticks was no problem for her. During the meal, an important conversation transpired.

First, Thomas handed her an envelope that contained her travel itinerary. He explained that her flight to Amsterdam would be on KLM, the Dutch national airline, and would depart at noon the next day, which was July 5. It was a 12-hour flight, and because Amsterdam was six hours behind China, she would arrive in Amsterdam around 6 p.m. on the same day. She would stay in the Netherlands for three days, then on Thursday, July 8, she would fly to Dublin on Aer Lingus, then take a commuter flight in Dublin to Kerry Airport in the west of Ireland, which wasn't far from Dingle. Thomas explained that there were no further flight arrangements made at that time because it was unclear where Emily would need to go next. But he emphasized that as soon as she had a plan for where she wanted to go after Ireland, she should email them, and they would make the reservations.

"Why are you doing this?" asked Emily.

"Because you V-I-P!" said Wilson, enthusiastically.

"But you owe me nothing," she replied. "You don't have to do this."

Thomas interjected.

"Yes, Miss Emily, we *do* have to do this."

"But why?"

"You seem not to believe what the monk told you at the temple. But we take it very seriously. The monk would not take your money because of what he see in the smoke of the incense you lit. He would not take your money because you are special person, a person that most monks never meet in their whole life. You are someone that Wilson and I want to make strong relationship with. The money we spend to help you is really to help ourselves. We invest in you because you will do great things, and we want to be part of it."

"Well, thank you," said Emily. "I don't really understand, but thank you."

"In time, you will come to understand," said Thomas. "For now, you must keep moving forward. You must take one step at a time. We help you take first step."

"I will do my best," said Emily, wondering what that really meant, but also excited about what might transpire during her next adventure.

Chapter 36

When Emily reviewed the documents that Thomas had given her at dinner, she was surprised to see they had booked her in business class on the KLM flight. This sped up her check-in, allowed her to go through special screening lines, and enabled her to board the plane first. She checked two items, her suitcase and the sample box, and carried on only her backpack, which had become a staple in her life over the past month.

The business class seat was wide and comfortable, and because she'd been seated in the center section, she had easy access to the lavatory and didn't have to worry about another passenger climbing over her. The food was quite edible. Emily was served as much wine as she wanted, and she wanted plenty. The events of her life over the past month were cascading over her in waves, creating confusion and exhilaration at the same time. She barely ever thought of the Projector Man anymore, although she *had* lodged in her mind, for future use, a reminder that she had unfinished business with him. But she needed to move forward before going back to where it all started.

Before Emily had departed for the airport, she'd checked her emails and found responses to each of the four she'd sent the previous day. The NSCD contact had expressed disappointment but wished her well and told her to please contact them if and when her personal issues were resolved because they would be happy to find a place for her. Her father had told her he was open-minded to her request but would like to speak further at her earliest convenience. John had been ecstatic, telling her he was leading a group on the Kerry Way that week but would be finished Friday. He asked her to please let him know her arrival details as soon as she had them. Anna was also pleasantly surprised and told Emily that whenever she arrived, they would be there to pick her up.

Emily had written a quick thank-you email to the NSCD, sent another short note to her father telling him she would call him later in the week, sent the details of her arrival to Anna, then told John she was arriving at Kerry Airport on Thursday afternoon and would book a room in Dingle and wait for his arrival on Friday.

The plane touched down at Schiphol Airport near Amsterdam at 5:45 p.m. on Monday, July 5. Emily disembarked, followed the signs to arrivals, and breezed through immigration much faster than she expected. The agent was friendly and barely glanced at her passport before stamping it and waving her through. The luggage also arrived quickly, and Emily loaded her suitcase and the sample box onto a trolley and proceeded to customs. The customs agent glanced at the cardboard box.

"What's in de box?" he asked.

"Trekking poles," said Emily.

"Okay," he said, smiling. "I didn't see them, right?" He waved her on through.

Emily wondered if the agent was supposed to stop her and inspect the contents of the box, but she didn't argue, pushing her trolley through the automatic door and out into the arrivals hall, which was a city unto itself. The signage in the hall had English directions, in addition to what she assumed was Dutch, so it was no problem finding her way to the passenger pickup area, although it took some time.

It was hard for Emily to manage the trolley with only one hand because she had to squeeze the hand brake at the same time she depressed the handle. Otherwise, the brake would engage, and the trolley would jerk to a halt. But Emily was accustomed to getting some help from her handless right arm, and she was using it for all it was worth during the slog through the hall, pressing it hard against the right side of the handle to help propel and stabilize the trolley. It took her nearly 15 minutes to get outside.

After a moment of waiting on the side of the road, a small van approached and came to a stop. Anna got out of the passenger seat. Willem came around from the driver's side, and they all hugged and greeted each other. Willem carried Emily's luggage to the back of the van and put it in, then returned to the driver's side of the vehicle and got in. Anna helped Emily get into the back, then climbed into the front passenger seat, and off they went.

As they drove, Emily explained to Anna and Willem

that she'd acted on an opportunity that had arisen in China and was seriously considering pursuing the trekking pole business. Willem, in particular, found the irony of this amusing because it was he who'd first introduced Emily to trekking poles. When queried by Anna as to how the opportunity had arisen, Emily made up a story about a business associate of her father having given her the lead. Emily had revealed her dreams to Woha, John, and Thomas and Wilson, but she saw no urgency to share them with Anna and Willem, at least not yet.

The drive to the farm took around two hours. According to Anna, the farm was around 10 kilometers west of a town called Venlo, which Emily recalled was the name she'd seen written on a road sign in her dream from a few nights ago. The farm consisted of a brick, two-story home and three outbuildings. Emily could see fields full of plants to the rear of the home and buildings, but no farm hands were present.

"Where are the workers?" she asked.

"They come by bus every morning and go back in the evening to the institution where they live," said Anna. "It's not far, just over in Venlo."

"What time do they start working in the morning?"

"Half past eight," said Anna. "And they depart at half past four. Here in Holland, we do not work ourselves to death!"

They went into the home, and Willem carried Emily's suitcase up the stairs, presumably to put it in the bedroom where she'd be staying, but he left the box of trekking poles sitting in the entry hall. Emily smelled something delicious immediately upon entering the house. Anna noticed her sniffing the air.

"It's called hachee," said Anna. "Beef and onion stew. Will be ready shortly. Are you hungry?"

"Getting there," said Emily. "The food on the plane was good, and they fed us twice, but I'm definitely able to eat, especially since it smells so good."

"We normally eat a few hours earlier than this," said Anna, "but we had a nice snack before we came to the airport, so no worries."

Anna gave her a short tour of the first floor of their home, showing her the kitchen first, which seemed very modern to Emily compared with what she'd expect in a farmhouse. Anna snatched a bottle of white wine from the fridge, then grabbed three wine glasses with her other hand and carried them upside down, holding them by the stems. She led Emily through the dining room and into the living room, where she invited her to sit down. Anna placed the wine and the wine glasses on a coffee table, also quite modern, and poured three glasses of wine. Willem returned from upstairs and sat down to join them. Anna raised her glass, and the other two followed her lead.

"Proost!" said Anna.

The other two repeated the word, and they all drank.

"Oh, wow!" exclaimed Emily. "Now that's a great white wine!"

"Only de best for de vorld traveler!" said Willem.

"Thank you," said Emily. "I wasn't able to find a wine that I liked during my short stay in China. This one is fantastic!"

"It's a common wine here," said Anna. "We Dutch like a good French wine from time to time. This one is from the Sancere wine-growing region."

The conversation carried on while the first bottle of wine was consumed, after which they moved to the dining room, where dinner was served and another bottle of wine was emptied. After the dishes were cleared away and the three were well into their third bottle of wine, Anna turned the conversation in an unexpected direction.

"Emily, I've made up my mind to tell you something," said Anna, her face serious.

"What?" said Emily, having no idea where Anna was headed with this. But it didn't take Anna long to reveal her secret.

"I know about the video," said Anna.

Chapter 37

Emily was stunned and confused. Could Anna be referring to one of the films she'd seen at the Projector Man's house?

"What video?" she asked. "I'm not sure what you mean."

"I mean the video of John walking in the mountains and leading the group through town and into the B&B," said Anna.

That was enough for Emily to conclude that Anna *was* speaking about the first *film*, but she wasn't sure why she referred to it as a video. But that detail was unimportant at the moment, so she decided to play this out as if she knew for certain what Anna was referring to.

"How could you possibly know about that?" she asked. "Did John tell you?"

"No," said Anna. "I didn't know John knew about the video."

"I told him. But how did *you* find out?"

"Because I made it," said Anna. "I made the video during a tour we did with John last year."

Another shock wave cascaded through Emily's nervous

system, but she fought to maintain her composure. She thought it through and didn't say anything. She reasoned that if Anna had actually shot the scenes in question, she would have undoubtedly used a digital device, most likely a phone, which explained why she was referring to it as a video. If it actually *was* her footage that Emily had seen at Fred Watts's house, Anna's video must have been somehow transferred to cellulose film. The picture *was* quite grainy, so it could be something as simple as taking a film of the video itself while it played on a screen. Emily glanced at Willem and saw that he had a serious look on his face, but he made no attempt to add to the conversation. This was obviously all about Anna, and it would be up to Anna to explain herself.

She better have a good explanation, thought Emily, *because otherwise I'm out of here.* Emily waited, and Anna finally continued.

"I will tell you what I know," said Anna. "It's not much, but it's something. I'm actually violating the confidentiality agreement I signed, but it doesn't matter. I can't let these secrets destroy our friendship. I've grown too fond of you to carry on with this charade any longer."

Emily experienced mixed emotions as Anna confessed her betrayal. She was upset that up until this point, Anna had deceived her. On the other hand, she was relieved that she was finally going to get some information that would help explain how her life had been turned upside down since viewing that first film.

"Please, Anna," she said. "Tell me what you know. I've been going crazy trying to figure this out."

"Very well. I have a friend, a woman I went to university with. We were both studying psychology, and after we graduated, she went on with her studies, obtaining a master's, and then went on to obtain her PhD in cognitive psychology, which is the study of brain processes such as perception, memory, language, problem-solving, and learning. The woman and I kept in touch over the years, but only casually. We never worked together at all, but then a few years ago, she called me and said she might have some freelance work I could do for a project she'd become involved in."

"What kind of project?" asked Emily.

"When I first met with her, she was somewhat evasive about that, but she *did* reveal that the project she was involved in was studying how people dream. I pushed her to tell me more, and she said that in order for her to say more, I would need to sign a confidentiality agreement, which I did. After that, she told me the project was focused on what she called 'future dreaming.'"

"What does that mean, exactly?" asked Emily.

"I don't know *exactly*, but from our conversations, and from the assignments I was given, I concluded that her group is trying to find ways to stimulate people's brains into dreaming about the future."

Anger swirled around inside Emily, but she forced herself to stay calm to learn more.

"What assignments did they give you?" she asked.

"My assignments were simple. I was to take videos of interesting things. My friend knew that Willem and I travel a lot, and that we are often in very remote and interesting environments. She asked me to make short videos when we were traveling and to send them to her. The video of John was one of them."

"How did you find out that I had seen the video?" asked Emily.

"If one of my videos is approved, I am paid 1,000 euros, which is good money for doing something I'd probably be doing anyway. On the other hand, I'd say that only one out of five of my submissions is approved."

"But that still doesn't explain how you would know I'd seen your video."

"Well, the video I made of John was approved, and I was paid. I thought that would be the end of it, but then I was contacted by my friend in early May of this year. She asked if I was willing to go on the Wicklow Way tour and make observations of a subject. The subject was you."

The emotions Emily was feeling rose closer to the surface. She thought back to their time along the Wicklow Way and remembered the afternoon in Roundwood when she'd seen Anna and Willem following her as she'd been walking to Byrne and Woods for dinner with John. She had no idea at that time that they were involved in her perplexing situation, and it angered her now to learn that they were.

"Why did you do it?" she asked.

"I was paid 10,000 euros," said Anna.

"Was it worth it?" Emily asked, sarcastically, feeling disgusted that someone she cared for would do this.

"No," said Anna. "It wasn't. So, I refused to file my report and sent the money back. I also told my friend I would no longer be submitting films to her. The whole thing smells bad to me. I care for you, Emily, and I am so very sorry to have betrayed you in this way." Tears leaked from Anna's eyes and flowed down her cheeks. She wiped them away with the back of her hand.

Emily refocused and continued asking questions.

"So, I'm a subject in some secret study? Is that what you're telling me?"

"Yes. And I don't like it. I will help you in any way I can to free yourself from these people."

Emily was somewhat appeased that Anna had confessed her role and that she had in fact rejected it and resigned. She was still upset, but not at Anna. Emily was upset that she was being used. The time had come to reveal everything to Anna and Willem so they could help her figure things out and get on with her life, on her terms.

"There's a man in Denver who pretends to be some old man selling a projector," she said. "He's the one who showed me the film of John in Ireland. Then I dreamed about it, in even more detail than the film contained, so I went to Ireland and actually met John. When I went back to the Projector Man and started asking questions, he showed me another film, of China. And now here I am selling trekking poles made in China. And I dreamed about *all* of it before I did it. I even dreamed about coming to see you here in Holland."

"So, you dream the future, and then you make it come true," said Anna.

"Yes. What does that mean?"

"It means you are a very special person, I think," said Anna.

"That's what the Chinese said, too. So, why don't I feel

that way? Why do I feel like I'm being used?"

"Because you *are* being used!" exclaimed Anna.

"Can you tell me who this woman is who is supposedly your friend? The one who hired you to participate in something that is unethical, and very likely illegal."

"I will tell you," said Anna. "But we have to be careful. My friend wouldn't hurt anyone, physically, but she's a very powerful person. We will have to approach this matter delicately if and when you decide to confront her. And let's not forget: The real perpetrator of the events that led to your future dreaming is the old man in Denver. I don't know him, but *you* obviously do."

"Oh, yes, I know him," said Emily. "And I won't forget about him—or your friend. But now that I know there's something going on behind the scenes, I will definitely wait for the right moment before I confront any of these people."

When Emily went to bed that night, she felt a sense of progress. She had no idea at that point if anything would pan out regarding the trekking poles, but she'd finally gotten some concrete information about the films—and her dreams. There were people out there—a group of people that included Fred Watts—who were operating a clandestine program designed to induce people to dream the future. And they'd succeeded. She was living proof that it could be done. And while the direction these future dreams had taken her had been mostly beneficial to her, it still wasn't right. These people had no right to take advantage of unsuspecting, innocent people like herself.

Yet Emily was conflicted. She realized clearly that one day she would need to confront these people, especially

Fred Watts, and bring them to justice if she could. But today was not that day, nor was tomorrow. Tomorrow she would begin the work to determine if Thomas and Wilson and the monk at the temple had been right. Tomorrow she would continue her quest to unravel the mystery of where her latest dreams would actually take her.

Chapter 38
February 2010

At breakfast the next morning, Anna and Emily were alone at the kitchen table. Willem had already gone out to manage the workers.

"I have another secret to tell you," said Anna.

"What?" asked Emily, hoping it wasn't that Anna had made the China video as well.

"My brother is the purchasing manager for Bever Outdoor."

"And *what* is Bever Outdoor?" asked Emily.

"It's the largest outdoor retailer in the Netherlands. It's like the REI of Holland."

"And that means?"

"That means I think we might have found a home for your first container load of trekking poles!"

"Are you serious?"

"The poles look good, and if you're going to sell them to my brother for 20 percent less than comparable products, he will probably buy them. If there's one thing you will learn about the Dutch, it's that we are frugal people.

We always like the lowest price—as long as the quality is good. And with a recommendation from me, your chances go up even further."

"That would awesome! Thank you. I didn't expect that at all."

"That's just the beginning," said Anna. "There's more. Venlo is one of the biggest logistics hubs in Northern Europe. It's right on the German border, and it's only four hours from Paris. A lot of big logistics companies there can hold your goods for you, and many of them will have contacts with the big outdoor retailers, especially the ones in Germany, which is the biggest market in Europe."

"Wow, this sounds too good to be true," said Emily.

"Actually, to me it sounds like you were *meant* to be doing this!"

"But why? I just don't understand the why!"

"Eventually, it will become clear, I'm sure. But for now, let's take it one step at time. Anyway, before we go out and introduce you to our workers, let's talk about something that's more important than *anything* we've talked about so far."

"What?" asked Emily, feeling as if she'd absorbed so much new and baffling information in the past 12 hours that she couldn't take any more.

"You and John. How's that going?"

"Oh, come on, Anna. Do we have to talk about this?"

"I think you *need* to talk about this. Do you know why?"

"No, why?"

"Because you are a human being, and John is a human being, and the most important thing in this world is the love two people can have together. I am lucky I found it with Willem, nearly 30 years ago."

"Was Willem involved in your spying 'mission'?" asked Emily.

"He knew about it, because there are no secrets between us. But he wasn't at all happy about it, especially after he got to know you. Willem and I never had children, so you very quickly became important to both of us. You are the kind of person we would have wanted our child to become. Willem was disgusted by what I was doing and was adamant that I discontinue my involvement not long after we met you."

Emily was touched by Anna's comments about her and Willem's feelings for her.

"I figured Willem wasn't involved," she said. "He just doesn't seem the type."

"And I do?" asked Anna, a little defensively.

"More so than him, I suppose. You seem quite worldly, with all your languages and sophistication. You're not really the farmer type, but Willem definitely is."

"He is," said Anna. "And it's true that I'm not that involved in the day-to-day operations of the farm. I really could use something more appropriate to my skill set, which could possibly be the trekking poles. But enough about that. What about you and John?"

"He and I only spent a few days together," said Emily, feeling some anxiety over the whole situation with John. "Yes, there *was* a connection, but we live 5,000 miles apart and have completely different lives."

"One thing you might not realize because you are so

young is that these 'connections' you speak about, they are very rare indeed."

Emily thought about what Anna was saying, and she knew in her heart that it was true.

"I suppose you're right," she agreed. "And if I'm honest, I would tell you that I've never had a connection like I had with John."

"I knew it! But why do you say 'had?' It doesn't go away, you know."

"It's just that I've had a lot going on. You would agree with that, wouldn't you?"

"Of course, Emily, of course. I know. But here in Holland, we *live* first, work second. We truly appreciate life and make it our highest priority to enjoy it."

"I understand, I think. And maybe that philosophy is the correct one. But in my country, we value achievement. People are free to decide what that means to them, and I've always considered helping others to be my way of accomplishing something important. I was hoping to serve others with my new job, but that's history now, so I'm going to have to accomplish something big, or I'll regret it for the rest of my life. That might not leave much room for a personal life."

"Well, my hope is that you can have your accomplishments and also find and share the love of another human being."

"I hope so, too," said Emily.

"Shall we go out and meet the team?" asked Anna.

"By all means."

They went out and joined Willem, and he introduced

Emily to the workers. They were people of all ages, both men and women, and all mentally challenged in their own unique way. Emily was moved, not by their limitations, but by their radiant smiles. Their smiles reminded her of Hannah Baxter, her student back at Winter Park. This brought on a wave of sadness and regret for what she'd left behind. But she recovered quickly and kept her own smile wide, experiencing profound joy as she witnessed the bliss of people who were at peace with themselves and the role they played on the farm.

Anna was watching her closely and leaned up to her ear.

"Glad to see you understand," was all she said.

After lunch, Anna drove Emily to Venlo while Willem stayed to manage the farm. They met with a logistics company that owned a huge warehouse and had distribution throughout Europe. They had two more meetings like that on Wednesday morning, then drove to the headquarters of Bever Outdoor and presented the trekking poles to Anna's brother, Robert.

Emily left trekking pole samples at each place they visited, and she still had two sets left to take with her. All the meetings were very positive, especially the one with Bever Outdoor, and one of the logistics companies had promised to make calls right away to some of the big outdoor chains in Germany. By the time Emily boarded the plane Thursday morning for Ireland, she was firmly convinced that the trekking pole venture could be successful, and she had yet to even test the waters in Ireland, which was coming next.

Chapter 39

Emily found Dingle to be a very lively, interesting town. After she checked in at her B&B, she strolled down to Dingle Harbor, a bright, cheerful place of gently bobbing boats, with a backdrop to the north which included the bustling village and vibrant rolling hills. She noticed an area with signage dedicated to "Fungie the Dolphin" and saw people boarding boats that guaranteed a sighting of the famous aquatic mammal.

It was late afternoon, and Emily was hungry, so she made the five-minute walk into town, chose an inviting pub, and sat down for a glass of wine and some fresh fish and chips, all of which were excellent.

Emily noticed people glancing at her right arm, reminding her she was different from them without intending to. It made her think of John. She wondered why her missing hand was such a non-factor to him. This warmed her heart in a way she hadn't had time to feel since the last time she was with him. She'd traveled almost around the world to return to Ireland, and her self-inflicted busy schedule had kept her from appreciating that she was connected with John in a way she'd never experienced before. As she sat there in the busy pub, alone with her thoughts, she considered the possibility that the human relationships she'd cultivated during her quest, including but not limited to John, had more value than anything else that had happened so far. She resolved to hang on to these connections—to nurture them and let them grow.

A day passed, and John joined her for dinner at a place in town he'd recommended. It was a rainy Friday evening, and John had just made the four-hour drive from the Dublin Airport after dropping off the people who'd walked the Kerry Way with him. They shared a long hug and a short electric kiss when he arrived, neither of them comfortable with ignominious PDA. After they sat and ordered drinks, Emily spoke first.

"How was the Kerry Way?" she asked.

"It was great!" he said. "It's the longest waymarked trail in Ireland, well over 200 kilometers, and very challenging. I love that walk. And the group was all experienced walkers, so we were actually able to complete some of the long days along the way. We didn't have time to go all the way round, which is a nine-day walk, but we gave them a good taste of it."

"Sounds like you really enjoy that walk," she observed.

"It's m'favorite in all of Ireland. Challenging, diverse landscape, ocean views to kill for, the whole lot."

"I hope we can do it together one day," she said, reaching out with her left hand and placing it on top of his. "I've missed you, John."

"And I you," he said, taking her hand in his and drawing in a deep breath, peering directly into her eyes. She loved it when he did this, his peaceful, intense blue eyes always calming and energizing her at the same time. "So, tell me all that's happened," he said. "Fill me in on the details."

"There's a lot to tell," she said and proceeded to cover the high points.

Emily explained that she'd given up the opportunity to work at NSCD, at least for now, and was pursuing the business venture of the poles, which looked very promising on the Continent, and hopefully might catch on in Ireland as well, with his help. But she didn't linger on this subject long. She wanted to speak to John about what she'd learned from Anna about the future dreaming program and her unknowing participation. She told him what she knew and waited while he processed it. After a few moments of reflection, he spoke.

"'Tis a strange thing indeed and a bit troubling in my mind," he said. "I don't like that these people have manipulated you without your knowledge."

"But if they hadn't, I would never have met you," she countered.

"Indeed," he said. "And for that, I'm grateful. But I wonder where all of this is headed, Em. It seems to me it could take you places you might not want to go."

"Maybe," she said. "But as of this moment, it's taken me to the exact place I want to be." She smiled at him warmly, and he returned it with an even warmer smile.

"Again, I can't argue with that! So, what will happen next?"

"I want to show you the trekking poles, which I think you'll be pleasantly surprised to see, for reasons I won't disclose at the moment."

"And why is that?"

"Just wait until I show you the poles, okay?"

"Very well," he said.

They finished dinner and drove the van back to John's small home, which was on the outskirts of town and sat at a higher elevation and provided a spectacular view of Dingle Bay and the Atlantic Ocean beyond. The summer solstice had not yet arrived, so the days in Ireland were still long. They sat out on the veranda in front of John's home, which had a roof over it so the beautiful view could be enjoyed even in the rain. Emily sipped wine, and John toyed with his stout.

Then Emily went to get the poles and brought them out to show him. It didn't take long for him to notice the name "Hill and Town" circling the top of the shaft.

"Well, then," he said. "That's a surprise."

"It was a-spur-of-the moment decision, but one I'm happy with. Are you okay with it?"

"I think so," he said. "I'll be selling these for you in Ireland, is that it?"

"I want you to point me in the right direction, that's all. Maybe accompany me on a few meetings, but I wouldn't want you to take time away from your work. Just help get me started, if you're willing. Do you know stores that sell equipment like this? I assumed you do."

"I'm happy to help," he said. "I know most of them, and I can't tell you the number of people we've sent into those stores to buy poles. And the best news is that I know many of the people inside these companies, since m'family's been involved in the tour business for so long."

"That's what I was hoping," she said.

"I'll point you in the right direction, then."

And he did. The following week, they had five appointments, and they would have had more if they'd been able to fit them into their schedule. The outdoor market in Ireland was much more fragmented than on the continent of Europe. There were literally dozens of retailers, some of which had only one store. But John had selected the five he felt were the largest, and they'd gone to see them together.

Four out of the five companies expressed sincere interest, excited by the fact that one of the local walking tour companies had their own brand of walking poles. Emily had only one sample left by their third appointment, so she held on to it and used it in all of the remaining meetings, promising to provide samples within a week. She emailed Thomas and Wilson to see if they could send more poles to Ireland, and they readily agreed to fly 10 more sets to them immediately.

As the week came to an end, John asked Emily if she could stay a while longer, and she said yes. They'd resumed their intimacies from the first night forward, and Emily was surprised that the intensity of their connection had not dissipated in the least. If anything, it had grown as they learned more about each other. And she didn't want it to end.

Emily said she'd stay a while longer, and John suggested they walk the Kerry Way together. It was a nine-day walk, and Emily thought that might be longer than she had, even though she still wasn't sure where she'd be going next. So, she tentatively agreed, with the condition that if something came up that required her attention, she might have to cut the trip short. John arranged to have one of his assistants handle the next group tour he was scheduled to lead and made the bookings at all the B&Bs along the Kerry Way.

The trip started off well. They began in the busy tourist town of Killarney and walked in a westerly direction for 22 kilometers (13.7 miles), through Killarney National Park and into the Black Valley. They stayed the first night at the home of an elderly couple who'd known John's family for 30 years. Next, they continued west, walking 20 kilometers (12½ miles) to Glencar, negotiating two difficult mountain passes and ending up in a remote farmhouse nestled in a beautiful forest but seemingly by itself in the middle of nowhere.

On the third day, they continued in a westerly direction, walking 20 kilometers (12½ miles) to Glenbeigh, and upon reaching the final summit of the day they looked north and saw the glimmering waters of Dingle Bay, which flowed into the Atlantic in the distance. Emily peered across the bay at the Dingle Peninsula, trying to pinpoint exactly where John's home might be. She gazed out at the endless sea, then slowly turned in a circle, taking in the views of green, rolling mountains to her left, behind her, and to her right. She'd always loved the mountains, but as she turned back to face the spectacular seascape in the distance, she nearly lost her breath at the diversity of beauty to be found on this ancient, tiny island. At that moment, she felt at peace and happy, reaching out to take John's hand in her own. Then her phone rang.

It was Anna. Emily told Anna that she and John were walking the Kerry Way together, then put the phone on speaker and explained that John was listening as well.

"Hi, John!" said Anna. "We hope you are well!"

"Very well indeed, Anna. It's good to hear from you."

"You might not think that after you hear what I have to say, but you never know."

"What's up?" asked Emily, a little worried.

"My brother called. He's ready to buy that first container load. And one of the logistics companies we met in Venlo also called. They said they have three customers in Germany who want to see you, and the poles, right away. So, it's good news and bad news, you might say."

"What's the bad news?" asked Emily.

"You need to come here right away. Your appointments are at the end of the week. Thursday and Friday. I'm afraid you'll have to cut short your walk on the Kerry Way."

Emily looked at John, who was keeping up the appearance of being happy for her, but she could tell he was disappointed, as was she. John nodded his head and spoke softly.

"We've some unfinished business with the Kerry Way, then," he said. Emily nodded to John and then addressed Anna.

"Okay," she said. "It's Tuesday, so I can probably get there by tomorrow night. I'll let you know my itinerary as soon as I have it."

"Great! But there's one more thing," said Anna. "My brother wants to know where to send the deposit."

Emily was stunned that things were moving so quickly. She hadn't even had time to set up a company. But John gave her the answer she seemed to be missing.

"My company name is 'Hill and Town,' ladies. So, why don't you have him send the money here. I operate in euros, and so does he. Unless Emily feels I'm not to be trusted, this seems the most expeditious solution."

"Yes!" exclaimed Emily. "That's the perfect solution!" Emily calculated that the Bever Outdoor deposit would be enough to pay for the first container load *and* to buy the second one, which meant she wouldn't need to take out the loan from her father. She was very excited, and she felt that John was stepping up in a big way to help her out.

"I'll send the wiring information when we get to Glenbeigh," said John. "Won't be long. We're almost there."

"Very well," said Anna. "I will wait to hear from you both."

Emily and John arrived at the B&B in Glenbeigh and informed the owners they wouldn't be spending the night, but would appreciate it if they could borrow their Wi-Fi to send some emails. John emailed the banking information to Anna while Emily emailed Thomas and Wilson to tell them the good news and that she would book and pay for the flights back to Europe. Then Emily and John took a taxi back to Dingle and spent one more night together.

The next morning when John dropped Emily off at the airport, he kept a stiff upper lip, but he also encouraged her to return soon.

"After all, I'll have your money in m'bank," he said, grinning. "If I have to use blackmail to get ya back, I'll do it!"

"That won't be necessary," she said. "I'll be back. As a matter of fact, I was wondering if you could start the paperwork to get me a work permit. After all, I'm bringing a lot of money into Hill and Town, right?"

"Are you serious?" he said.

"Indeed I am. Looks to me like I'm going to be working in Europe for a while, so why not spend that time with my best buddy over here."

"Well, I hope I'm more to you than just a buddy, Em."

"You *are*," she said, pressing forward and kissing him deeply. "Much more."

And then she was gone, into the airport, chasing a dream with an ending that was unknown to her.

Chapter 40
September 2013

Emily and John lived and worked together for the next three years. They were building a good life, or so it seemed to all who knew them. John and his attorney had helped Emily set up a new company named Hill and Town Trekking Poles and hired some administrative staff to handle the incoming orders and the purchases from Thomas and Wilson in China. They shared office space with his tour company. Overall, Emily's operation was a very low overhead enterprise. Anna had begun working for her full time, helping to manage the logistics company in Venlo and playing a customer service role with the largest customers on the Continent, including Bever Outdoor, while Willem continued to manage the farm.

The company had grown rapidly and was now selling more than 5 million euros per year of trekking poles. The popularity of the Hill and Town Trekking Poles in Ireland also had a halo effect on John's tour company. He was expanding rapidly and had hired three new guides and purchased three new vans to handle the increased business.

Then one day, in September of 2013, Emily received a call from Anna that changed everything.

"Hi, Em," said Anna. "Something's come up."

"What?" asked Emily, concerned by the tone in Anna's voice.

"I've just been contacted by a large camping supply company that wants to purchase Hill and Town."

"Well, that's good news, right?" said Emily. "We're always interested in selling more poles."

"They want *more* than the poles," said Anna. "They want to buy the company!"

"Oh," said Emily, unsure of what this would mean if she let it happen.

"Emily, are you there?" asked Anna.

"Yes, I'm here."

"What do you want me to tell them?"

"Well, I suppose we could talk to them. Where do they want to meet?"

"They want to meet in China. I think it's the China production that interests them the most, plus your distribution in Ireland and the U.K."

"Okay," said Emily. "I'll let Thomas and Wilson know, and I'll figure out a date to go over."

"Are you sure you want to do this, Em?" asked Anna. "This company has been great for all of us."

"It has," said Emily. "But there are other things we can do after this. And it probably won't happen anyway."

"If you say so," said Anna.

Emily went to China and met with the suitor. They traveled together to the production site, along with Thomas and Wilson. After the China trip, the company conducted additional due diligence and then sent Emily a letter of intent to purchase. On December 31, 2013, she sold the company for a price she couldn't refuse—7 million euros, which at that time, was equal to nearly 10 million U.S. dollars.

Immediately after the sale, Emily had to shut down the Hill and Town Trekking Pole Facebook page that had been linked to her personal Facebook profile, but before doing so, she prepared a post that she put on the company page *and* on her personal profile. The post announced that the company had been sold and that she would keep her friends updated on what she'd be doing next through her personal Facebook profile.

After the sale closed, John offered jobs at Hill and Town Walking Tours to all of Emily's employees, and three of them accepted. He also asked Anna if she'd like to open a Hill and Town Walking Tours office in Europe to help the company expand onto the Continent, which she accepted. As for Emily herself, she asked John if she could become a tour guide for the disabled, the job he'd originally offered her when they'd first met, and he readily agreed.

Emily and John had been living together at that point for three and a half years, in his home in Dingle, and they were very, very close. Emily's dad and mom visited every year, separately, and John's parents came to visit often. Everything seemed perfectly aligned for a marriage between the two. But then something started happening to Emily that would upset the equilibrium she had achieved in her life.

During the entire time she'd owned and operated her trekking pole company, Emily hadn't remembered her dreams. The last dream she'd remembered had been the one of her meetings with Anna and John while she was still in China. For several months after the sale of her company, the welcome absence of remembered dreams continued—until a beautiful spring morning in May of 2014. That morning, Emily awoke, noticing that John wasn't beside her. She assumed correctly that he was up making coffee, but then her mind suddenly flooded with images from a dream that was unlike any she'd ever had before.

The first difference was that there'd been no film viewing to stimulate the dream. Emily had not returned to see the Projector Man since her second visit, four years previously. She rarely even thought of Fred Watts, had made it a point not to actually, even though she had vowed to one day approach him and seek final clarity regarding his role in the future dreaming enterprise that Anna had spoken about. The second difference was that the dream was so far afield from any dream before that Emily wasn't certain it had any meaning at all.

Emily saw herself on a stage, giving a speech. Behind the lectern where she was speaking, a large banner read "Emily Noland for Congress." After the speech, the scene shifted to backstage, and Emily saw herself in an intense conversation with an attractive woman with red hair, who appeared to be her campaign manager. Then the dream ended.

The following day, Emily was guiding a tour on a day trip along the Dingle Way, the walking trail that circled around the Dingle Peninsula. This was a group of people without disabilities. Her program of guided walking tours for the disabled had been slow taking off. They had only conducted a few of these tours so far, but Emily and John were hopeful they would eventually grow in popularity.

The group Emily was leading that day was on a trail that traveled through some farms in the mountains, so several stiles needed to be crossed. When Emily approached the first stile, she experienced a panic attack, nearly fainting. She asked the group to take a break and called John on her cell phone. Luckily, he was in town and was able to drive to the area where they were located and track them down. He made sure Emily was okay, gave her his keys, told her to drive home, then took over the guidance of the tour. Emily drove back to their home in Dingle, depressed that her fear of ladders had returned.

Emily came to the unfortunate conclusion that it was related to her recent dream. She'd realized some time ago that the only time her fear of ladders returned was when she resisted the process of turning her dreams about the future into reality.

The next morning, she woke remembering another dream. She'd been in a very statesmanlike office holding court with a few advisors, one of whom was the pretty woman with the red hair. In the next scene, Emily was seated in an armchair in a large assembly room. Her chair sat on one of several tiered platforms and faced a large desk where a man with short dark hair was sitting, wielding a wooden gavel. There was a large American flag draping the wall behind the desk. Emily had seen images of this room before. It was the House Chamber in the Capitol Building in Washington, D.C. Emily concluded that she had won the election to Congress that she'd been running for in the previous dream.

Later that day, Emily received an unexpected FaceTime call. She was still at home, waiting for John to return from a day hike he'd taken over for her. Emily answered the call. On the screen of her phone, a person she'd never met in the physical world appeared. It was the woman with red hair, from her dreams.

Chapter 41
May 2014

"Hello, Emily, my name is Lydia Dench. I'm a political consultant here in Colorado."

"Why are you calling me?" asked Emily, already knowing the answer. "And how did you get my cell phone number?"

"We tracked you down through your friend Woha. We consulted with him on his campaign for a seat on the Tribal Council of the Cherokee Nation."

Emily was well aware of Woha's successful run for one of the 17 seats on the Tribal Council, the legislative branch of the Cherokee Nation government, but she didn't know he'd hired consultants to help him.

"What has that got to do with me?" she asked, trying to delay the inevitable.

"It has nothing to do with you," said Lydia, her voice crisp and professional. "It's simply the truth about how we found you."

"Why did you want to find me?"

"Because we'd like to engage you for a run for the U.S. Congress," said Lydia.

"Why? I don't even live in the United States anymore."

"Yes, we know. But that's something that can be easily rectified."

"What if I don't want to rectify it?" asked Emily.

"That's solely your decision. We just wanted you to know that the news of the multi-million-dollar sale of your company went viral in the district we want you to run in. You've become a bit of a rock star up there as a result of your accomplishments on the international stage. I'm sure you've seen that on your social media accounts."

Emily *had* seen that people all over ski country in Colorado, and also in Boulder, had become enamored with her success story, especially since she was a person with limitations that were expected to keep your accomplishments in check. But she didn't want to give the red-haired woman the satisfaction of acknowledging it.

"What district is that?" she asked.

"The Second District, which not only includes Boulder, where you went to college, but also Grand County, where you taught skiing to disabled people for many years, plus Summit County and Eagle County, also ski country. The more heavily populated parts of the district, like Jefferson County, will catch on quickly to your story."

"I made my living there as a bartender," said Emily. "How will that go over with the constituents of the Second District?"

"Quite well, I'm sure. It makes you more relatable to everyday people."

"I'm sorry to disappoint you, but I'm not interested."

"Please hear me out a little bit further, Emily."

"If you insist. But I have to get off soon, if you don't mind."

"All right," said Lydia. "I'll make this quick. Here's the story that will get you elected. Disabled woman becomes expert snowboarder and skier, then passes on her skills to other disabled people for seven years. Graduates from college with a 3.9 grade average, with a minor in business, then uses her intelligence, knowledge, and courage to found an international company that she ultimately sells for $10 million. Decides to run for Congress back in the district that made it all happen for her so she can help the less fortunate on a broader scale."

"Nice story," said Emily. "But it just seems to be a path I'm not ready to walk."

"I understand," said Lydia. "I *can* tell you, however, that you wouldn't be campaigning in earnest until the latter half of 2015, which is more than a year away. The election is in November 2016, and the term begins in January 2017, so you have plenty of time. Please keep my number, will you?"

"I'll save you as a contact, but please don't count on me to change my mind. What was your name again?"

"Lydia Dench."

"Okay, Lydia, thanks for your call. Have a good day."

"And you as well. I hope to hear from you again, Emily. Please give my proposal some thought."

"Bye," said Emily and hung up the phone.

Chapter 42
May 2015

A year passed. Emily remained in Ireland, although her fear of ladders curtailed her ability to be a walking tour guide. John accommodated her by sending her on walks that didn't include stiles. While this reduced the diversity of tours she could do, it didn't substantially diminish her contributions to Hill and Town Walking Tours. What bothered Emily was the fact that *accommodations* had to be made at all. Her firmly entrenched need to overcome all obstacles, with no special treatment, was severely compromised by *accommodations*. And she didn't like it. What kept her in Ireland was her love for John and the beauty of the country and its people, sprinkled with a disabled walking tour group every now and then.

But the most severe problem for Emily was the relentless dreams, which had evolved into scenes not only portraying the intricate details of campaigning, but the actual day-to-day responsibilities of serving in Congress and beyond. In Emily's dreams, she served two terms in Congress, her second one ending in January 2021. But before her second term came to an end, she was already campaigning for an open Senate seat, which she secured in November 2022, beginning her six-year term in January 2023. Well before her Senate term ended in January 2029, Emily was being courted for a run for President in 2028. She would enter office at the age of 43, the youngest President to be elected since John F. Kennedy and the first woman President *ever* elected in the United States of America.

Emily understood that these experiences were just dreams from the night, and she strove to believe they were simply wild fantasies rampaging through her mind as she slept. But Emily's experiences over the past five years gave credence to the idea that these dreams could actually become reality.

The thing that finally tipped the scales for her was a speech she remembered from her dreams of her Presidential campaign. Emily had discovered that, apparently, she was a good public speaker, and after a dozen years of giving speeches prior to her run for President, she'd become *exceptionally* good at it. In the speech that caused her to seriously consider pursuing these political dreams, she was in a large stadium, filled with tens of thousands of people. As she looked out at the crowd, she saw people in wheelchairs and on crutches, hundreds of them! She saw Native Americans, some of them in full headdresses and traditional garb. She saw people of all creeds and colors, each one having come to that stadium to see and listen to her. And as she spoke of the things she believed in from the deepest recesses of her heart—equality for all, helping each other, aspiring to greatness of your own definition—the crowd roared with an intensity that still rang in her ears even after she'd woken from the dream. And that was when she knew that the time had come to find out, once and for all, what her destiny truly was.

That very evening, Emily approached John at their home on the outskirts of Dingle. John was sitting out on the front veranda, sipping from a pint of stout while gazing out at Dingle Bay. It was around 8 p.m. and wouldn't get dark for quite some time. Emily sat beside John, a glass of Sauvignon blanc in her hand.

"What are you thinking?" she asked, reaching over and touching him with the end of her right arm. One of the many beautiful things about her relationship with John was that he so genuinely loved every aspect of her being that the missing hand never entered his mind, and this in turn had led Emily to overcome all insecurities regarding her deformity, at least when she was with John. He set his glass down on the small table to his right and reached over and rubbed her arm.

"I'm wondering when you'll be leaving me," he said, his expression grim.

"We've never discussed that possibility before," she said, stalling for time and hoping he'd make this easier for her. And he didn't disappoint.

"No, Em, we haven't. But I know you. You won't be pinned down on the ground when you know you can fly."

Emily had been forthcoming with John regarding the details of her ongoing and increasingly disturbing dreams. He'd reacted generally in a neutral way, neither encouraging her to pursue them nor to reject them, but their discussions about her dreams nearly always put him in a somber mood, as if he knew it was only a matter of time until she ran after them. And now that time had arrived.

"I love you, John," she said, fighting the tears. "I want to be with you, always. Won't you please come with me?"

He didn't hesitate.

"You know I cannah do that, m'love. We have no children, but we've built a family nonetheless. I have a dozen people working for me now, and their own families depend on the money they earn working for Hill and Town. And we've hundreds of loyal customers who come back ev'ry year because they love what we help 'em find out in the green spaces of Ireland, and beyond. I love you more than anythin' in the world, Em, and I promise to wait for you 'til I'm old and gray, if that's how long it takes you to come back. Because I believe in m'heart that you *will* come back. I have to believe that, or my heart would break and not be mended."

Tears were flowing from John's eyes as he gave the speech he'd undoubtedly given to himself many times before sharing it with her. It moved her to a full flood of tears herself, and as was often the case with Emily, they were complex tears. First and foremost, they flowed as tears of sadness for the pain she was inflicting on the one person in this world whom she'd shared everything with. But on the other side of her tears was profound joy that John loved her so much that he was releasing her to follow the path her inexorable dreams had laid out for her. Emily hoped that one day soon she would discover a way to end this seemingly never-ending pattern of dream-determined future events that kept returning to haunt her. But to have any chance of doing that, not only must she pursue the dreams, she also needed to confront the man who'd started it all.

Chapter 43
Late May 2015

Emily approached 22 Maple Street in Edgewater, Colorado, for the third time in her life. Nearly five years had passed since her first visit, and a lot had changed for her—mostly for the better. She'd met John, and she'd gotten rich because of the films she'd viewed at 22 Maple Street. And while she *had* concluded, based on what Anna had told her, that Fred Watts was somehow connected to a clandestine organization that had dedicated itself to the pursuit of future dreaming, she knew very little about how they actually caused their subjects to dream the future and pursue it. And now the new dreams of her political successes had become her remembered dreams and there had been no film viewing to induce them. Her mind was doing it by itself now and this new "phase" was very disturbing to her. She intended to get answers this time, and she had a very specific plan as to how she would do it. The first part would be easy because her anger and resentment toward Fred was real.

Give him a gut punch, then ease up and become his

friend, she thought.

Promptly at the 2 p.m. scheduled time for the meeting, Emily scaled the two steps and prepared to knock on the door. As always, just as she was about to knock, the door opened, and Fred appeared.

"Hello, Emily," he said. "It's been a long time."

"Too long," she said. "Too long without any answers from you!"

"Well, now, let's not get huffy!" said Fred, with as much animation as she'd ever seen from him. "Why don't you come in and see what's playing?"

"That's the problem," she said. "I don't need to see what's playing! Because I'm already seeing it, in my dreams!"

"Oh, I see," said Fred, with no hint of surprise in his voice. "Okay then, why don't you come in and tell me about these dreams."

Fred opened the door and let Emily in. Instead of going to the dining room, he took a seat in the living room, beckoning her to sit across from him on the couch. She sat on the old sofa, wondering once again what he did all day without a television.

"Would you like something to drink?" he asked. "A soda? Some water?"

"No, thank you. All I want are answers!"

"I can't answer anything until you tell *me* somethin', young lady!" said Fred, with as much gumption as he could put into it.

"First of all, I sold my trekking pole company for $10 million. So, I have the money to buy the projector if that's what it comes to."

"Fine," he said, seemingly unimpressed, as if he already knew what had happened in her life. "Just tell me about these dreams."

Give him what he wants, she thought.

"Before I came back from Ireland in 2010, I stopped remembering my dreams—until I saw the film of China. Then before I left China, I stopped remembering my dreams again. And then I sold my business."

Fred didn't hesitate.

"And then you started remembering your dreams again," he said, as if he knew already what she was going to say.

Okay! she rejoiced in her mind. *I think he's taking the bait!* She noticed that Fred's voice had changed with his last comment. He didn't sound like the grumpy old man anymore. He sounded more ... professional. His diction was clear, and he seemed more focused on *her* than ever before. In the past meetings, he'd always acted like he didn't know what was going on and didn't really care. But now he seemed intensely interested, which made sense, based on what Anna had told her. He'd *always* cared because he'd known what he was doing to her from the beginning. His indifference and feigned ignorance in the first meetings were purely an act.

"Yes," she said. "I started remembering my dreams again, a few months after I sold the business."

"And was it one dream, or several different ones?" Again, the professional manner, like a doctor asking questions of a patient.

"It was one dream that had different ... different

episodes, as time went by."

"Did you remember your dreams every day?"

"No, I didn't. They were sporadic. Unpredictable."

"But they told a story to you over time, did they?" he asked.

"Yes."

"And what was the story?"

"The story was I was running for Congress. And I won!"

"Oh, my," he said.

"What do you mean, 'oh, my'? What's going on Mr. Watts?" Emily had made up her mind not to reveal what she already knew about the future dreaming program unless circumstances developed during the meeting that called for it. Her ruse was to play the innocent victim, which wasn't hard to pull off because that's exactly what she was. The hard part was keeping her outrage in check.

Fred cupped his chin in his hand, obviously pondering. He went on like this for some time. Finally, he spoke.

"So, you've got the million dollars then, do you?" he asked.

"Yes. I'm ready to buy the projector if you're unable to help me figure this out."

Fred laughed.

"What are you laughing at?" she asked.

"Well, first off, it's not the projector you want. It's the films, but you've already seen the ones that matter, and they've had their desired effect."

"I want the two films you showed me, too, of course," she said, improvising, not caring anymore about the projector *or* the films. She knew that Fred never intended to sell the projector, but she needed him to say it.

"Neither the projector nor the films are for sale," he said.

Emily continued pretending she knew nothing.

"What? Why?"

"I put a price of a million dollars on it because no one will pay a million dollars for a projector that's worth only one percent of that. Not until *you* that is. But you won't be buying it because it's not worth a million dollars. Trust me."

"But it changed my life!" she said, really getting into her performance of the innocent victim.

"Like I said, it was really the films that did that."

"How did they do that, Fred? What was in the films that caused me to start dreaming the future?"

"Okay, look. I can explain all of this. I *will* explain it. Because now that you've started having future dreams without the catalyst, we need to start working together more closely."

Chapter 44

Emily was excited that Fred was apparently going to come clean. She was finally going to understand everything, but she still didn't let on that she already knew about the existence of the future dreaming program.

"What? You mean you intended for all this to happen to me?"

"Well, yes, we did. Are you sure you don't want something to drink, Emily, because my explanation is going to take some time."

"I'm fine," she said casually. "Please just tell me, Fred, because I need your help. I promise to cooperate with you if I can just learn more."

Fred cupped his chin in his hand, making a decision about how much to reveal, no doubt. Emily tried to put on a countenance of humble acquiescence to follow whatever advice he would provide. And then, he complied.

"Emily, I'm not who I appear to be," he said.

"I see," she replied, trying to remain calm. "So, who are you?"

"I'm several things. First, I'm an oneirologist. That's a scientist who studies dreams. But I'm also a theoretical physicist. I received my PhD in oneirology first, and it gave me a basis for the dissertation I wrote for my PhD in theoretical physics. I proposed that the B-Theory of Time—which posits that time does not flow, in other words, that the past, present, and future exist at the same time—can be proven when people dream. My research involved the study of time through people's dreams.

"We brought in dozens of subjects. The first thing we did was teach them how to remember their dreams. We then exposed them to a variety of stimuli. This included interesting stories and articles about marvelous people and places, and these stories sometimes included pictures—articles and pictures from *National Geographic*, for example. We then measured their brain activity while dreaming, but most importantly, we had them give us detailed descriptions of their dreams after they woke up. A few of them dreamed about the stimuli. Most didn't. We then had them report back to us for several months as to what had been going on with their dreams and in their lives. In a few cases, the subjects had actually lived out some of the events they had reported to us from their dreams—you know, going to those places and experiencing what they'd read about and dreamed about.

"And while my research was inconclusive, primarily because we didn't have enough funding to get the number of subjects we needed to make firm conclusions, my dissertation attracted the attention of a well-funded international program that was studying the ability of the brain to predict the future, through dreams. They called it future dreaming. And they hired me to continue my research.

"The first thing I was tasked with was to identify the kind of people that were predisposed to seeing the future—people who have what we call *precognition*, or *prescience*. To tell you the truth, we made only limited progress in identifying a 'type' of person who was predisposed to seeing future events. But there was *some* evidence that people who'd experienced a major trauma in their past were slightly more likely to have prescience than your average subject. Eventually, after a lot of failures, I decided to make a bold hypothesis about people who'd experienced trauma because they were the only sliver of hope we had for a breakthrough."

Fred paused to take a sip of water from a glass that was sitting on the coffee table in front of him.

"I started with the research objective from my dissertation that the past, present, and future exist simultaneously, and that this could be proven through people's dreams. I further theorized that we could tie the past, present, and future together while people dream and that we could do that most easily with people who were predisposed to higher levels of precognition, i.e., people who've experienced trauma. These people are inextricably tied to the past. They keep getting thrown back to that terrible moment when the trauma originally occurred, reliving it over and over. Certain things trigger them to do that, but they do it nonetheless. So how could people who are consumed by the past predict the future? I theorized that these people—people who couldn't shake the past because of the trauma they'd experienced—were desperately seeking the future, *subconsciously*, in order to rid themselves of the trauma that anchored them into the past. I further theorized that these subjects could somehow be stimulated to *bounce* their minds into the future—like a rebound off a backboard.

"We tried a lot of things, including using the triggers, but that didn't work. The subjects had their normal PTSD episodes. And that's when I stumbled onto the idea of the projector. I had studied film theory in one of my oneirology classes, as I'm sure you did as part of your major in cinema studies, which means you will fully comprehend what I'm about to say. There are many different scholarly approaches in film theory, but the one that interested me most was called apparatus theory. The essence of apparatus theory is that when people are in a theater, passively viewing a film on a screen, with the lights dimmed, they are essentially in a dream state. They experience the film in exactly the same way they experience a dream—as if it were reality."

Emily did indeed remember apparatus theory from her film theory class. Although she had been fascinated by it, she never thought it was something that could actually affect her life. But there was obviously a lot more involved here than just apparatus theory, so she said nothing, wanting to hear more. It was all starting to make sense to her now, and Fred's information was flowing like a stream swollen by a downpour.

"So, now we have a medium that is in essence a dream," he said. "We combine that with a subject who desperately wants to leave the past behind and a theory that the past can be linked to the future in the dream world. The practical question was how to get the subject to start connecting the past and the future in their dreams. We needed their minds to take something they saw in a film, something from the past, and process it, then extend it into a future event, all while in a dream state.

"To do this, we needed to plant the subjects firmly in the past without traumatizing them, establishing a dream state with the projector, screen, and dimmed lights. And we needed to do it in a way where the subject had absolutely no idea of what we were doing. My past research had proven that was important. Now it's a given that a cellulose film projector is old, and that the movies it plays are also old. So now we have a person who subconsciously doesn't want to be in the past, who's willingly, unsuspectingly viewing a film on a projector that's most definitely from the past. But there were still two more things we needed. The first is that the people needed the right catalyst."

"What do you mean by catalyst?" asked Emily, fairly certain she knew the answer.

"The *film* is the catalyst. And it has to be chosen carefully."

"So, you're saying that the first time I came in here, you'd already selected a film clip specifically for me?"

"Yes, I *am* saying that."

"But you didn't even know me. We had a brief conversation on the phone, and I showed up. There's no way you could do any analysis that would help you select the right film for me."

"That's actually not true, Emily."

Chapter 45

While Emily was absolutely furious about Fred taking advantage of people, especially trauma victims, she was pleased with the amount of information she was receiving from him. He seemed to be completely convinced that she wanted his help, or maybe he was just as tired of the game he'd been playing as she was. Whatever the reason was, Emily was not inclined to interrupt him. Instead, she listened while he continued spewing out intelligence that she could use.

"The first thing you need to know," he said, "is that 30 years ago, I was asked to leave the program. I was fired. That was the year 1985. I was a 40-year-old hot shot with PhDs in both oneirology and theoretical physics, and I'd become the driving force behind the future dreaming program."

"Why did they fire you?"

"Because I discovered a way to dramatically improve our ability to unlock the potential of our subjects."

"Why would they fire you for that?"

"Because it was illegal, basically."

"What? That's not cool, Fred." Emily said this calmly, not wanting to sound the way she felt.

"Now let me finish. You can judge me for yourself. What I discovered is that the subjects responded much better when they didn't know they were subjects."

"You mean you didn't tell them why they were there?"

"Essentially, yes, although because the people were paid participants in our studies, we had to tell them something. So, we lied. We told them we wanted their opinions on the films we were showing them. And the results were good. A few of the subjects responded well. But then I was fired. Because of my methods."

"What do you mean by 'responded well,' Fred?"

"I mean they started dreaming about the films, and a few started extending their dreams to include things that weren't in the film."

"Just like I did."

"Yes, that's right."

"Wait a minute. You said you were fired. But you continued your research anyway?"

"Absolutely," he said. "For the past 30 years. You see, by the time I was let go, I was affiliated with a network of scientists and politicians, literally around the world, who believed in what we were doing. Several of them have continued working with me. And a few of them are wealthy people who were willing to fund my continued research. I realize this shabby little house makes it look as if I'm operating a low-budget operation, but I don't actually *live* here. I live in a very nice home in another part of town.

"My office is downtown, in a prestigious location, and

I have a significant staff working there as well. We have a very professional practice over there, with consenting subjects and full disclosure. The 'Projector for Sale' angle is my own pet project. Only two people at the main office even know about it, although some key individuals in my international network know, mainly the ones who manage the people taking the videos that we convert to films. If I catch a fish over here, I do all the inputting of data myself in a user field that's reserved exclusively for me. And then the algorithm works its magic."

Emily was stunned and overwhelmed by the amount of information Fred was providing. She was particularly interested in finding out more about the algorithm he'd just mentioned, but he was talking so fast that he'd either forgotten to explain how he'd selected the films she had viewed or didn't want to. She needed that information, and much more, so she augmented her ploy of wanting to work with Fred.

"I need your help, Fred. I want to learn how to control what's happening to me. Can you help me? Can you bring more resources to bear on my case?"

"Of course," he said. "That's what we want to do!"

"That would be great," she said. "What's the name of your company?"

"FDI," he said. "Stands for Future Dreaming, Inc. It's a nonprofit company. We're not in this for the money, Emily. We want to help people—to help the world."

Emily took in this information and continued probing.

"How did you find out things about me that were useful to you so quickly?" she asked.

"That was easy," he said. "In the old days, it was harder and involved a lot of guesswork on my part in terms of what film to select. But with the advent of social media, we can instantly acquire important personal details about many of our subjects. Several of us have made a point of becoming adept at social media and can easily uncover information that is often very useful to us. In your case, you told me over the phone that you lived and worked in the mountains and loved it. And you told me your name, which was the real key to uncovering what we needed to know. We easily determined from pictures you had posted that you were very likely a victim of a traumatic accident, which is our number one marker for good subjects. But the second thing we need, which we rarely find, is someone who will *act* on their dreams. That's where your friend Wohali came in handy. With a quick study of him on social media, plus my own knowledge of the Cherokee belief system with regard to dreams, bingo, we had all that we needed. Wohali's your best friend, plus he believes that dreams are real and that people should try to bring their dreams into the physical world whenever possible. Wohali could be counted on to encourage you to follow your dreams. All of this information suggested that you were a high potential subject."

So, Fred is just another abuser of social media, thought Emily. *He takes advantage of a medium that was meant to build connections and community by using the information people willingly provide to manipulate them.*

This infuriated Emily, and she wanted to slap Fred in the face for his arrogance and insensitivity. But she had him where she wanted him, pouring his guts out, so she continued her subtle interrogation. She knew the answer to her next question but asked it anyway.

"How did you get that film of John? And the one of my Chinese suppliers at the Great Wall?"

"As I said, we have a network of people around the world. They make short digital videos about every imaginable subject. We then film these videos with our cameras and put them on reels, to make them seem to be older than they really are. Then we catalog the films and put them onto a huge database. We have thousands of them, a lot more than what's stored in the dining room here. Another important thing we do is conduct social media research, when possible, on the key actors in the films, which is useful at the next stage, especially when we encounter a high potential subject, like you. Our social media findings and other key information are fed into the database, and a film is selected by our algorithm software. Here's a fun fact: You actually know the person who made the first film we showed you."

Even though Emily already knew that Fred was referring to Anna, she feigned ignorance.

"How would I know that person?" she asked.

"Because you met her on your guided tour of the Wicklow Way. Her name is Anna. She loves walking in Ireland and has made some films there, one of which is the film we showed you. It's also interesting that you and Anna became friends and that she's been working for you and John. We assumed she had told you what she knows about our program, but it appears she may not have."

"She didn't say anything," said Emily, wanting to protect Anna and to keep the conversation moving. She came up with a question to help him proceed and asked it.

"So, you know about me and John—that we're living and working together?"

"Of course, you told us yourself, on your social media accounts."

Emily felt she'd gathered enough information to execute her plan, although she still had more questions, but Fred's audacity was so enraging it was increasingly difficult to keep her emotions in check. She was angry, but she'd been angry at Fred for a long time, and she *did* have more questions, so she kept her cool.

"But how could you predict that I'd have such good chemistry with John?"

"Personal connection is part of the algorithm we use, which is very powerful. We had data on both you and John, and the algorithm obviously figured out there would be a connection."

"And in China? All you filmed were two men at the Great Wall and then in their showroom. How could you predict that I'd go into business with them and get rich?"

"That one was a lucky roll of the dice by the algorithm, if I do say so myself. The first bit of luck was the film we got on the China guys. We have several people making videos for us over there, but you never know which one might be useful. And since neither Thomas nor Wilson uses social media, we had to send in an operative to get a tour of the showroom. They provided a list of detailed observations, not only about Thomas and Wilson, but also about the products they observed, which included the trekking poles.

"The other lucky thing that was in the database, which the algorithm easily picked up, was that Anna's brother was a purchasing agent at Bever Outdoor. And of course, Anna had no idea of the role we had planned for her in the walking poles venture. But it was a no-brainer for the algorithm to match you up with the film of the guys in China, especially since your risk profile, which our research also quantified, was a good predictor that you would make a great entrepreneur."

"But how did all of that make any difference?" she asked. "How did that make me dream the future?"

"That, my dear, is what I will explain next."

Chapter 46

"The algorithm is the key," said Fred. "It's designed to create conditions that enable the brain to rewire itself to dream the future. But it's a two-part process. First, we plant the memory of the film in your subconscious mind. The algorithm selects the films that the subject can relate to and therefore remember. The subconscious is comfortable with these films and begins the process of rewiring immediately, embedding the contents of the film in your brain. The brain is quite plastic. It rewires itself all the time, so we take advantage of that. And as I said earlier, a film is the perfect medium for doing this because when you're watching the film, you are basically dreaming already. But the algorithm goes further. It wants you to *act* on the dream—to make it become real."

"Why is it important that a person follows the path your algorithm selected?" she asked.

"That's important because when you follow the dream, your subconscious recognizes this and wants to do it again, especially if the outcome has been positive for you, which we make sure will happen. After a few sessions, the sub-conscious of a gifted subject learns how to dream the future by itself. As I said, it essentially rewires itself to do this. And in so doing, it detaches your subconscious link to the past that your trigger accesses when it throws you back to your trauma. But if you don't follow the path your dreams have predicted, the rewiring of your subconscious begins to un-ravel. And the triggers become active again."

"So, that's why my fear of ladders returned?"

"I wasn't aware that you had a fear of ladders, but if that's your trigger, then yes, your subconscious is telling you that by refusing to pursue the future dream, you are es-sentially retrenching back into the past and all that resides there. The return of the PTSD trigger is the first sign to the subconscious that things are not going as it planned. It then accelerates its predictive dreaming in a desperate attempt to reorient the subject back onto the path that it has chart-ed. The subconscious is extremely powerful, Emily. It's the most powerful part of the brain, by far."

Fred's description of accelerated predictive dreaming was consistent with Emily's experience over the past year, when the dreams kept stretching further and further into the future, luring her to follow them. But it was all so infu-riating that she could no longer maintain her patience. She couldn't help but express her true feelings at that moment.

"This is crazy, Fred. It's wrong for you to do this!"

But Fred was not deterred. He was so deeply into his explanation at that point that he seemed unable to stop, no matter what she said.

"Please, Emily. Let me explain the *why* about what we

do. Imagine a world where people can predict their own destinies with a high level of certainty—where they can dream big and know they can make their dreams come true. The world will be a better place if we can get to that point. But that's just the beginning. Imagine if we can learn how to get people predicting things that are bigger than themselves—things that involve all of us, like climate change. We can use what they tell us to help prevent these things from happening."

"But do the ends justify the means, Fred? I don't think so. And what if people have dreams about bad things, and they go out and make *them* happen. How will that work?"

"We make sure that *can't* happen. We realize that many trauma victims aren't stable and might eventually have misdirected dreams, so we avoid that kind of person altogether. We only move forward with people who are stable and want to do good in their lives—people like you. When *you* look forward, you look to do *good* things, positive things, because you want to leave the bad in the past.

"Another extremely important aspect of our program is that the algorithm is programmed to seek only *positive* outcomes. It's taken our programmers years to develop and refine, and it's become highly reliable."

"But what about my latest dreams?" asked Emily. "They weren't even influenced by one of your films. Have you lost control of one of your subjects, Fred?"

"No, of course not! I've already told you that after a few sessions your subconscious teaches itself to dream the future without the catalyst. Did you miss that? And by the way, all of us at FDI have been down this path before, and in every case, the high-performing subjects have ended up improving their lives and doing positive things for the world. You'd be amazed at some of the people who've gone through our program."

"But you won't reveal *their* names because of doctor-patient confidentiality, right?" she said, sarcasm in her voice.

"Yes, that's right. You can make fun of what we do, Emily, but you can't deny that the things that have happened to you since you got involved in our program have been extremely positive, for *you!*"

"But that's the point, Fred! You say I got involved in your program, but it wasn't *my* choice to do that!"

"I don't see it that way. When you answered the ad, you got involved."

"I got involved to look at your projector, not to unknowingly submit to a project that rewired my brain against my will! You've really lost touch with reality, Fred. You just don't seem to understand that what you're doing is simply not right! But the people who fired you 30 years ago *did* understand. That should have brought your crazy program to an end right there!"

"Maybe you're right, Emily. I don't know for sure. But one thing I *do* know is that we need to continue this conversation because you're at a crossroads, my friend. You need to decide what to do next."

Emily was worried that her aggressive behavior might shut Fred down, but his comments suggested otherwise. He still seemed to want to work with her to further his research, so she forced herself to calm down. Perhaps she could extract information from him that might help her to break free of this whole mind-bending game.

"So, you're saying I could actually end up a congress-woman?"

"You've said you're dreaming it, right? So, if we rely on what's happened in the past when you've dreamed something and remembered it, the likelihood that it will happen is extremely high."

"Does it *have* to happen, Fred?"

"I don't think so, no. If you're willing to live with the consequences, i.e., the dreams of your unfulfilled future will continue and so will your fear of ladders. But why wouldn't you want it to happen? You want to help people, right? That's what government is for. Unfortunately, not enough politicians do it for the right reasons. Our government needs people like you, Emily!"

"How can I stop these dreams from coming, Fred?"

"Why would you want to do *that*? Your dreams have produced so much good. Why stop them?"

"That's my business, Fred. Just tell me. How do I stop them?"

"You already know the answer to that, don't you?"

"What?"

"It's the old cliché, Emily. 'Follow your dreams.'"

Yes, of course, she thought. When she was pursuing her dreams, the next set of future dreams was put on hold. But when she concluded living out her previous dreams, the new ones started.

"How do I stop them if I don't *want* to pursue them?" she asked, desperate now.

"I don't know, Emily. But if you would agree to let us

take this study to the next level, we could probably figure it out. That's what you said you wanted, right, for us to help you? We'll pay you good money to study your brain while you're dreaming. Please!"

"I don't need the money!" she screamed. "What you're doing is wrong, Fred. I could sue you!"

"You could try," he said. "But my version of the facts is that you answered an ad I ran in the paper, I showed you the machine, and you decided not to buy it. You kept coming back to try to negotiate, but we could never strike a deal."

"Okay," Emily said. "You're right." She got up to leave.

"Wait, where are you going? We need to talk! We need to do more together!"

"Go to hell, Fred."

Emily ran out of the house, jumped in her car, and sped away. After she got back to her hotel, she kept the car running and pulled out her phone. She opened the Voice Memos app on her phone to check the recording she'd made of the entire conversation with Fred. His voice was clear, and so was hers.

Chapter 47
May 29, 2015

Emily checked in at the Hard Rock Hotel and Casino in Tulsa, Oklahoma, in the afternoon. It was one of several hotel casinos that were owned by the Cherokee Nation and was about a one-hour drive from Woha's home in Tahlequah. He'd highly recommended the hotel and explained that he'd already made a reservation for three at the best restaurant in the hotel for that evening. The third person would be Woha's fiancé, Kamama. He suggested that on Saturday they could drive up to Tahlequah, and he'd show Emily around. He'd also booked a room for her, and when she checked, in she found that it was a complimentary room, requiring a credit card imprint only for incidentals.

Emily took the elevator up to the restaurant, McGill's on 19, at 6:55 p.m. It was a steakhouse on the top floor of the hotel with panoramic views of the surrounding area. Woha arrived at 7 p.m. and introduced her to Kamama, which he explained means *butterfly* in Cherokee. She was very beautiful, tall and slender, with smooth brown skin, and straight, silken black hair, like Woha's. She extended her hand in greeting, and Emily reached out with her left hand and squeezed Kamama's hand warmly.

"I'm so pleased to meet you," said Emily.

"And I you," said Kamama. "Although I must admit I'm somewhat nervous, considering you will be a congress-woman soon."

"Well, I haven't completely made up by mind about that yet."

Emily raised her eyebrows at Woha, a little peeved that he would share her personal information with someone else. Woha responded calmly.

"There are no secrets between Kama and I, which is why I was comfortable bringing her tonight," he said. "I hope you can respect that, Em."

Woha was telling her, indirectly, that he wanted to hear everything and that Kama could be depended on to keep it all confidential. Emily understood and said so.

"Okay, sounds good," she said.

"Shall we all have a seat?" asked Woha.

Emily noticed a subtle difference in Woha from back when they knew each other at CU and up in the moun-tains. He was more confident and assertive. He was now in the second year of a four-year term on the Tribal Council, and he had obviously embraced his role as a leader of his people. She also noticed that he ordered a Sprite, and she wondered if she should avoid drinking wine, but Woha re-lieved her of the need to decide.

"Please, Em, feel free to have a drink. I'm quite used to others around me drinking, including Kama, who's been known to tie one on every now and then."

Kama smiled, blushing slightly, but she ordered a glass of wine and Emily joined her.

"So, what's new in your life, Em?" asked Woha. "I think I'm up to date on all of the dreams, but what about your meeting with the Projector Man? What's his name again?"

"Fred Watts," said Emily. "And yes, I have a lot to tell you. Perhaps the best way is for you to simply listen to the conversation. I recorded it. It's a little long, but I think you'll find it very revealing."

"By all means, please play it," said Woha.

Emily set her phone on the table, making sure the volume was at the right setting to be heard by the three of them but not by others in the restaurant. They all leaned forward toward the phone. Emily pushed *play* and watched the expressions on Woha and Kama's faces as her conversation with Fred played. As always, Woha remained stoic throughout the playing of the tape, but Kama's face was very expressive, showing signs of fear, anger, and amazement as the conversation proceeded and then came to its abrupt ending.

"So, what do you think?" asked Emily, addressing her question to Woha.

Woha cupped his chin in his right hand, thinking, and after a moment he returned his hand to rest on his leg under the table.

"I think the guy is crazy," he said.

Emily didn't hesitate.

"There's no doubt about *that*," she said. "But what about this program of his? Do you think it really works the way he says it does?"

"About that, I'm not sure."

"What do you mean?" she asked.

"My thinking on your dreams has always been that you would have had them anyway, even if you'd never seen the films."

"I find that hard to believe," she said. "I mean it all started with the film of John in Ireland, and my dreams came immediately after that."

"I understand," said Woha. "I just believe what I believe. It's not for me to tell you what you should believe."

"But I want you to help me decide what to do!" she exclaimed, exasperated by the calm demeanor of her best friend.

"Regarding what?" he asked.

"First, regarding Fred Watts. I want to take this tape to the authorities. He needs to be stopped. Do you think I should do it?"

Woha thought on this for a moment, then made his opinion clear.

"I think Fred Watts doesn't matter," he said. "I think what matters is your dreams and how you react to them."

"But he shouldn't be doing this!" she said. "Are you saying I should just let him continue taking advantage of unsuspecting people?"

Woha looked directly into her eyes, and she saw intensity there but no commitment.

"I think *that* is your decision. If it gives you some closure to turn him in, then you should. But as I said, in my opinion, he doesn't matter."

"Okay," she said. "In that case, I'm going to do it. I'll

take this tape to the FBI as soon as I get back to Denver."

"The trial might interfere with your campaign," he said.

"True," she replied. "But first, I haven't even decided on whether or not to run, and second, I don't care if it affects the campaign or not. Right is right, and wrong is wrong. Period."

"Spoken like a true leader," he said.

"And what's *that* supposed to mean?" she asked.

"It means you were born to do this, Em, just as I was born to lead my people."

"So, you think I should run?" she asked.

"In my mind, you have no choice."

"It's that *simple* for you?" she asked.

"Yes. It is your destiny."

"What about John? Is he part of my destiny?"

"Have you seen him in your recent dreams?" asked Woha.

"No, I haven't."

"So, there's your answer."

"But what if I don't want that to be the answer!" she wailed, frustrated with Woha's steadfast adherence to the validity of her dreams.

"I'm not trying to hurt you, Em," he said. "I know you love John, and I hope that somehow you can get back together. John seems to be a good man, and I hope I can meet him in person one day rather than over a FaceTime connection. But my interpretation of your dreams is pretty black and white—even if neither of us is happy with my conclusions."

"I understand," she said, regaining control of her emotions, then redirecting the conversation. "What do you think of Lydia Dench?"

"She's good at what she does. She will leave no stone unturned. She will represent you well."

"Is she an honest person?"

"Yes. She always did what she said she would do."

"Okay, thanks," she said.

"Now, why don't we take a look at the menu and have a great dinner?" suggested Woha. "I'd like you to get to know Kama a little better before we are married."

"When is the wedding?" she asked.

"Soon," he said. "We are hoping you can come. Will you be staying in the U.S. or going back to Ireland?"

"As you said, I'm not sure I have a choice," said Emily.

Chapter 48
November 8, 2016

At 8:55 p.m., Mountain Time, CNN projected that Emily would be the winner of the race for the Congressional seat representing the Second District of Colorado, winning in a landslide. The crowd in the banquet hall of the hotel erupted in cheers and celebration. Soon after that, 31-year-old Emily appeared on stage to give her victory speech. It was short and to the point, but filled with a current of emotion that always ran under the surface of her words.

"Thank you, my friends," she said. "Thank you all, for your support. And a special thanks to my family—my dad, my mom, and my brother, Sam—for their tireless efforts on my behalf. But most all, I thank the people of the Second District of Colorado for giving me a chance!"

The crowd cheered. Emily paused, her silence bringing the crowd to a hush, foreshadowing something important and causing emotions to build.

"I'm just one person," she said. "And as you know, I look a little bit different than most of you. But I'm glad you figured out that the way someone *looks* does not determine the way they *think*! That the way someone *looks* does not determine the way they *work*!! That the way someone *looks* does not determine what they can *achieve*!!!"

The applause and cheers from the crowd burst out. But Emily lowered her voice, engaging the crowd to listen carefully to what she said next without having to say so.

"I believe in my heart that I am here for a reason—that somehow I was destined to be in this place, at this time."

The volume of her voice began gradually rising.

"But it will take *all* of us to make a difference! It will take *all* of us to make change happen!! It will take *all* of us to make our dreams come true!"

The crowd was on their feet now roaring its approval. Many people began stomping their folding chairs on the floor. The noise went on for a long time.

"I thank you once again for your support. And I pledge to you now: I will give it my all to deliver on the promises made during this campaign! Thank you!"

The cheering continued while Emily brought her family out on the stage, along with Lydia Dench and a few key members of her staff, and the celebration got under way in earnest. After around 20 minutes, Emily waved goodbye to the crowd and retired to her penthouse suite for a more intimate celebration involving her family; some close friends, including Woha and Kamama; and the staff of Lydia's firm. They celebrated until 2 a.m., when the crowd finally began to thin.

After everyone had gone and Emily was alone in her suite, she went behind the bar and poured herself a cold glass of Sauvignon blanc. She thought about her speech, knowing in her heart that it was no different than so many other speeches she'd heard from politicians over the years. And she wondered if she truly *could* make a difference. She certainly wanted to. She *had* to. Otherwise, she would regret the decision to leave Ireland for the rest of her life.

As Emily sipped her wine, lounging on the sofa now, she reminisced about all that had happened during the 18 months that had led to this night. The never-ending meetings, the relentless campaigning, some of it in the sub-zero temperatures and heavy snow of her old stomping grounds up in the mountains. And all of this was complicated by the trial of Fred Watts, at which Emily was a key witness. Luckily, the judge had granted her request for the trial not to be public. This helped minimize any fallout that her involvement with Fred might engender.

After Emily had handed over her recording to the local FBI office, they'd been able to secure a warrant and had raided the headquarters of Future Dreaming, Inc. in downtown Denver, as well as the little ranch home on 22 Maple Street in Edgewater, and Fred's *real* home, which turned out to be in the exclusive, high-end town of Bow Mar. A treasure trove of case reports and computer records had been secured, including the infamous algorithm software that Fred was so proud of. And while the situation was somewhat unprecedented, government lawyers identified a variety of state and federal laws that had been broken. The charges included several forms of malpractice and numerous counts of failure to provide informed consent.

Fred had been convicted and sentenced to 20 years in prison. Furthermore, the international network of his colleagues had been uncovered and exposed, many of whom were government officials. The "friend" who paid Anna for the videos was actually the Minister of Health and Human Services for the Netherlands, who had been forced to resign and was awaiting trial.

Emily was glad she'd been able to put an end to Fred's reckless and irresponsible future dreaming program, but as she sat alone in the room, she was acutely aware of the irony of how she had gotten to where she was at that moment. In spite of Woha's beliefs to the contrary, Emily was firmly convinced that the path of her entire life had changed forever when she watched that first film back in April 2010. Her mood was further dampened by the lingering doubt in her heart that *this* path, the one she was on, was the right one for *her*.

As Emily sipped her wine, she pictured herself working behind the bar at the Oasis in the Cold. She remembered pouring beers for Woha and also for Tommy, Brian, Reenie, and so many other kind souls from that innocent time in her life. And she remembered Hannah Baxter, and Hannah's supportive parents. She felt certain that most of the people she'd known in her life in the mountains that were of voting age had cast their ballots for *her* in this election, and she believed that they would vote for her in the ones yet to come. But it wasn't their *votes* she coveted. It was knowing they were all okay and doing well, especially Hannah. She made a mental note to find out.

Emily's reminiscing shifted to Ireland, and she recounted her first trip there—meeting Tim and Nancy at the train station in Dublin, the beautiful train ride south, and then

John emerging from the van and shaking her hand with an electricity that had never faded in all the time they'd known each other. She thought of Anna and Willem, Babette and Paul, Nadine and Helmut, and all the others, wondering what they were doing in their lives and if she'd ever see them again.

She remembered Thomas and Wilson and the monk who had predicted her rise to power. It seemed so long ago. She hoped all was well with Thomas and Wilson, and she knew from her dreams that she would see them again soon when she traveled to China on a diplomatic mission.

But most of all, she thought of John. She pictured him in Dingle, sitting out on the veranda of his wonderful little house, gazing with his peacefully intense, ocean blue eyes out toward the sea. She wondered if he was alone, and suspected he was, and she also reflected that he was probably quite sad, just as she was at that very moment. She'd won the election, but she'd lost so much in the process.

Emily finally went to bed around 4 a.m., quite drunk from a night of celebrating followed by solitary reflection and additional imbibing. Eventually, she dozed off to sleep, but just before she slipped into a restless slumber, she *hoped* that she would dream, and she *hoped* she would remember at least one dream in the morning.

Chapter 49

Unfortunately, Emily awoke the next morning remembering nothing from her dreams, which had always been the case when she was pursuing the path previous dreams had predicted for her. She was sworn into Congress on January 3, 2017. During her first 17 months in office, she sponsored and cosponsored numerous bills that helped the disabled, and most of them passed and were signed into law by the President. Even though partisan politics had reached an all-time high while Emily was in Congress, helping the disabled was a bi-partisan priority. There was already a lot of legislation in this area, including the Americans with Disabilities Act, so Emily focused on bills that funded programs centering on training disabled people for careers and jobs that were in demand, and on placement programs that helped them secure employment in the fields they were trained in. And while her legislative accomplishments were deeply fulfilling, the empty spot in Emily's heart remained.

She missed John, and she missed the feeling of being *present* when she personally helped people, especially disabled people, to overcome their fears. There was no feeling like that. Knowing that her legislative agenda was helping others was rewarding, but there was no replacement for actually being there and doing it. Each night she *hoped* she would wake up in the morning remembering something from her dreams that was new and different from what she had dreamed before, something that would lead her back to what she'd lost. But she was always disappointed. She remembered nothing from her dreams.

John never came to visit her in the U.S., and she never went to visit him. The love was still there, but the *hurt* was also painfully present, as was the fear of *regret* surrounding any temporary reunions that might occur. So, they never saw each other, not even on FaceTime. They emailed and spoke on the phone from time to time, but that was it.

Emily was beginning to realize that the word *hope* had a different meaning than the word *dream*. She knew in her heart what she wanted but was held back by her inability to dream it. Her accomplishments provided full justification for the choices she'd made, but what no one except Emily clearly understood was her desperate need to remain protected from the excruciating pain that she relived every time she slipped back to that horrible moment when she was 11 years old. She'd been unable to find a way to break the cycle other than pursuing the dreams. And with this clarity came terrible guilt and heartache. She had left the man she loved and the *life* she loved to help herself. Yes, she had helped others along the way, many of them, but the harsh reality of the truth sat like a stone in her gut.

Emily began to wonder if she actually *was* dreaming

about all that she had lost but simply couldn't remember it when she woke up. She researched how to teach herself to remember her dreams and made some adjustments to her sleeping regimen. First, the last thing she did before she fell asleep at night was to tell herself to remember her dreams. She repeated it over and over in her head—*remember your dreams, remember your dreams, remember*—until she fell asleep. Second, she kept a notepad and a pen beside her bed to record anything she remembered if she woke up during the night or immediately upon waking in the morning. And finally, when she *did* wake up for the day, she stayed in bed longer, trying to make her mind think of nothing that was upcoming in her schedule or that needed to be done, waiting for something to come, hoping that a memory of a dream would surface. But nothing ever came.

One day in the spring of 2018, Emily's chief of staff and campaign manager, Lydia Dench, came into her office at the Capitol Building and sat down in front of Emily's large oak desk.

"What's up, Lydia?" asked Emily.

"We need to start campaigning—soon," said Lydia. "We should have started already."

"I know," she said. "But I'm way up in the polls. If it ain't broke, don't fix it, right?"

"Wrong," said Lydia. "Jeb Parsons is a local hero just like you, and he's got a huge campaign war chest. He's been out on the trail for months now, and the gap is closing. We've got to get out there, Emily, yesterday!"

The truth was that Emily was conflicted about her future. She was well aware that her dreams had predicted she would run again, and win, then run for Senate, and win, and then run for President, and win. And so far, she *had* made a difference—no doubt a much broader difference than she could have made as a client coordinator for the NSCD. She was helping *every* client coordinator in the country with funding for their programs, and she was helping the disabled people the coordinators served with that same funding. But she just wasn't ready to pull the trigger on the re-election campaign. She *still* wondered if all of this had been *her* choice, or not, and that was important to her. She wanted to know! Was this *her* life or some life that had been manufactured by that cursed algorithm?

Emily went to bed that evening feeling the pressure of deciding. She followed her normal procedure of reminding herself to remember her dreams. She checked to make sure the notepad and pen were beside her bed. She tossed and turned for what seemed hours and finally fell into a deep slumber. She awoke the next morning and relaxed, wiping any thoughts about upcoming obligations from her mind. She breathed deeply, nearly falling back asleep, but then something came into her mind. It was a memory of a new dream! And it was different from any dream she'd ever remembered before.

Chapter 50
Thursday, June 14, 2018

Emily settled into her room, unpacking a few things, but left most of them in her bag. The room was somewhat spacious for this kind of place and had a nice double bed in it. She reached for her backpack and removed the water bladder, went to the sink and filled the bladder, then returned to the bed and secured the bladder back into the pack. She put the pack on, grabbed her walking pole, the same one Willem had gifted to her eight years ago, then strode purposely out the door.

The weather in Glenbeigh that early afternoon was nice. The morning clouds and mist had cleared, and a bright, blue sun warmed the land to a pleasant 63 degrees Fahrenheit. Emily walked down the busy road that passed through Glenbeigh, but she soon turned east and headed up into the hills. She remembered the way quite clearly, although she'd never walked it in this direction. The normal route was to walk west out of Glencar, negotiating the beautiful countryside and ending up in Glenbeigh after covering the 20 kilometers of wilderness between the two. This time, however, she was going in the opposite direction, hoping that her scheme would pay dividends soon.

She reached the trailhead and left the rural, surfaced road, then began climbing up the long, winding slope to the summit of the mountains that fronted the sea to the west. It was a pleasant walk, with numerous switchbacks to reduce the angle of the ascent, but Emily found herself breathing hard at times, due to the life she'd led for the past three years—endless meetings, dinner engagements, and speeches, with little time to exercise. She hadn't done a proper walk since she'd left Ireland, and while tired, she was ecstatic to be here. But as she approached the summit, she became anxious.

When she arrived at the top, she turned around and looked to the northwest. She saw the glimmering waters of Dingle Bay, which flowed into the Atlantic in the distance. She surveyed the Dingle Peninsula, trying to pinpoint exactly where John's home might lie. She looked out at the endless sea, then slowly turned in a circle, taking in the views of the green, rolling mountains on three sides of her. She'd always loved the mountains, but as she turned back to face the spectacular seascape in the distance, she nearly lost her breath at the diversity of beauty to be found on this ancient, tiny island. She remembered a thought she'd had, just briefly, during her first day ever walking in Ireland, when they were going down through the forest on the way from Glenmalure to Glendalough. *I could live my life doing this,* she'd thought. And she'd done that, for a while. But then she'd thrown it away. This tragic realization caused the serenity and happiness she'd been feeling to be replaced by an emptiness that she yearned to fill. The anxiety returned.

Emily walked back down the trail toward Glenbeigh, removed her walking pole from her hand and took a seat on a rock around 25 feet from the summit. She used her left hand to place the valve of her water hose into her mouth, taking in a deep draft. She focused her eyes on the trail at the top of the rise and waited. A half hour passed, so she stood up and removed her pack, then sat back down on the rock and placed it in front of her. She unzipped a pocket on the pack, removed an energy bar and munched it down slowly. She'd skipped lunch because her planned schedule for this tenuous rendezvous was tight, so she was quite hungry. She washed her mouth out with water and swallowed the mixture of crumbs and water down. She waited another half an hour, becoming more despondent with every passing minute.

Suddenly, she saw someone coming up over the rise in the east. It was a solitary man with his head bent down. When he reached the summit, he raised his head and looked out at the sea, not noticing Emily sitting on the rock 25 feet away. A slight smile came to his lips as he gazed out at the water with his peacefully intense stare. Then he glanced down and spotted her. The emotion Emily felt at that moment was a combination of exhilaration and terror, because she didn't know how John would react to seeing her there. She was afraid to move, so she just sat, waiting, her heart beating faster than it had been on the climb up.

John didn't move either, but he spoke to her.

"How'd you know you'd find me here?" he asked.

With a little shakiness in her voice, Emily answered, "I

called the office, and they said you were on your annual walk on the Kerry Way—a walk you'd started making by yourself after I left."

"And they gave you the details of my itinerary?"

"Yes."

John remained where he was, and Emily stayed where she was.

"We never got to finish this walk, not together at least," he said.

Emily was afraid to ask the next question, but she asked it nonetheless.

"Can we finish it now, John? Together?"

John took one step forward, then another, and he came to stand in front of her as she sat on the rock, waiting for his answer.

"We've some unfinished business here on the Kerry Way, have we not?"

"Yes," she said, trembling now.

"Well, stand up then. Let's get to it."

He reached out, took her hand, and helped her to her feet. Then he embraced her, squeezing tightly. She squeezed back, tears rolling down her cheeks. He continued to hold her but wasn't finished talking yet.

"I invented this fantasy after you left: If I walked the Kerry Way each year, by m'self, one year you'd show up as I came over that rise. This is my third time doing it, and here you are."

"Did you dream about it?" she asked.

"No. Just *hoped*. What about you? Did you dream about it?"

"I *did*," she said. "But it was *hope* that made the difference. I was able to turn my hope into a dream, and then I taught myself to remember my dreams, and I finally started remembering dreams that were truly *mine*. I'm free now, John. I broke the Projector Man's spell. And I want to come back. Will you have me?"

"What about your job, Em? And the future your dreams have predicted for you? You must be campaigning for re-election by now."

"I'm not going to run for re-election, John. I'll finish my term, but then I'm done with politics."

John released her and stepped back but his eyes never left hers. She saw tears on his face and felt the ongoing flood streaming down her own.

"This is where I want to be," she said. "I need so very much for you to want me here, too."

John didn't hesitate. "Emily Noland, I'll wait for you 'til I'm old and gray. That's what I said three years ago, and I meant it. But 'tis good news I won't have to. Seven months seems only a few seconds compared to that."

Emily lurched forward, embracing John with all her strength. He reciprocated. The electricity flowed, just as it had done from the first moment they'd met. After a long time, they separated, and John helped Emily get her gear back on. They walked back toward Glenbeigh, enjoying the spectacular view together. As they descended, John asked a question.

"What will happen if you have new dreams, Em?"

"I've already had some," she said.

"Do they involve me?" he asked.

"Oh, yes, they very much involve you."

"But what if one day they don't?"

"Not a problem," she said. "I've finally learned that *hope* and *love* are the foundation of life—not *dreams*."

The End

Epilogue
Early June 2028

Emily pulled the Hill and Town van off the road and onto the small car park alongside the entrance to the Wicklow Way. The group had voted to drive the 3 kilometers from Roundwood rather than make the walk on the surfaced road. John was in the passenger seat beside her. Their two children, Jonathan and William, plus three families occupied the 12 seats in the back of the van.

Each of the three families had a disabled child with them. One family was from Germany, one from England, and one from America. The German family was composed of a father, a mother, and a 10-year-old-boy with a missing arm. The family from England was a father, a mother, and an 8-year-old girl with a missing leg, plus her 11-year-old brother. And the family from the States was a mother, a mother, and a 12-year-old girl who was missing a foot.

The Hill and Town Disabled Walking Program had been refined over the years and was now marketed as a family vacation, and this tweak had produced amazing results. Hill and Town was now conducting as many guided tours for families of the disabled as it was for people with all four appendages intact and functioning properly. It was rare for Emily and John to do a tour together, but the Wicklow Way tour had special meaning for both of them, and the trail they were about to walk was a particularly important part of their past.

They got out of the van, put on their gear, and got ready to walk. Their son Jonathan, who was eight, and his little brother William, who was six, helped the other kids with their stuff. Emily and John then led them the 250 meters to the stile, the same stile that John had helped Emily climb over 18 years ago. John was 47 now, and Emily was 43. They were both still in great shape because they made their living walking in the beautiful hills and towns of Ireland. John had a few streaks of gray in his reddish-brown hair, but Emily's short, dark bob still shimmered in the light of the sun. Emily addressed the group.

"This thing right here is called a stile. It's a way to get over the fence without opening the gate. Now if you don't want to go over the stile, that's no problem. We can open the gate and get you through that way. John will show you how to go up and over and then we'll see who else wants to try."

John removed his walking poles, holding them in one hand, then went slowly up and over the stile.

"Okay," said Emily. "Let's get Bernhard, Betsy, and Erin up here near me first."

The three disabled kids made their way to the front. Jonathan and William accompanied them. Bernhard, the 10-year-old-boy from Germany with a missing arm, went up and over and down the other side. Betsy, the 12-year-old girl from America with the missing foot, went up and over next. Emily looked closely at Erin, the 8-year-old from England with a missing leg, and saw that she was scared.

"Hey, Erin," she whispered. "Why don't I hold onto your right hand while you go up. You hold onto the stile with your left hand. Is that okay?"

"I guess so," peeped Erin.

Erin had a prothesis attached to her right leg, and she was very good at using it. But this was something new, and she needed some help. Emily took Erin's walking poles from her and removed her own pole, then approached the fence and handed them over to John. She returned to Erin, who was holding onto the stile with both hands. She took Erin's right hand with her left and squeezed tightly.

"I've got you, honey," she said. "Okay, up we go!"

Erin climbed slowly up the stairs of the stile, holding tightly to Emily's hand. As Erin approached the top platform, Emily scooted around to the ladder and took a few steps up so she could continue holding Erin's hand. When Erin reached the top, Emily released her hand.

"That was great!" she said. "You'll want to use two hands to go down, okay?"

"Okay," said Erin, excitement in her voice.

Erin easily negotiated the steps down the other side, and Emily quickly followed her. They faced each other, and Emily raised her hand for a high five, which Erin promptly returned, the slap of their hands memorializing their mutual joy. Erin was beaming, obviously proud of what she'd done. Emily leaned close to the little girl's ear and whispered. "I wouldn't tell just anyone, but the first time I went over this stile I needed John to help me, just like I helped you," she said.

"Really?" asked Erin.

"Really, really," said Emily. "But then I learned that people like me, and like you, can do anything we want to if we just believe in ourselves. Do you understand that, honey?"

"I hope so," said Erin, putting her fingers up to her mouth.

"Well, you're on the right track because *hope* is the key. Let's walk a little further, okay?"

"Okay."

They slowly ascended, and eventually they could see Roundwood Village and the reservoirs around it. Emily explained that the reservoirs had been built in the 1860s and still supplied water to south Dublin. Further up, she pointed out two beautiful lakes, Lough Tay and Lough Dan, lying in the left side of a beautiful valley. Next, she pointed at a huge building in the top right of the valley, noting that this was the Guinness family summer residence, which was built in the 18th century and was still owned by a family member. She explained that it was in this area that most of the movie *Braveheart* was filmed. She then suggested they stop for an early lunch because this was such a beautiful site. People pulled off their backpacks and took out their packed lunches. Emily sat beside Erin.

"It's really awesome up here, isn't it?" she asked the little girl.

"Beautiful," said Erin. Her English accent caused the word to come out as "BYOO-tuh-ful."

"And you know we would never have been able to fully appreciate this beautiful view if you hadn't gone over that stile, right?"

"What about the gate?" asked Erin.

"Yes, we could have used the gate," she responded. "But that's not really what you wanted, was it Erin? That's not what you *hoped* you could do. You wanted to go over that stile, didn't you?"

"Yes," came the sheepish reply from the little girl.

"And if you hadn't gone over that stile, when we got up here to this beautiful spot, all you would have been thinking about was how much you regretted not going over that stile, right?"

"Yes, I think that's right," said Erin.

"You see, Erin. If you *hope* for something, truly *yearn* for it from deep inside yourself, you have to try everything you can to make it come true. That's the key to life, my young friend. You won't always succeed, but knowing you've tried your best will carry you through. And sometimes, when you *do* succeed in making your hopes real, it allows all the beauty of being here on this earth to fill you up with joy—just like you and I felt when you went over that stile. Do you understand, honey?"

"I think I do," said the little girl.

"So do I," Emily reflected. "So do I."

Acknowledgments

I want to thank my lifelong friend Scott Hardy for giving me the idea to write this book. And my heartfelt thanks to my daughter, Paige, who reminds me every day that *hope* keeps us all going. Paige is also my biggest critic and pushed me to get this book right, just as she did for my first novel, *Distant Finish*. I also want to thank Jennifer Bright and her staff at Bright Communications for making everything perfect, at least we hope so! Jennifer is the Book Doula of all book doulas. Finally, I'd like to thank Christopher and Teresa Stacey of Footfalls Walking Holidays in County Wicklow, Ireland, who helped me discover the beauty of Ireland and its generous people. I know I may not have gotten every turn of the walks exactly right, but I hope I've conveyed how special a walk in Ireland can be. May we all walk in peace and harmony for the rest of our days.

CPSIA information can be obtained
at www.ICGtesting.com
Printed in the USA
BVHW041735130122
626144BV00014B/587